ALSO BY CONSTANCE SANTEGO

FICTION
The Nine Spiritual Gifts Series:
Journey of a Soul – (Vol. 1 Michael)
Language of a Soul – (Vol. 2 Gabriel)
Prophecy of a Soul – (Vol. 3 Bath Kol)
Healing of a Soul – (Vol. 4 Raphael)

NON-FICTION
The Intuitive Life, The Gift of Prophecy, Third Edition
Fairy Tales, Dreams and Reality… Where Are You On
Your Path? Second Edition
Your Persona… The Mask You Wear
Angelic Lifestyle, A Vibrant Lifestyle
Angelic Lifestyle 42-Day Energy Cleanse
Archangel Michael's Soul Retrieval Guide
Secrets Of A Healer, Series:
  Magic of Aromatherapy (Vol. I)
  Magic of Reflexology (Vol. II)
  Magic of The Gifts (Vol. III)
  Magic of Muscle Testing (Vol. IV)
  Magic of Iridology (Vol. V)
  Magic of Massage (Vol. VI)
  Magic of Hypnotherapy (Vol. VII)
  Magic of Reiki (Vol. VIII)
  Magic of Advanced Aromatherapy (Vol. IX)
  Magic of Esthetics (Vol. X)

FOR CHILDREN
I am big tonight. I don't need the light!

COOKBOOK
All My Favorite Recipes, *with a hint of giggle*

Published by
Editor: ChatGPT and Grammarly
Interior Layout: Constance Santego
Book Layout: ©2017 BookDesignTemplates.com
Cover Design: Jennifer Louie
Soft Cover ISBN: 978-1-990062-12-4
eBook ISBN: 978-1-990062-13-1
Created and published in Canada. Printed and bound in the United States of America
Ordering Information: csantego@gmail.com

Constance Santego

Miracles of a Soul

Constance Santego has been practicing and teaching *The Nine Spiritual Gifts, Granted From Spirit,* for over twenty-five years. She lives in British Columbia, Canada with her husband.

www.constancesantego.ca

Cast of Characters

Some of the Residents of New York City, USA, and other places.

Alexandra (Lexi) Elizabeth Constantine: Fashion designer in Upper East Side Manhattan. Daughter of Olivia and Marcus Constantine (Italian). Fiancée to Reverend Edward Julien Hawthorne. Her boss is Sebastian. Friends with co-worker Southern belle, Sherie.

Susannah Grace Constantine: Lexi's belated sister and now guardian angel. Lived in Dumbo (Down Under the Manhattan Bridge Overpass). She was an antique collector for Aryeh Jacob Kofman and dated Billy Randazzo.

Olivia Sarah Constantine (Maiden name, Austin): Mother to Lexi and Susannah. Widowed housewife. Parents were from England. She lives in Dyker Heights, Brooklyn, NY.

Reverend Edward Julien Hawthorne: Mortician and minister of a funeral home in Brooklyn. Fiancé to Alexandra (Lexi). Casandra is his secretary.

Tamara Reeve: Psychic medium and teacher of many of the Spiritual Gifts. Fiancée to Greg Masones. Now owns her grandmother's brownstone in Brooklyn Heights.

Detective Ferguson "Red" Redington: 1st-grade homicide investigator, Manhattan Bureau – Midtown South Precinct, Shield number 1323, NYPD. Lives in Far Rockaway Beach, Queens, on Long Island, NY. His family comes from England.

Greg Masones (AKA Julian D'Angelo): At large. Accountant for the Genovese crime family. Italian immigrant. Son of Serena D'Angelo. Was Tamara's fiancé.

Isabella Jackson: Famous actress. She moved around to wherever her next movie was being filmed. Friends with Lexi, Edward, and Redington. Girlfriend of belated Hans (now Erland, an Elf) and mother to Aias.

Hans Magnusson (Erland): Lawyer. He lived in Switzerland but was from Sweden. He inherited his family's fortune, and his grandfather was Olof. After he died, he became a walk-in soul to Erland in the Elemental Realm of Alfheim, Still communicates with Isabella.

Aias Jackson Olof Magnusson: Son of Isabella and Erland. He was a half-elf with many gifts, the main one being able to heal.

Kesia Bango: Gypsy tarot card reader. Daughter of Florence. Ancestral Granddaughter of Tatiana Masones and Clementina (Tatiana's mother). Related to Greg, he is her uncle.

Luna: Kesia's Wiccan friend from high school. She lives in Jersey Shore.

Doctor Neo Singh: Edward's Neurosurgeon at Brooklyn Neurocritical Care. His Greek mother is Naida, and his East Indian father is Paal. Sister to Evangeline and uncle to her son, Todd.

Evangeline Singh: Neo's sister. Massage Therapist. Her son is Todd, and her fiancé is Jeff.

Delish Chakladar: Acharya Shri Sharma's assistant and devotee at Aias's gurukala (spiritual school) in Puttaparthi India.

Main Angel of each Novel

Book 1 – Archangel Michael
"Warrior"
Companion Book – Archangel Michael's Soul Retrieval Guide.
Book 2 – Archangel Gabriel
"Messenger"
Companion Book – Your Persona... The Mask You Wear.
Book 3 – Bath Kol
"Daughter of the Voice," the Holy Ghost, and Gabriel
Companion Book – The Gift of Prophecy.
Book 4 – Archangel Raphael
"God Has Healed"
Companion Books – Secrets of a Healer Series.
Book 5 – Archangel Hamied
"Miracles"
Companion Books – Secrets of a Healer, Reiki, and Secrets of a Healer, The Gifts

Miracles of a Soul

The Gift of Miracles

A Novel
5th in the series, The Nine Spiritual Gifts
'The Gift of Miracles'

Constance Santego

Vol 5

Dedicated
to Jesus, Dr. Mikao
Usui, and Sri Sathya
Sai Baba!

Miracles of a Soul

The Nine Spiritual Gifts

In the New Testament, my favorite story is
"The Gifts."
Corinthians 1, Chapter 12, Verse 4-11
*(Maybe a little differently worded
depending on which Bible you have).*

The variety and the unity of gifts
There are many different gifts, but it is always the
same Spirit; there are many different ways of
serving, but it is always the same Lord. There are
many different forms of activity, but in everybody,
it is the same God who is at work in them all. The
particular manifestation of the Spirit granted to
each one is to be used for the general good.
To one is given from the Spirit the gift of utterance
expressing **wisdom**; to another the gift of utterance
expressing **knowledge**; in accordance with the
same spirit, to another, **faith**, from the same Spirit;
and to another, the gifts of **healing**, through the
same Spirit; to another, the working of **miracles**;
to another **prophecy**; to another, the power of
distinguishing spirits; to one, the gift of **different
tongues**; and to another, the **interpretation of
tongues**. But at work in all these is one and the
same Spirit, distributing them at will to each
individual.
The New Jerusalem Bible

Awaken to the spirit world, for there lie your gifts granted by Spirit.

~ Constance Santego

Fact:

All biblical references, science, legends, and myths are real *(slightly changed to fit the character)*. This novel was written as a story inspired by Spirit to give you, the reader, a new perspective, a new way to learn, and a new opportunity to empower your life.

All characters are fictional, but the locations are based on reality.

Prologue

$\mathscr{I}$have been studying Reiki since 1999, became a Reiki Master in 2000, and achieved Grand Reiki Master status in 2010.

My Lineage

I was initiated into Reiki Levels 1 & 2 in September 1999 by an American lady named Nefertiti.

In 2010, as Constance Santego (formerly Connie Brummet), I was attuned to Grand Reiki Mastery by Spirit. In 2000, I attained Reiki Mastery through Margaret Ripple, a Canadian practitioner who herself was attuned in 1998 by Wendy Koenig. Wendy, in turn, received her attunement in 1997 from Laurie Allen Grant.

In 1989, Laurie Grant was attuned by James P. Davis, whom Dr. Arthur L. Robertson had attuned in the 1970s. Dr. Robertson's initiation into the Reiki system occurred under the guidance of Master teacher Virginia W. Samdahl, who holds the distinction of being the first Occidental Reiki Master initiated by Hawayo Hiromi Takata.

In 1938, Mrs. Takata received her master's attunement from Dr. Chujiro Hayashi. Dr. Hayashi is believed to be the last individual to receive Reiki Mastership directly from Dr. Usui in 1925. Dr. Usui, in turn, received his attunement from Spirit on Mount Kurama in the early 1920s as a result of his quest to discover the healing method within ancient Sanskrit texts.

Interestingly, Iris Ishikuro, one of Mrs. Takata's Reiki Master students, and her cousin also received training in the Johrei Fellowship, a practice involving healing with energy projected from the hands. Iris gained additional insights into Reiki from her sister, who worked in a Tibetan temple in Hawaii, and she explored another type of Reiki that later became known as Raku Kei. Iris is renowned for her contributions, including changing Mrs. Takata's fee structure, and she actively shared her knowledge with Dr. Robertson.

**From my book,
Secrets of a Healer – The Gift of Reiki**

Constance's Reiki Interpretation

I love to use this simplified story to explain to my students what Reiki energy is and how it works.

Imagine a lamp in your home; it can be any size or color. Most lamps have an electrical cord, a lamp fixture, and a light bulb to use the lamp properly.

Imagine you are the lamp fixture, the client or person you will work on is the light bulb, and God, Spirit, or your Reiki Master is the Ki (Chi) energy that flows through the electrical cord to light the bulb.

You are the facilitator—the lamp—yes, an essential item needed to light the bulb, but without plugging in the lamp to an electrical socket in the wall to receive the energy required, no matter how nice or expensive the lamp is, the light bulb will never work without an energy source.

Also, it is useless and a waste of energy to plug the electrical cord in without the bulb in the lamp. Ensure you always have a reason and the client's permission during a Reiki session. When your Reiki Master in Spirit comes to help you, do not waste their time.

I remember doing a science project where we had a potato and a small flashlight bulb. I was amazed that a potato had enough energy to light the bulb for a few seconds. Just like the potato, I do not have enough energy to heal my client. And if I tried, I would burn out quickly. Only the Universal Life Force Energy, Source, God, Creator, or whatever other name you call it, has all the healing energy needed at the correct frequency to heal.

If you ever feel drained after a session, you gave your energy away instead of using the Cosmic energy granted through the Source. My point is you are the facilitator, not the energy source itself.

As a healer, almost every miracle I witnessed was during a Reiki session, from hearing coming back to cancer disintegrating. But it is not me. Instead, it is the healing energy flowing through me from the Spirit.

Constance Santego

~

Archangel Hamied, the Saint of Miracles, carries the essence of Christ's Light and is such a dazzling white that you can only see his incredible eyes shining through. As Archangel Hamied watches over you, he waits for opportunities to create miracles in your life.

He has a mission, and it is to spark the memory of your divinity, spirituality, and holiness through his examples.

Through being a witness to a miracle, one becomes enlightened. Miracles can be as simple as getting a promotion at work, a mother lifting a car off her child, or a deathly ailment being cured.

Archangel Hamied's Christ's Light was there when Jesus, Dr. Usui, and Sathya Sai Baba performed miracles. So, the only thing you need to do to witness a miracle is BELIEVE.

6   Constance Santego

Chapter 1

 In the luxurious confines of first class, Lexi found herself accompanied by Aias, Kesia, and Luna. She had graciously accepted the role of chaperoning this trio. Despite Aias being twenty-one and technically an adult by societal standards, Lexi couldn't help but view him as Isabella's toddler half-elf. The conversion of elven years to human ones still confounded her. The haunting realization struck her that while she would age and grow frail, Aias would remain eternally youthful, his age forever frozen in time.

Seated between Aias and Luna, Kesia, her wise eyes often seen peering behind tarot cards, met Lexi's gaze. With a thoughtful but playful nod, she said, "Hey, Lexi, seriously, thanks for joining us. My mom would have firmly said 'no' to this trip without you. It's going to be amazing!"

"Ditto," Luna agreed. "This promises to be an unforgettable summer vacation before we embark on college this fall."

Nodding in agreement, Aias chimed in, "Ditto to your ditto. I'm really glad my mom allowed me to explore my personal quest for the hidden secrets of my healing ability before starting University in September."

The reason they were all on this trip was that Aias had pursued a lead discovered by Kesia regarding a hands-on healing technique. He had determined that the best way to unravel the mysteries of his healing powers was to travel to Japan and delve into the teachings of a technique called Reiki, which meant "universal life force energy."

Aias playfully bumped Lexi's shoulder and said, "Thanks again, Lex. Although I could have gone alone, and my mom couldn't have legally stopped me, I'm genuinely pleased you're coming with us. This adventure should reignite your excitement for your spiritual journey."

"Thank you, guys. I'm genuinely excited to be traveling with you. I've always wanted to explore Asia," Lexi replied, closing her eyes briefly as she heard Kesia teasing Aias.

Giggling, Kesia teased, "If your mom weren't so famous, I don't know if I'd be friends with you. You're kind of ugly, you know."

"Ugly? Are you kidding me?" Aias retorted with a hint of pride, slightly puffing out his chest.

Luna rolled her eyes, amused by their banter.

Kesia leaned back, her face adorned with a radiant smile. *Holy Hanna, he's absolutely stunning! His flowing jet-black hair, captivating green eyes, skin that shimmered like the moon, and those adorable pointed ears.*

"Wait, I don't recall any of you mentioning that your mother is famous," Luna commented. "Who is your mom?"

Kesia turned to Luna and replied, "Isabella Jackson."

Luna blurted out, "The movie star?"

Kesia nodded.

"How did I not know that I'm friends with the son of a famous movie star? Well, I'll be," Luna exclaimed.

"Hey, you two. Just because my mom is famous doesn't mean I am," Aias interjected. "In fact, most people don't even know she has a son."

Curious, Luna inquired, "What do they think?"

"My mom had to come up with a logical explanation for her two-year-old baby suddenly being twenty-one, so she told the world that I died."

"Harsh!" Luna exclaimed.

"It makes sense to me," Kesia reasoned. "Could you imagine what scientists would do if they knew you existed?"

"I know, right? That's what my mom was worried about."

Kesia slipped her arm through Aias's. "Besides, it would look pretty weird if I were in love with a two-year-old."

Aias gazed into Kesia's eyes, searching for the truth. "You're in love with me?"

As she rested her head on his shoulder, Kesia chuckled softly, "Of course, silly."

Luna rolled her eyes, inserted her earbuds, and remarked, "Ugh. Get a room, you two."

Aias whispered to Kesia, "Kesia, you don't think of me as a baby, do you?"

"No, why would I?"

"Well, I am only two human years old."

"Exactly. Human years."

"You don't care that I'm a half-elf?" Aias asked as he leaned his head against hers.

"No. I kinda think it's sexy."

"You do?"

"Yep."

Aias turned his head and planted a gentle kiss on the top of Kesia's head. "You're amazing."

Kesia snuggled in closer, her voice soft and teasing, "So are you."

Chapter 2

After arriving in Tokyo, the four spent a few days sightseeing before delving into the mystery of Aias's healing ability.

They started their first day with a fun visit to DisneySea, one of the best Disney theme parks in the world.

A shiver ran down Kesia's spine when she saw their first ride, the Tower of Terror. Its intimidating façade was a throwback to a bygone era of elegance and splendor in 1912 New York. But now, it loomed over her like an ancient relic, tinged with a sense of foreboding. Each gothic spire seemed to reach for the skies, and the empty windows appeared as if they concealed untold secrets of those who had once resided within.

The group entered, and a rush of cool, stale air greeted Kesia. The dimly lit lobby was like stepping into another world, with every detail seemingly trapped in time. She felt the weight of the dusty chandeliers' ornate crystals and the piercing gaze of the vintage portraits on the walls. The mournful sound of a gramophone echoed a ghostly melody that tugged at her heartstrings. It felt as if the past had gripped the very fabric of the place, refusing to let go.

The elevator doors closed with a finality that made Kesia's stomach churn. The metallic taste of fear lingered on her tongue. In an instinctive search for comfort, she sought Aias's hand, their fingers intertwining. His familiar warmth offered a fleeting sense of safety, starkly contrasting the unease that knotted her insides.

Silence enveloped them, broken only by the elevator's soft humming. As they ascended, Kesia's thoughts raced, the anticipation threatening to overwhelm her. And then, with no preamble, the world turned upside down. The elevator halted, casting them into a heart-stopping stillness.

The drop was unexpected, a gut-wrenching freefall. Kesia's heart raced, mirroring the rapid descent. Holding onto Aias's hand became her lifeline, the anchor amidst the whirlwind of sensations. As Luna and Lexi's terrified screams blended with her own, the rush of wind and speed became an all-consuming force.

And then, as abruptly as it started, it was over. As the elevator steadied, Kesia tried to catch her breath, her chest heaving. Luna and Lexi looked equally shaken, their expressions reflecting their shared ordeal. They had faced the terror together, and in that shared experience, a bond had solidified.

Stepping back into the sunlight felt surreal. The everyday sights and sounds of the theme park were a stark contrast to the tumultuous emotions they had just weathered. Her hand still interlocked with Aias's. They made their way out, the indelible mark of their shared experience forever etched in Kesia's memory. That day, reality and fantasy intertwined, culminating in an adventure that forever held a special place in her heart.

"How were you not scared?" Kesia asked Aias.

Squeezing her hand, he said lovingly, "One of us had to be brave."

After the adrenaline-pumping experience at the Tower of Terror, Kesia and her friends found themselves standing before the entrance to another enticing attraction - The Journey to the Centre of the Earth. The ambiance shifted dramatically; where the Tower had been eerie and foreboding, this entrance was a symphony of mystery and wonder. The dark cave-like tunnel beckoned, its very essence hinting at hidden realms and long-lost secrets deep within the Earth's core.

Kesia's heart thrummed with anticipation, the lingering thrill of their previous ride melding with the intrigue of this new adventure. The unique design caught her eye as they approached the subterranean vehicle—like something out of a Jules Verne novel. The intricate details, the dim ambient lighting, and the distant echoes gave her the sensation that they were about to embark on a real-life expedition to the world's core.

Kesia made a beeline for Aias, ensuring they were seated beside each other. Their shared experiences from earlier had created a subtle connection, and Kesia wanted to continue this journey together.

As the vehicle started moving, the surroundings began to change. What started as a gentle, mesmerizing exploration took a sudden twist. Kesia barely heard Luna's voice, filled with awe, comment on the enchanting scenery. "This is pretty," she whispered, her voice echoing the sentiments of everyone aboard.

But, just as they were settled into the beauty of it all, an abrupt and thunderous eruption broke the serenity. A volcano, alive and angry, sent magma flying. Without warning, their vehicle accelerated, rocketing them through the tunnel with such force it stole their breath away. Kesia's eyes widened, her grip on Aias's hand tightened, her heartbeat matching the roaring speed of their descent.

Time melted into a vortex of dazzling sights and intense sensations as they plunged through the depths, creating a surreal blend of reality and fantasy.And then, as suddenly as it began, it was over.

Emerging into the daylight, the rush of the experience still coursing through her veins, Kesia let out an exhilarated laugh. "Holy Hannah, that was awesome!" she exclaimed. Aias grinned in agreement, the thrill evident in his eyes. Luna and Lexi, still recovering from the sudden eruption and ensuing dash, shared facial reactions mixed with shock and elation.

Together, the group shared a moment of collective awe, their adventure through the earth's center solidifying yet another unforgettable memory in their DisneySea journey.

After their exhilarating trip to the center of the Earth, the group was buzzing with excitement, eager for the next thrill. Luna, her eyes dancing with joy, posed the question to Kesia, "What ride should we do next?"

Lexi, looking a shade paler than before, responded, a hint of queasiness evident in her voice, "You kids go ahead. I think I've had enough rollercoasters for one day. Text me when you're done, and I'll meet you for dinner."

Kesia watched as Aias leaned down, planting a playful kiss on Lexi's cheek, his tone light and teasing, "You are the best chaperone a two-year-old could have!"

Kesia smiled as Lexi attempted a weak smile, knowing that her unease momentarily clouded her usual joviality.

Armed with their Fastpasses, the remaining trio made their way to the Raging Spirits ride.

The anticipation built as the line inched forward. Kesia, curiosity piqued, turned to Luna. "Luna, what happens on this ride?"

With a twinkle in her eye, Luna shared, "The ride description said it's an outdoor rollercoaster that goes upside down with a 360° inversion."

"Lit!" Kesia exclaimed, excitement mounting.

As the ride commenced, Aias dropped an interesting tidbit. "Did you guys know that in Ayurvedic medicine, it's believed that if a person loves rollercoasters, the thrill produces chemicals in the body that can cure cancer?"

Luna, always curious, probed further, "What happens if they don't love rollercoasters?"

Aias replied, "Then the body won't produce the healing chemicals needed."

With a laugh, Kesia quipped, "I love roller coasters, so I should always be cancer-free!"

The high-energy ride left the trio on an adrenaline high. To commemorate the moment, Aias treated the girls to "fun-designed curry popcorn buckets." The three wore them proudly around their necks, munching away contentedly.

The sun began its descent, casting a warm glow as they strolled leisurely toward Ristorante di Canaletto. Situated overlooking the Venice canals, the restaurant offered a taste of Italy amidst the Disney magic. As they savored their pizza slices, the tranquil view transported them, making them feel as if they were truly in the heart of Venice.

Their day neared its conclusion, but not before one final ride. Much to Lexi's delight and relief, it was the gentle Sinbad's Storybook Voyage—a perfect blend of Pirates of the Caribbean and It's a Small World. As the melodies from the ride serenaded them, they were all reminded of the magic that DisneySea held: a perfect blend of thrill and comfort.

The night culminated in a magnificent fireworks display, painting the sky in hues of gold and violet, a fitting end to an unforgettable day.

Chapter 3

The subsequent day ushered them to the hallowed grounds of the Meiji Shrine, a cornerstone of spirituality in bustling Tokyo. As they approached its imposing torii gates, a profound sense of reverence permeated the air.

Observing the individuals ahead, they noted a ritualistic sequence: two bows, a pair of claps, a silent wish, followed by another bow. Embracing the spirit of cultural immersion, Aias's group mirrored the actions, feeling a deep connection to the traditions of the land.

Wandering further into the shrine's expanse, they were rendered speechless by the sheer majesty of the environment. A dense forest comprising a staggering 100,000 trees enveloped them in an embrace of tranquility. The mesmerizing inner garden beckoned with its serene beauty, while the enigmatic Kiyomasa's Well promised energies as rejuvenating as a mystical vortex. Their journey of discovery was further enriched by the twin Meiji Jingu Museums, their treasures painting tales of epochs gone by.

Near the shrine's main entrance, rows of sake barrels caught Kesia and Luna's eyes, making for a picturesque backdrop for their selfies. The wooden casks, draped in colorful fabric, were symbolic offerings to the deities.

The day held more surprises in store. Fortuitously, their visit coincided with the weekend, granting them the privilege to witness a heartwarming sight—a traditional wedding procession. The bride, groom, and their entourage, resplendent in their elegant kimonos, added a touch of timeless grace to the shrine's courtyard.

Concluding their shrine visit, they made a pit stop at the Shiseikan, a beacon for martial arts enthusiasts, where disciplines were honed and legacies were crafted.

The sun dawned on another day, and Tokyo's skyline awaited them from a different perspective. Boarding a helicopter, they soared over the sprawling cityscape, the world beneath reduced to a breathtaking patchwork of structures and nature. The highlight of the aerial tour was the iconic Mount Fuji, standing sentinel in the distance, its peak crowned by snow.

Kesia, ever curious, sought insights about the revered mountain from her "almighty oracle" - her smartphone, no doubt. She shared her newfound knowledge and informed the group, "Mount Fuji is not just a peak; it's steeped in legends. It's believed to be the sanctuary of the mountain gods and is revered as a portal to the afterlife."

As the helicopter continued its course, the tales of Mount Fuji, intertwined with the experiences of the past days, made the journey all the more memorable.

Peeking over Kesia's shoulder, Luna asked, "The mountain is a god? How is that possible?"

Kesia read more, "It says here that Mount Fuji is a highly personified entity. The mountain is believed to be a god that watches over the whole country, bringing prosperity but at times also calamity and destruction."

Staring at the mountain, mystified, Luna said, "Hmm, who knew that a mountain could be a god?"

The helicopter's trajectory offered them a bird's-eye view of the Tokyo Imperial Palace. This sprawling edifice, surrounded by moats and massive stone walls, stood as a testament to Japan's rich heritage and history. Built on the grounds of the former Edo Castle, the palace was an architectural marvel and a symbol of Japan's continuity, bridging the old with the new.

As they hovered over the palace, its lush gardens and courtyards, interspersed with historical buildings and modern residences, painted a harmonious blend of tradition and progress. Kesia, Luna, Aias, and Lexi gazed in awe at the sprawling grounds below, absorbing the sheer magnitude of the palace's significance. The juxtaposition of this serene oasis against the bustling metropolis of Tokyo created a mesmerizing contrast that resonated with the group.

The Tokyo Imperial Palace, with its storied past and its role as the residence of Japan's Imperial Family, added another layer of depth to their journey, a tangible link to the nation's cultural tapestry and legacy.

As they flew back to the helicopter pad, and as Luna looked at the city, she commented to the others, "Tokyo seems to go on forever."

Still researching her oracle, Kesia added, "It says that almost thirty-eight million people live here."

Lexi answered, "Wow, that is the same amount of people living in the state of California or the whole of Canada."

Luna laughed, "They must be crammed in there like sardines."

"I'll say, "Kesia nodded.

On the last day of touring Tokyo, the group visited a Buddhist Temple, San'en-zan Zōjō-ji.

As she walked through the main gate, Kesia informed the group, "As it was constructed in 1622, it is the oldest wooden building in Tokyo."

"Lit!" Luna said as she touched the structure, trying to feel the memories of that time.

"Hey, get this," Kesia said halfway through the gates. "It says that if someone passes through this gate, they can free themself from three passions—ton, shin, and chi."

"In English," Luna laughed.

"Greed, hatred, and foolishness."

Luna ran back and forth through the gate. "I have to ensure every cell in my body receives this boon."

Aias laughed at her silliness and asked, "What does boon mean?"

Lexi answered, "Boon implies a beneficial gift or something advantageous bestowed upon someone."

"Thanks for clarifying, Lex."

As they walked the rows of stone statues of children in the Sentai Kosodate Jizō—*Unborn Children Garden*, Lexi had an unexpected moment of sadness, and a tear escaped.

Luna asked Kesia, "Please, look this place up on your oracle and tell me what it represents."

Moments later, Kesia informed her, "It represents unborn, miscarried, aborted, and stillborn children."

"What is Jizō? And why red clothing?" Luna asked.

Kesia looked it up. "Jizō is the guardian of the unborn children. It says that any parent can choose a statue in the garden, decorate it with a small red hat and scarf, and leave toys in memory of their lost child. Occasionally, the baby's loved one will pile stones to symbolize Jizō and dress the stones near a statue in the graveyard, at a busy intersection, on the roadside, in a temple, or along hiking trails. It also says that a small gift is usually left for Jizō to ensure that the prayed-for baby's soul is brought directly to the afterlife."

Aias noticed Lexi's mood, went over to her, and hugged her. Then, as he moved away, he placed his hand on her tummy and said, "You must believe in miracles to receive one."

Lexi moved his hand away and answered, "I don't think God has that planned for me."

Aias smiled and said, "Lexi, you are looking at a two-year-old. Trust me when I say God has all kinds of miracles up his sleeve. You have to have faith."

Chapter 4

Before embarking on his journey from the United States, Aias had delved deep into the origins of Reiki. His studies led him to Dr. Mikao Usui, who was often hailed as the modern-day proponent of this ancient healing art. Intriguingly, it was said that in the late 1800s, Dr. Usui claimed to have unearthed the very hands-on healing techniques that Jesus once practiced.

While Aias struggled to find concrete evidence of Dr. Usui's academic credentials, he stumbled upon information suggesting that Dr. Usui had been associated with Doshisha University in Kyoto, Japan. Some sources even attributed a Doctor of Theology degree to him from the University of Chicago Divinity School and labeled him a Christian minister. What piqued Aias's curiosity the most was the striking parallel between his own question and Dr. Usui's quest: the enigma of how one could potentially heal with mere touch.

But beyond historical facts and stories, Aias was driven by a more profound question. He yearned to understand the mechanics behind such healing. Was it merely a matter of will, where one could think and manifest the healing? Or was there a tangible process, an unseen force, or specific rituals that, when harnessed correctly, resulted in these miraculous healing outcomes? The philosophical and practical implications of these questions fueled his intrigue even more.

On the fourth day in Tokyo, Aias's anticipation was palpable. Together with the girls, he embarked on a deeply personal journey to delve into the roots of Reiki by visiting the birthplace of Dr. Mikao Usui—the village of Yago, nestled on Japan's main island.

As they traveled, Kesia, always eager to learn more, dug into her "oracle"—her trusted smartphone—to gather more insights about Yago. To Aias's amusement, she found a connection between the name 'Yago' and a type of dragonfly nymph. More intriguing was the symbolic representation of the dragonfly: it stood for transformation and metamorphosis, a fitting symbol given Dr. Usui's own transformative journey with Reiki.

As the landscapes changed and they drew closer to Yago, the weight of their journey's significance settled upon them. For Aias, it wasn't just about retracing Dr. Usui's footsteps; it was about understanding the essence of Reiki and the power of transformation that lay within one's grasp. The symbolism of the dragonfly, with its life of change and adaptation, seemed to echo the very questions that stirred within him.

Aias's journey into the life and teachings of Dr. Mikao Usui deepened as he unraveled more about the man's early life. It became apparent that Dr. Usui hailed from a well-to-do family, affording him the privilege of a holistic education. This foundation was laid in a Buddhist monastery, where young Usui was not only immersed in spiritual teachings but also acquired skills in martial arts, swordsmanship, and the Japanese form of Chi Kung—known in the Western world as Qigong. These disciplines, which harmoniously blended physical prowess with spiritual depth, likely laid the groundwork for Dr. Usui's later explorations into healing and energy work.

Their journey then led them to the picturesque city of Kyoto, specifically to Doshisha University. As they walked its sprawling campus, Aias and the girls were captivated by its serene beauty—a harmonious blend of ancient architecture and modern facilities. The university had a distinctive reputation for being one of the pioneering Japanese institutions advocating Christian teachings, adding another layer to Dr. Usui's diverse educational tapestry.

The following dawn painted the sky in hues of gold as the group set out for Mount Kurama, a place shrouded in spirituality and legends. Opting for an immersive experience, they decided to stay overnight at the venerable Kurama Temple, which had stood since the 770s. With its rich history and spiritual aura, the temple offered them a sanctuary from the outside world.

Within the embrace of the temple's ancient walls, the group spent their time in introspection. They indulged in meditation sessions, seeking inner peace and clarity, and penned down mantras, encapsulating their thoughts, prayers, and hopes. This retreat wasn't just a physical journey for Aias and the girls but a spiritual odyssey, allowing them to connect with something much more significant than themselves.

Mount Kurama resonated with a spiritual ambiance that beckoned its visitors to connect deeply with its essence. Luna was particularly taken by the experience. The act of writing mantras was reminiscent of crafting chants for spells, and she reveled in this familiar yet novel exercise.

The group's walk towards the main hall was accompanied by a chorus of birds and the distant murmur of water. Breaking the serene silence, Aias posed a reflective question to the girls, "Do you all feel the spiritual power here?"

Lexi took a deep breath, her lungs filling with the crisp, cedar-scented air, and remarked, "Whether we sense the spiritual energy or not, the sheer natural beauty of this place is undeniably breathtaking."

Ever reliant on her 'almighty oracle,' Kesia fumbled with her phone, seeking an elusive connection in this sacred enclave.

Luna, in contrast, paused and grounded herself, standing still amidst the ancient trees. Eyes closed, she sought to tap into the unseen energies of the mountain. After a quiet moment, she opened her eyes, a touch of disappointment evident as she confessed, "I don't feel anything specific." But, ever hopeful, she added, "However, I would love to encounter the Tengu or any of the mountain spirits said to inhabit this region."

The journey through Mount Kurama was turning out to be as much about personal introspection and exploration as it was about the location's rich legends and spiritual heritage.

Amidst their discussions, the soft tread of a monk approached. Cloaked in saffron robes and exuding a serene aura, he chimed in, "Tengu, often termed as 'Heavenly Dog' or 'Heavenly Sentinel,' are enigmatic entities, representing the mountain's mystic force. They're painted with distinct long noses and a fiery countenance in our folklore."

Having finally secured a connection to her digital oracle, Kesia inquired, "I've come across tales that they're known to abduct monks. Is there any truth to that?"

With a nod, the monk responded, "The lore is rife with tales of Tengu's complex relationship with Buddhism. They've been depicted as creating illusions of the Buddha to mislead the devout and, indeed, spiriting away monks to forsaken lands. Stories also tell of their penchant for possessing women, aiming to tempt those of devout disposition." He paused, adding, "Some even attribute temple thefts to them, and it's believed that those who worship them might be granted malevolent powers."

Luna's gaze darted around, her curiosity tinged with apprehension, "Given their reputation, should we be concerned about them lurking within your temple's bounds?"

The monk's lips curled into a mysterious smile, "Though they are known to masquerade as monks or nuns, it's said their true essence mirrors that of a kite."

Misunderstanding, Luna's eyes shot skyward, "A kite, like the one in the sky?"

Aias, sensing an opportunity for playful teasing, quipped, "Why are you gazing upwards? A Tengu might very well be standing right before us."

Luna's eyes widened, realizing Aias's jest implied the monk might be the Tengu in disguise. Not wanting to take any chances, she darted past the monk, making a beeline for the temple's main hall, maneuvering between the grand tiger statues guarding its entrance.

The monk's laughter, gentle and good-natured, echoed in the backdrop as Kesia, Aias, and Lexi, chuckling at the playful scare, trailed behind Luna into the hall.

Chapter 5

The morning dawned clear and bright, the sun casting dappled patterns of light and shadow across the temple grounds. Reconvening at the main hall, the group prepared to descend the mountain, their starting point marked by the Kongoshō—a distinctive star symbol crafted from stones on the ground.

The familiar monk from the day before approached them, drawing their attention to the star. "This Sonten trinity here represents both the trinity and the Lotus Sutra. The six points, radiating outward, symbolize the six mediums through which we perceive and engage with our surroundings—eyes, ears, nose, mouth, body, and heart."

Her brow furrowed in confusion, Luna leaned towards Kesia and whispered, "Do you see six sides?"

Peering down at the main triangle, Kesia replied, "No."

As if reading their minds, the monk elucidated, "Standing on the triangular stone at the heart of the innermost star and facing the main hall is believed to channel a surge of energy."

Grasping the monk's explanation, Luna mused aloud to Aias, "Ah, he's referring to the six triangles formed outside the pebbled circumference."

Gazing down, Aias recognized the shape—a Star of David, crafted intricately from cement and pebbles.

As Luna stepped onto the triangle, she felt a subtle pulse, an energy coursing through her. "Kesia, give this a shot!" she exclaimed, intrigued by the sensation.

Watching with a gentle smile, the monk remarked, "By connecting with this energy, you come to recognize the potent power residing within you."

Aias, his eyes twinkling, quipped, "See, Luna, magic isn't just about spells. You, yourself, are magical."

Beaming at the sentiment, Luna stepped off the stone and began navigating the sandō path— a trail weaving between the temple and Kibune Village. Along the route, they stumbled upon the Maō-den, a spiritual site venerating Maōson, a deity believed to have descended from Venus nearly six million years ago.

As they continued, the uniquely twisted wisteria trees caught their eye, their forms and colors a testament to nature's artistry.

Aias gazed at the trees, saying, "These trees would've enchanted my mom."

Seizing the moment, Lexi suggested, "Pose by that tree. I'll snap a picture and send it her way."

Grinning widely, Aias obliged, allowing the beautiful backdrop to encapsulate the moment.

Their journey took an exciting turn when a fellow traveler shared a tale of a Chinese monk named Ganchō. He spoke of a dream that directed Ganchō northward, towards a realm pulsing with spiritual energy, the domain of the Tengu and other mountain spirits.

Engrossed in his tale, the group paused, the ancient stories of the mountain weaving seamlessly with their own experiences, creating a tapestry of old legends and new memories.

The group stood transfixed, every word painting a vivid tableau of Ganchō's perilous quest. The man's voice, filled with passion, recounted Ganchō's trials and tribulations.

"Tragically, Ganchō's search for power led him astray," the man narrated. "Yet, hope appeared in the most unexpected form. The god Kibune Myōjin graced his dreams, directing him to gaze eastwards towards the heavens. There, he beheld a divine sight—a resplendent white horse, its saddle vacant, beckoning him. Though mounting the creature proved elusive, Ganchō's determination saw him trail the celestial guide to this very part of the mountain."

The tale's landscape shifted, casting a shadow of foreboding as the man continued, "As dusk settled and Ganchō erected his camp, his solitude was shattered by a menacing presence. A female oni, a formidable demon revered as the 'Bringer of Doom,' emerged, her intent malevolent—she sought to consume the monk."

The listeners could almost hear the rustle of leaves, the monk's desperate breaths, and the oni's menacing approach.

"The battle of wills that ensued saw Ganchō narrowly escape her clutches. Desperate and fearing for his life, he sought refuge within a hollow tree trunk. In his dire state, prayers for deliverance poured forth, echoing with fervor in the silent night. It was then that salvation manifested. The Guardian of the North, Bishamonten, descended, vanquishing the demon and sparing Ganchō's life."

The atmosphere was thick with reverence, the group's attention unwavering.

"In gratitude and inspired by his otherworldly encounter, Ganchō erected a humble hermitage at the very spot. Leaving behind worldly distractions, he embraced the life of a hermit. His days were dedicated to meditation, seeking enlightenment, and venerating the Heavenly King who had, against all odds, granted him a second chance."

As the man's story concluded, the air seemed to hum with the weight of ancient tales and powerful deities, a reminder of the mountain's rich spiritual tapestry.

After finishing his tale, the man paused to gaze into the distance. The trees whispered secrets as a gentle wind rustled their leaves, and the atmosphere around them was thick with the weight of the ages.

Turning to Aias and the group, the man said, "You see, young travelers, a profound lesson is woven into Ganchō's journey. It speaks of the relentless pursuit of power and the dangers it can bring. Power alone, without guidance, can lead one astray, into the very jaws of peril."

He leaned in closer, his voice soft yet compelling, "But the story also tells of hope, of redemption, and the miracles that faith can bring. Even in his darkest hour, trapped and seemingly at the mercy of a powerful foe, Ganchō's prayers and unwavering faith called forth a savior. It is a testament to the strength that lies in humility, seeking help when overwhelmed, and the belief that even in our direst moments, we are never truly alone."

The man's eyes twinkled with wisdom as he concluded, "In essence, young ones, the tale teaches us that true power does not lie in external forces or worldly pursuits, but within— within our faith, our humility, and our ability to recognize and lean on the greater forces that watch over us."

The group, enveloped in reflective silence, pondered upon the depth of the message, understanding that some stories carry wisdom far beyond their tales.

Nodding appreciatively, Aias responded, "That was truly a fascinating story. Thank you for sharing it." Pausing briefly, he then inquired, "By the way, do you know the way to Dr. Usui's meditation site?"

The man momentarily considered the question, then pointed down the mountain. "Indeed, you'll want to follow the sacred path known as Kinone-michi. Pursue that route, and it will lead you to Osugi-gongen, where Dr. Usui often meditated."

"Much appreciated," Aias said with a grateful smile. Turning to the girls, he motioned in the direction the man had pointed. "Alright, let's head this way."

The group, invigorated by the tales and the promise of discovering more about Dr. Usui's legacy, embarked on the next leg of their journey toward Osugi-gongen with a renewed sense of purpose.

The meditation site radiated a tangible energy. The knotted roots sprawled out in every direction, their twists and turns a physical testament to the swirling energy they said was the vortex's doing. The atmosphere was thick with a meditative silence, broken only by the soft, rhythmic breathing of those engrossed in their inner worlds.

As Aias took his place among them, he felt the cool texture of a small stone beneath his hand. Instinctively, he picked it up, allowing its weight to settle in his palm. As he closed his eyes, his thoughts centered on Dr. Usui, seeking a deeper connection to the legacy and wisdom the revered healer had left behind.

Almost immediately, a powerful surge of energy emanated from the stone, causing his heart rate to quicken and his senses to heighten. A magnetic pull beckoned him inward, deeper into the recesses of his consciousness.

When Aias finally opened his eyes, the disorientation was immediate. The familiar paths, sculpted by countless pilgrims over the years, were replaced by untamed wilderness. The murmurs and soft movements of the Usui followers were conspicuously absent, replaced by nature's raw symphony. The girls—Kesia, Luna, Lexi—all traces of their presence had vanished.

A heavy realization settled over him: he was utterly and profoundly alone.

Panic began to bubble within him, but then he took a deep breath, trying to harness the teachings and inner strength he had been nurturing on this pilgrimage. The stone had transported him somewhere—or somewhen—

else, and he needed to find out why and, more importantly, how to return.

Chapter 6

*A*ias scrambled to his feet, his eyes darting around, searching for the girls. His steps led him to a babbling creek, and as he bent down to quench his thirst, a startling reflection met his gaze. Instead of his familiar visage, the water mirrored back the face of a middle-aged Japanese man standing about five feet tall.

Bewildered, he stammered, "What the Billi—Heck?" The Hindi exclamation slipped out in his confusion and disbelief. This new reality was proving to be even more mysterious than he could have ever imagined.

As Aias made his way back to his initial meditation spot, his eyes were drawn to the multitude of small pebbles surrounding him. As he settled down, a compulsion took over. He started counting the pebbles beside him—one, two, three... ten in total. Glancing over, he noticed another set slightly apart—eleven of them—combined, there were twenty-one.

The significance of that number triggered a rush of memories, and in an instant, a profound realization dawned upon him. He hadn't merely traveled back in time; he had become Dr. Mikao Usui.

The weight of this newfound identity was immense. Memories not originally his, flooded in, vivid and clear. Aias, now known as Dr. Usui, remembered growing up in a bustling household with his parents, two brothers, Kuniji and Sanya, and a sister named Tsuru. The tender moments with his wife, Suzuki Sadako, came to him, and the joyous memories of his two children, Fuji and Toshiko, played out like a cherished film reel.

The line between Aias's memories and those of Dr. Usui blurred, melding two lifetimes into one intertwined existence. The realization of his unique ability to traverse time and embody another's life was both awe-inspiring and overwhelming. The journey ahead promised to be an exploration of self, legacy, and the bounds of what was considered possible.

With the melding of memories and experiences, Aias could vividly recall the recent tumultuous events of Mikao's life. The sting of illness, the debilitating fever brought on by an epidemic, and the haunting brush with death. That near-death experience wasn't just a fleeting moment for Mikao; it was a profound juncture that shook the very foundation of his beliefs and life's trajectory.

In that fragile state, between life and the beckoning abyss, Mikao had wrestled with existential questions. The transient nature of life, the elusive essence of true healing, and the narratives of great healers from the past weighed heavily on his mind. Chief among these was the story of Jesus Christ, a figure renowned for his miraculous healing abilities. How did Jesus heal? Was it pure divinity, a hidden technique, or perhaps a universal energy that anyone could tap into?

This contemplation was not merely intellectual for Mikao—it was deeply personal. He felt a burgeoning need, an insatiable quest, to uncover the secrets of such profound healing. Could he, too, harness such a power? Could he bring solace and healing to the ailing, much like the biblical savior?

Caught in this confluence of past and present, Aias struggled to discern where his own thoughts began and Mikao's ended. *Is this what it's like to truly walk a mile in someone else's shoes?* He pondered. The vivid sensations, from the chill of the mountain air to the intricacies of the fabric draped around him, felt both foreign and intimate.

He wondered, *Do I still have control? Or am I just a vessel for Mikao's spirit now?* The ambiance of Mount Kurama was overwhelmingly intense. Every rustle of the leaves seemed to whisper secrets of ages past, and Aias felt the urge to comprehend every word.

The weight of Mikao's attire, every fold and seam, made him ponder the societal expectations and duties that Mikao might have borne. *How different were his responsibilities from mine? And yet, how similar might our internal struggles be?*

Feeling Mikao's heartbeat synchronizing with his own, Aias reflected on the essence of life and existence. *We're separated by centuries, yet our hearts beat in unison. Is this the shared human experience across time?*

With every moment he spent melded with Mikao's consciousness, Aias felt a growing reverence for the man whose life he was reliving. *What lessons, I wonder, is Mikao's journey meant to impart to me?* The realization dawned that this wasn't just about understanding Mikao's quest for spiritual healing, but perhaps it was also a profound exploration of Aias's soul.

Retracing the steps that led Mikao to this sacred spot, Aias—through Mikao's senses—relived each moment. Every thought, every decision, every doubt, and every revelation played out, allowing Aias an unprecedented insight into the life and journey of Dr. Mikao Usui. The tapestry of memories and emotions vividly depicted a man's pursuit of a higher calling and the universal quest for healing and understanding.

The rich tapestry of the past unfurled before Aias, immersing him in an ancient Zen Buddhist monastery. The atmosphere was charged with scholarly devotion. Aias could see monks and scribes, deeply engrossed in their studies, reading from massive tomes, each page filled with Sanskrit writings that held secrets of the past.

As Aias delved into the scriptures with Mikao's eyes, a flurry of introspective thoughts enveloped him. *It's strange,* he mused, *how my past choices—as in studying in India—have led me to this exact moment. Every decision I've made has brought me closer to understanding Mikao's quest.*

The Sanskrit characters, once just elegant squiggles to many, revealed profound truths to him. He was reminded of the countless hours he had spent in classrooms and libraries grappling with the complexities of this ancient language. *All that effort wasn't in vain,* he realized. *It was preparing me for this very moment.*

As the tales of Jesus and his miraculous healing abilities unfolded before him, Aias felt a pang of familiarity. *Across cultures and times,* he reflected, *we all seek some form of healing, whether physical, emotional, or spiritual. Mikao's quest isn't so different from my own journey of seeking understanding and purpose.*

Aias began to see parallels between his life and Mikao's. While the contexts were different, the essence of their quests had striking similarities. *Both of us,* he thought, *are driven by an insatiable hunger for knowledge, a desire to heal, and to connect with something greater than ourselves.*

Each revelation in the scripture felt like a piece of a puzzle fitting into place, not just for Mikao but for Aias as well. *Is this serendipity? Or is it destiny?* he wondered, feeling an overwhelming sense of interconnectedness with the universe and every soul within it.

With each page he turned, Aias felt the thrill of discovery and the weight of anticipation. Amidst the ancient sutras, he found symbols, formulas, and intricate writings that seemed to provide the much sought-after answers. The key to healing was unveiled: the harnessing and channeling of the universal life-force energy. As he traced the diagrams with his fingers, he unraveled the specific hand positions that were integral to the process.

It's like having a jigsaw puzzle but missing that one crucial piece, Aias thought. Or being handed an intricate device, yet clueless on how to operate it. Even if I stumble upon the instructions, there's always that essential spark missing. It's not just about grasping the concept but finding how to ignite and channel that profound, innate universal energy.

The vision faded, but Aias's newfound knowledge, intertwined with Mikao's experiences, resonated deeply within him. More than ever, he was determined to delve deeper into this profound art of healing. The journey had only just begun, and Aias was eager to unlock the remaining secrets that would bring him closer to truly understanding and harnessing this divine energy.

Chapter 7

The tapestry of memories transitioned again, and Aias felt himself transported to another, more tranquil chamber within the monastery. The room was filled with the soft glow of candlelight, and a fragrant blend of incense permeated the air. He felt Mikao's reverence and anticipation as he sought guidance from the esteemed Abbott.

Listening intently, Aias heard the Abbott's words, rich with wisdom, "You must journey to the sacred Mount Kurama, located outside Kyoto in the Kuriyama district. It stands majestically in the heart of Hokkaido. Commit yourself to a twenty-one-day fast, meditating and seeking the answers that elude you."

The mention of 'Kuriyama' elicited a feeling of warmth in Aias, reminiscent of Mikao's appreciation for the literal translation of the name: 'Chestnut Mountain.'

Suddenly, the monastery's ambiance faded, and Aias was enveloped in the cold, crisp air of Mount Kurama. No longer burdened by the ascent, his consciousness jumped right to the heart of Mikao's spiritual quest. Wrapped in warm robes, Mikao would begin his day at the break of dawn, signaling the passage of each day with the symbolic act of tossing a pebble.

Today marked the twelfth day, as evidenced by the twelfth stone that left Mikao's hand to join the others on the ground. A pang of disappointment coursed through Aias, mirroring Mikao's feelings. The elusive knowledge, the key to harnessing and activating the healing energy, still remained just out of reach. But hope wasn't lost; nine days remained. Each sunrise brought with it another chance for revelation and enlightenment. Determined, Aias—imbued with Mikao's spirit—braced himself for the challenges and insights that the coming days would bring.

Besides tending to his basic needs, foraging for roots, and sipping on fresh mountain water, the majority of Mikao's time was consumed by deep meditation.

As dawn broke on the 21st day, Aias, living through Mikao's experiences, felt the weight of disappointment. Despite their diligent efforts, the much-desired insight remained elusive. Aias could almost feel the words of Mikao's prayer resonate within him, a deep yearning evident in each word. *Please, show me the light. Guide me to understand the 'keys to healing' I've uncovered in the scriptures.* With a heavy heart, he tossed the final stone, marking the culmination of the three-week-long quest.

Aias sat very still all day as Mikao continued to pray and meditate. That evening, Aias felt how disheartened Mikao was for not accomplishing his quest. As Mikao stood up to leave, Aias noticed, as Mikao did, a tiny beam of light way off in the horizon that was moving towards them. As it came closer, it became bigger and bigger. Aias could feel the fear that Mikao was experiencing. The eerie luminescence light was nearly frightening him to death. Luckily, Mikao had spent years on this quest and was not about to run away.

As Mikao did, Aias braced himself as the light struck them in the middle of Mikao's forehead and knocked them out cold.

In a dream state, Aias was experiencing everything Mikao was, and at this moment, they were experiencing a rainbow of colors. Aias was surprised that drawn in the sky were some Sanskrit symbols he had not seen before. Fortunately, their use and meanings were also provided. Aias watched as Dr. Usui received all the keys to healing at once in this attunement.

Aias was also granted the celestial attunement, being that he was in Mikao's body.

During his stay in India, Aias had learned that attunement was the ability to sense others kinesthetically and emotionally. It was the ability to metaphorically be in their skin and experience what they were. Aias knew that an attunement meant going beyond empathy to create a two-person experience. An attunement is an unbroken connection that provides a shared effect, also called an echoing response.

Aias honored Mikao's vow never to forget the sacred symbols and never to allow them to be lost.

As Mikao excitedly went down the mountain back to Kyoto and the monastery, Aias could feel his joy of having this newly found knowledge. But to Aias's horror, Mikao tripped and fell down the mountain. Dazed, Mikao sat up and noticed blood coming from his foot. Aias could feel the pain in Mikao's toe. As Mikao grabbed his toe and held on to it, the pain subsided to Aias's amazement. Aias was as shocked as Mikao when he removed his hand. His toe was intact, with no cut or blood.

Mystified at the heat penetrating from his hands, Aias watched as Mikao opened his palms and stared at them.

Aias intuitively knew that he had just witnessed Mikao's first miracle. *Heat is produced when the sacred energy surges.*

Gloriously, Mikao got up and continued to descend the mountain.

At the bottom of the mountain was the most delicious aroma of onions, meat, and other wonderous cooked foods that instantly had Mikao salivating. Aias was now as hungry as Mikao and was delighted that Mikao went inside the Inn and ordered an entire meal from the owner.

As the innkeeper's daughter delivered Mikao's food, Aias noticed, just as Mikao had, that she was suffering terribly from an abscessed tooth.

Mikao's hands became hot just thinking about the girl's pain. Insisting that she sit, Mikao stood up and placed the items she held in her hands on his table. Without thinking, Mikao put his hands on either side of her jaw, barely touching her. Aias felt his hands go even hotter. He could also feel a slight tingling sensation as the universal life force energy flowed out of Mikao's hands.

Within moments, the girl grabbed Mikao's hands and said, "How did you do that? The pain, it's gone."

"I have done nothing. The healing power of the celestial world has healed you, not I."

Aias knew that Mikao had just performed his second miracle *when the life force energy flowed out of Mikao's hands.*

As Mikao continued his journey back to the monastery, Aias noticed that Mikao wasn't sick from breaking his fast with a full meal. From his time living in India, Aias had done a fast and knew that one could never introduce a full meal back into the body for many days. Instead, he knew that you must start eating again with broth and work your way back to solid foods. Thus, Aias experienced Mikao's third miracle *of having a full meal without complications.*

As Mikao entered the monastery, he was told that the Abbott was bedridden due to arthritis.

Aias could feel the panic in Mikao as he ran to his friend's bed-chamber. Upon entering, even Aias was concerned with the Abbott's welfare, for he looked like he was on death's bed. So Aias wasn't surprised when Mikao casually touched the area of pain while sharing his experiences with the Abbott.

Aias quickly noticed that the Abbott's pain expressed on his face had disappeared, and he excitedly sat up, saying, "Mikao, you did it. You found how to activate the healing power. What will you do now?"

As it was part of the Japanese culture to look after people with deformities, missing limbs, and diseases, and after much meditation and consulting with the Abbott, Dr. Usui decided that he would use his new knowledge of healing, that he called Reiki, on the poor, diseased, and crippled.

Mikao went forth happily with this new purpose in mind.

Like fast-forwarding a movie, Aias watched the next seven years of Mikao's life as he worked with these people in the slums, giving them healing.

One day, to Aias's surprise, Mikao noticed that many of the people he had healed returned to their lives as beggars, and Aias was just as interested in answer to the question Mikao asked the beggars, "Why do you continue this life when you are healed?"

Many people replied with the same answer that it was a much easier life with no responsibilities to go on begging than to start over.

Aias could consciously understand, see, and feel everything that Mikao was, and at this moment, Aias could feel Mikao's disappointment and feelings of failure.

Soon after, Mikao concluded that even though he had healed the sick, he had not taught them any responsibility. So, he pledged that an equal energy exchange must be provided, whether monetary or other, from that day forward.

Time fast-forwarded again as Aias followed Mikao's pilgrimage through Japan, lecturing on the 'Five Principles of Reiki.'

Just for Today,
I will not worry,
I shall do my work honestly,
I shall accept my many blessings,
I shall deal with anger appropriately,
I shall show love and respect for everyone and everything.

Just before Aias's consciousness teleported him back through time to the present moment,

Aias's sci-scan past life mediation quickly showed him the rest of Mikao's life, right up until Mikao's death in 1926. His first Reiki clinic, his school in Tokyo—where he trained approximately sixteen Reiki Masters—and even where his ashes were buried in his family's gravesite in a cemetery at the Saihoji Temple in the Suginami district of Tokyo.

Chapter 8

Opening his eyes, Aias was happy to see that the girls were exactly where they were sitting when he had teleported back through time.

Aias waited patiently for the girls to finish their mediation.

Lexi was the first to open her eyes.

Aias smiled at her and whispered, "I have so much to share."

Hearing Aias's voice, Kesia and Luna opened their eyes.

Luna said, "Well, don't keep it a secret."

Some of Dr. Usui's followers hushed the small group, so they got up and walked down the mountain. During the journey down the mountain, Aias said, "You won't believe what happened in my meditation."

Lexi smiled at his excitement.

And Luna said, "Well, don't keep us waiting."

"I was Dr. Usui."

Confused, Luna asked, "What does that mean?"

"It means that I was inside of Mikao's consciousness. I experienced whatever he did. I witnessed his memories and life right up until he died."

"How did he die?" Luna asked.

"He died of a fatal stroke."

Not knowing what else to say, Luna uttered, "Oh."

"Don't you all want to know how he healed?" Aias asked excitedly.

Keisa wrapped her arm through his and said lovingly, "Yes."

Aias beamed from the sexy smile Kesia had on her face and said, "Let's rest here, and I can tell you all about it."

Lexi was happy to take the break because her feet were hurting.

Noticing, Aias sat down in front of Lexi and gently picked up a foot. Then, taking off her shoe, he lightly placed each hand on either side of her foot. "The Reiki energy comes from the cosmos. It is a life force energy with a high frequency that can shift and alter many forms of energy, such as thermal, nuclear, chemical, electromagnetic, sonic, gravitational, kinetic, and ionization."

"Isn't that all the types of energy?" Luna asked, trying to remember what she had learned in high school.

Aias answered, "I haven't decided yet if it has potential energy. Wait, no, it doesn't. So, no, that is not all types of energy."

"Fine, but that doesn't tell us how he healed," Luna said, a bit cocky.

Aias looked at Luna as he switched to Lexi's other foot. He closed his eyes and said, "First, you must go inside your mind. You must have the ability to quiet your mind and focus on your intention. Next, you set your intent. One must take a deep breath and imagine that for an instant, they are going up into the cosmos through their crown chakra at the top of their head and bringing back with them the Reiki life force energy."

Aias watched as Luna closed her eyes. He knew she was practicing what he was saying. "I sense this energy surge coming back down through my head and into my body, then out through my hands."

Luna peeked an eye open and asked, "Through the center of your palms?"

"Yes," Aias answered.

"It tingles," Luna said as she placed her palms on her heart.

Aias watched as Kesia closed her eyes and said, "It is also kind of warm."

"Yes. I thought so, too," Aias said excitedly.

"Aias, I think that is enough," Lexi said, panicky.

"What? Oh, sorry." He removed his hands.

Lexi leaned down and lightly massaged her foot. "It felt great, up until you got excited. Then the heat was way too much."

"Noted," Aias said, lightly flicked his fingers to the ground to release the excess energy, then rested his arms on his legs.

Luna explained her experience to the group, "When I started, I closed my eyes and saw darkness, but soon after, my eyes became light, and I knew that the Reiki energy had done its magic."

"Fascinating," Aias said.

Kesia asked, "How do you think the Reiki energy works? I mean scientifically."

"Good question," Aias said, not knowing the answer.

Kesia checked her oracle. "Here is what I found on the internet."

Luna laughed, "Of course you found a signal up here."

"Lucky we are almost at the bottom," Kesia said smugly, then told the group what she found. "The scientific understanding of how Reiki works is limited, as current scientific models do not fully explain the mechanisms behind its effects. However, there are a few theories and considerations. Here they are. The Placebo Effect: Some skeptics suggest that any perceived benefits from Reiki are due to the placebo effect. The belief and expectation of the patient can influence their perception of pain and relief, leading to actual physiological changes.

Quantum Physics: Some proponents of Reiki draw parallels with concepts from quantum physics, suggesting that the interconnectedness of all things at the quantum level can account for the effects of distance healing and other Reiki practices. However, this is a speculative theory without concrete evidence linking Reiki to quantum mechanics.

Biofield Energy: The idea is that the body has an "energy field" or "biofield" around it, which energy healers can influence or balance. While some devices claim to measure this field, the empirical evidence still needs to be more conclusive.

Biological Mechanisms: Stress reduction is one of the common claims associated with Reiki. The relaxation response from Reiki treatment might reduce stress, leading to various physiological benefits like reduced heart rate, lower blood pressure, and increased immune function. The body's relaxation response can stimulate healing and well-being.

Electromagnetic Fields: Everything that has electricity also produces a magnetic field, including our bodies, specifically our heart and brain. Some suggest that Reiki practitioners manipulate or interact with their patient's electromagnetic fields.

Social and Emotional Factors: The act of touch, being listened to, or being cared for can all produce therapeutic effects in and of themselves. This interpersonal interaction might play a role in the reported benefits of Reiki.

Aias thought about what she read, "All I know is that when I touch a person, their physical, mental, emotional, and even spiritual issues disappear."

"What is that old saying? If it ain't broken, don't fix it. If Reiki works, who cares why," Luna responded.

Aias nodded but knew that there was more to Reiki than a placebo effect. His best guess would be a combination of the other theories.

The group finished the day by eating at a restaurant at the bottom of the mountain.

"Do you think this is the same place where Dr. Usui broke his fast?" Luna asked as she took a bite of her food.

"Wouldn't that be coincidental," Kesia said, smiling.

"Hey, Aias, where are we going next," Lexi asked just before she took a bite.

Aias smiled and said, "Ah, where we are going next is one of the most famous places that some of the oldest miracles were written about."

Luna looked at him inquisitively and asked, "Where is that?"

"Egypt."

Chapter 9

Aias was fascinated to learn that a student's question about how Jesus could heal was what sparked Dr. Usui's journey into hands-on healing. Inspired, Aias decided his next course of action would be to take a pilgrimage to the most famous person in history who could perform miracles, Jesus Christ.

After arriving in Cairo, Egypt, the group chose to see the historical sights, and of course, the mystical pyramids were one of them.

A few days after they arrived, while sitting at a café, Luna asked Aias, "Why are we starting in Egypt? I thought Jesus was born in Bethlehem,"

"In my research on his life, I discovered that Mary and Joseph fled to Egypt with Jesus to escape King Herod's order to assassinate all children under two years old, and they didn't return to Israel for almost ten years. I want to see what healing gifts Jesus may have acquired during his time in Egypt."

"Where did you hear that Jesus could heal before he was baptized?" Lexi asked.

Kesia and Luna were listening to their conversation.

Aias answered, "Just as Moses brought the Torah and Jesus the Bible, Muhammad brought the last book, the Quran. The Quran mentions Jesus as a miracle-working boy who could create birds from clay and raise the dead to life."

Kesia consulted with her oracle, "Here is what it says on the internet—Then will Allah say: "O Jesus the son of Mary! Recount My favor to thee and thy mother. Behold! I strengthened thee with the holy spirit so that thou didst speak to the people in childhood and maturity. Behold! I taught thee the Book and Wisdom, the Law and the Gospel, behold! Thou makest out of clay, as it were, the figure of a bird, by My leave, and thou breathest into it and it becometh a bird by My leave, and thou healest those born blind, and the lepers, by My leave. And behold! Thou bringest forth the dead by My leave. And behold! I did restrain the Children of Israel from (violence to) thee when thou didst show them the clear Signs, and the unbelievers among them said: 'This is nothing but evident magic.' Qur'an, Surah 005.110."

"Wow, I didn't know that Jesus is talked about in anything other than the Bible," Lexi said to the group. "Hey, isn't the Quran the Islamic sacred scripture?"

Kesia had already researched it. "It says here that the Quran is filled with messages from Allah."

"Who is Allah?" Luna asked.

"Allah is the common Arabic word for God," Kesia said.

Lexi added, "I remember Edward telling me that the Islamic Holy Books are the records that most Muslims believe were dictated by Allah to various prophets."

"Isn't the Bible also many books written by different authors?" Kesia asked innocently.

Lexi answered, "Yes. The Bible is made up of many scriptures written by many different authors."

"I heard the Bible has many different versions, but I didn't know it had many different authors," Luna remarked.

Kesia looked at her oracle and read, "It says that the Bible is made up of two main Testaments, the old and the new."

"What is the difference? Luna asked.

Kesia answered, "The Old Testament is before Christ was born and is considered the Hebrew Bible or Tanakh, and the New Testament documents the life and teachings of Jesus while he was alive."

"Why would that matter? "Luna asked, a bit confused.

Kesia consulted her oracle. "Hmm. Let me look. It says here that some Christians only believe in the twenty-seven books found in the

New Testament and nothing from the Old Testament."

Lexi exclaimed, "What! I'm Christian, I believe in God, and I grew up with both."

"What religion did you grow up with, Lexi?" Kesia asked.

"Catholic."

"I found a reference stating that some people believe Catholics aren't considered true Christians because they accept the stories in the Old Testament, which other Christians find implausible. And that a Catholic Bible not only has both the Old and New Testament, that it also holds nine books written that have nothing to do with God or Jesus."

Curious, Luna asked, "What are these nine stories about then?"

"It says here that they only tell about the times of old," Kesia answered.

"So, you are telling me that because Jesus wasn't alive and talked about in the Old Testament, Christians don't believe anything written?" Luna exclaimed. "But don't all these stories originate from the same place?"

Kesia quickly researched, "No. Over 1,000 years, the Old Testament had thirty-three authors who helped write the thirty-nine books. Pretty much, it tells one story—how God created the world, grew a nation, and began to use it to bless the world."

"But where did these stories come from?" Luna asked again.

"You're not going to believe this, but from monumental inscriptions that were preserved on rock walls, stone slabs, clay, and wooden tablets, broken pieces of pottery, papyrus manuscripts, scrolls, and parchment made from tanned animal hides."

"What! Really?" Luna exclaimed. "What about the New Testament? Where did those stories come from?"

"Mostly from one man, and get this, he wasn't even born when Christ was alive," Kesia read.

"Who was that?"

"Paul," Lexi said. "And I find him a bit sexist."

"What does that mean," Luna asked her.

"I find that he didn't speak about women very highly," Lexi said honestly.

Kesia said, "Get this, they found some Dead Sea Scrolls."

"What are those," Luna inquired.

"Found in an Israeli desert, they are ancient fragments of biblical texts dating back almost two thousand years ago."

She showed the group a picture of many men using tweezers and magnifying glasses, trying to unroll the ancient parchment paper without it falling apart into a million pieces.

Aias finally spoke up, "The point is, Dr. Usui studied many of these scripts, Greek, Hebrew,

Aramaic, and Sanskrit scriptures, to find out how Jesus could perform his miracles."

"Right, the reason we are here in Egypt," Luna said, trying to stay focused on his quest.

Chapter 10

The next day, the group headed down to the Nile River. There, they sat and listened in on stories about the miracles performed in Egypt.

The person telling the story was a young female Egyptian historian. Covered from wrist to ankle, she was modestly dressed, including a hijab headscarf. Aias could tell that her hair was jet black, and her eyes reminded him of his mother's when she was acting as Cleopatra in one of her films.

In a thick Arabic accent, she said in English, "The story that many of you have heard in the book of Exodus is about a Jewish man born in Egypt to Hebrew parents, who set him afloat on the Nile in a reed basket to save him from an order calling for the death of all newborn Hebrew males."

Aias was fascinated to find that even though he was here in Egypt to research the miracles that Jesus performed, there were others before Jesus.

"In the Jewish religion, Moses is revered as the greatest prophet and teacher. Not only did Moses part the sea and turn the water red, but he was also gifted the knowledge of the Ten Commandments. The first being, thou shalt not have any gods before me. The second one is, thou shalt not take the name of the Lord thy God in vain. Then, the rest, remember to keep the Sabbath day holy. Honor thy father and mother. Thou shalt not kill. Thou shalt not commit adultery. Thou shalt not steal. Thou shalt not bear false witness against thy neighbor. Thou shalt not covet thy neighbor's wife. Thou shalt not covet thy neighbor's goods."

Lexi whispered to the other three, "Could you imagine what kind of world we would be living in if people just followed these ten simple rules."

Kesia nodded as she listened to the lady say, "There is a belief that Moses' staff was originally crafted by Adam from the Tree of Knowledge in the Garden of Eden and used as a shepherd's rod when he and Eve left. That all he had to do was lift his staff toward Heaven whenever the Lord commanded, and then the Lord's Holy Miracles would be accomplished."

Aias whispered to the girls, "So Moses didn't possess any power on his own. All his miracles were achieved by using the staff."

Kesia added, "In the Tarot Deck, the suit of wands represents communication. The staff, rod, or wand represents words. The words you use to hold all the power or magic."

Lexi looked at her, "Interesting. It's the words spoken that hold all the power."

"Spoken, written, seen, felt, and even thought holds power," Kesia clarified.

"Well, I know the words spoken are the most important part of any spell that I chant," Luna stated.

The group listened to the historian say, "The Pharaoh's magicians could reproduce many of the miracles that Moses could perform. As in the story of when Aaron, Moses' brother, threw the staff down, it turned into a serpent. The Pharaoh's magicians could do the same with their scepters."

"Interesting," Aias said.

Lexi was shocked at what the historian said next, "One of the most well-known Pharaohs is Tutankhamun, also known as King Tut. There is a belief that the Pharaohs were half-human and half-god and that the crown worn by the Pharaoh was thought to evoke the divine power they possessed. Where others believed it just concealed their large egg-shaped alien brains."

Laughter was heard among the listeners after the historian's last words.

"Am I hearing this correctly? Is she saying that the Pharaohs were aliens?" Luna said quietly to the group.

Kesia chuckled and said, "That explains how the pyramids were built."

The historian continued, "Legend has it that a planet called Nibiru, or Planet X, has an elongated orbit around our sun and travels in the reverse direction than the rest of our planets rotate. Also, the Mayan calendar marks this planet's rotation around the sun once every few thousand years. The Mayan Long Count calendar ended on December 21, 2012. This planet is ten times larger than the Earth and has life on it. It is believed that these aliens are God-like."

Lexi whispered in disbelief to the other three, "So, let me get this straight. Is she implying that the planet the Pharaohs came from rotates around our sun once every few thousand years?"

Luna said, "I think she means that the Egyptian gods were from Nibiru?"

Aias answered with, "Right. So maybe the Egyptian gods—Ra, Horus, Isis, and Osiris, must have been the original aliens from Nibiru."

The four of them listened on as the historian said, "Now, what makes this story fascinating is that Nibiru needs gold in its atmosphere. Legend has it that the gods of that planet needed to harvest enough specific purity of gold and mix it into their atmosphere to survive. The gods found that the planet Earth had an endless supply, and as the element of gold ages, it eventually creates the perfect purity needed."

"Okay, this is ludicrous," Lexi quietly commented. "The purity of gold can change, really? I've never heard of that."

Aias whispered, "Crystals continually grow—it may take eons, but they do. So, why is it hard to imagine that gold could change?"

Lexi didn't know what to answer, so she just shut her mouth.

"These gods, knowing that their planet only traveled a short time in the vicinity of Earth, had to come up with a plan to harvest the gold even when they were not near. They bred and tried many combinations of creatures, half-ape half-goat, half-bird half-lion—but none of the creatures had enough brains to carry out the task. Finally, they mated their females with some of the creatures from Earth and created the Pharaohs. The Pharaohs mated with terrestrial primates from Earth and created man, which became the perfect miners for their gold."

Lexi just shook her head in disbelief.

"Fascinating story," Luna said.

The four listened as the historian continued. "Now, the story goes even further. In 2012, it was believed that the residents of the planet Nibiru were close enough to retrieve the gold they needed. They did this by using a landing site for their ship on the moon and then landing on the pyramids here on Earth. So, if you don't believe what legend says, ask yourself this—what is all the hype about the conspiracy theories and the missing gold reserves?"

"Ah, now I understand why they say the moon landing was faked and that they have never shown us another landing, even with all the advancement and new technology. It's all because there is alien activity that they don't want us to know about," Luna said, thinking about the conspiracy theories.

After the lecture, as the four of them walked back to their hotel, Lexi remarked, "Aliens, gods, gold, not what I expected to hear."

"I found it fascinating," Luna commented. "She went from talking about the miracles performed by Moses to the magic of the Pharaoh's magicians to the origin of the Pharaohs themselves."

Aias paused, looking into the distance, then turned to the group with a contemplative expression. "The universe holds countless mysteries," he mused. "And perhaps the greatest of them all is the boundless capacity for miracles beyond our understanding."

Chapter 11

Sitting at the café the following day, waiting for the girls, Aias saw the young historian who had spoken at the river.

"Miss? Over here," Aias called out, waving at her.

She responded, "Yes, May I help you?"

"If you are not busy, I would love to buy you a cup of coffee. I loved your speech the other day."

Looking around, she said, "Um, I guess I can sit for a moment."

"Perfect." Aias got up and pulled a chair out for her to sit down. "I am Aias, and you are?" Knowing some Egyptian customs, Aias waited to see if she would offer her hand to shake. As she did not, he bowed.

"I am Rana."

"Nice to meet you. I was fascinated with what you had to say the other day. Is it true that Ancient Egyptians were obsessed with death?"

"I've heard you Americans are direct. Very well. I presume you're referring to the tales of mummies, curses, enigmatic gods, and rituals that history books and films often showcase?"

"Yes," Aias said, nodding.

"Numerous Egyptians hold the belief that birth on earth is granted by the grace of the gods, particularly the deities called The Seven Hathors. These divine beings determine one's destiny post-birth, deciding whether the soul will continue to live a life as virtuous as it did in the earthly vessel it was bestowed."

"Is it true that Egyptians believe that death is only a transition to another realm?" Aias asked.

"Yes, it's a deeply ingrained belief in Egyptian culture that death isn't an end but rather a passage to another dimension or realm," she replied. "Every ancient Egyptian aimed to make their life worth living eternally. If justified by the gods, one would transition to a paradise known as The Field of Reeds or A'aru. It's a journey to another phase of existence, not a final cessation."

"Justified?"

"Yes, the soul needs to make its way toward the Hall of Truth in the company of Anubis, the guide of the dead, where it would wait in line with others for judgment by Osiris."

"What type of judgment?"

"The Negative Confessions is a list of forty-two sins against oneself, others, or the gods which one could honestly say one had never engaged in."

"Confession?"

"Yes, if one's confession was deemed acceptable, the soul would present its heart to Osiris to be weighed on golden scales against the white ostrich feather of truth. The individual would progress to the next phase if the heart were lighter than the feather. However, if the heart were heavier, it would be cast to the ground and devoured by Ammut—the female devourer of the dead."

"So, Egyptians don't believe in Hell?"

"No, there is no Hell in the Egyptian concept of the afterlife. Non-existence is considered a far worse fate than any eternal damnation."

"What happens if one's heart is lighter than the feather? What happens next?"

"If the soul passes the Weighing of the Heart, it proceeds along a path leading to Lily Lake. Once there, the soul is ferried across the waters to the Field of Reeds, where it lives in eternal bliss. Once in the Field of Reeds, the soul enjoys an eternal existence free from suffering, living in a paradise reflective of their earthly life."

"Is that the reason Pharaohs were entombed alongside their servants? To guarantee they succeeded in all the trials?" Aias inquired naively.

Rana let out a gentle laugh. "No, that's actually a misconception."

Lexi, Luna, and a jealous Kesia walked up to their table.

"Well, hello," Lexi said, offering her hand to the girl. "I am Lexi, and this is Kesia and Luna."

Shaking Lexi's hand, Rana said, "Hi, nice to meet all of you. I am Rana."

Aias noted that Rana didn't hesitate to shake Lexi's hand. *It must be because she is of the same sex.*

Pulling up a chair to their table, Luna said, "Loved your lecture yesterday. Especially the part about the aliens."

Kesia pulled up a chair and sat as close as she could beside Aias.

"No, really, I loved the part about the aliens," Luna said again. "Is there any proof of their existence?"

Rana smiled and inquired, "Have you ever heard of the Anunnaki?"

"No," Luna answered.

"How about the Sumerians?"

Kesia chimed in, "Weren't they the people of southern Mesopotamia?"

"Yes, and the descendants of the advanced race of human-like extraterrestrials called the Anunnaki that lives on Nibiru. The missing link in Homosapiens evolution. It is believed that these aliens were the Annunaki mentioned in the

Sumerian scriptures and the Nephilim mentioned in the Hebrew Bible."

"Oh right, these are the gods that mated with creatures from Earth and created man," Luna said, repeating what she remembered from the lecture.

"If you do not believe me, how do you explain a three-thousand-year-old hieroglyphic plane etched on the ceiling of the Temple of Seti in Abydos?"

"You're telling me that there is a picture of an airplane on the ceiling?" Luna said, fascinated.

"Not only modern-day flying machines such as helicopters and airplanes but also a submarine."

"How is that possible? They hadn't been invented yet," Lexi commented.

Rana looked over and replied, "Gods can create anything."

Chapter 12

On a low hill just outside what is now modern-day Cairo, the sun rose for the first time. On this day, the chief Egyptian sun god, Ra, often carrying a staff, first appeared and held court for a millennium.

Ancient Egyptians believed that Ra created all the animal life on the planet by whispering their secret names and created man from his tears and sweat.

To honor Ra, the Egyptians constructed their most revered and sanctified city, known as the City of the Sun or Heliopolis, a place frequently referenced in the Old Testament. Over many generations, numerous pharaohs erected magnificent temples within it.

Worshiped at Heliopolis were nine deities: the sun god Atum, also known as Ra; his children Shu and Tefnut; their children Geb and Nut; and their children Osiris, Isis, Set—also known as Seth—and Nephthys.

These gods were seen holding the w^3s scepter—a long straight staff with a forked end and an ornate animal head at the top. It symbolized authority and divine power. The belief was that the person who held the scepter had control over the forces of chaos.

The staff Ra carried symbolized power and divine guidance. The headpiece of the staff was supposed to be a guide to the Ark of the Covenant, and if one held the staff correctly, the sun would shine through the headpiece and lead the person to the burial site of the Ark.

Ancient Egyptians carved the symbol of the w^3s scepter in their tombs and sarcophagi, hoping it would serve as a beacon for Osiris during their journey in the afterlife. This significant emblem ensured that the god would recognize and grant them safe passage and well-being as they navigated the underworld. The importance of Osiris in Egyptian mythology is evident in the tale of his ascendancy. The myth goes like this: being the eldest brother, Osiris was destined to marry Isis, his oldest sister, while his younger brother Set was paired with their youngest sister, Nephthys.

Set was jealous that his brother got to marry the more beautiful sister and rule over a larger area of the world. His envy became a deep, dark rage, and he murdered his brother, chopping him up into fourteen pieces and scattering him across the lands.

More consumed with sorrow for her sister than being a queen, Nephthys devised a plan with Isis to bring Osiris back to life. They collected all the pieces of Osiris's body and stitched him back together, breathing life back into him once more. But Isis's magic was not powerful enough to grant him eternal life.

During Osiris's short time back on Earth, he and Isis conceived a child so their bloodline would live on. After her magic had run its course, and Osiris was transported into the underworld where he would stake new rulership, a pregnant Isis went into hiding, where she bore their child, Horus.

Horus was raised and trained in secret until he entered manhood. To avenge his father's death, Horus went to Ra for justice to be served, for he, being the heir to the throne, should be ruler instead of his uncle Set.

Ra found Horus too young and would not grant his request.

Horus was determined to prove his worth and continually dueled with his uncle. Unfortunately, in so doing, he lost an eye.

Isis determined to end this madness, disguised herself as a beautiful young woman and threw herself at Set's feet.

Set's weakness was longing to love a beautiful woman, so her crying before him softened his heart, and he asked her what the cause of her tears was.

Weeping, she answered, "My husband was killed by a most wicked man—his brother! He took my husband, and he took our lands, and now my son and I are left to the swamplands in exile."

Set, angered by her story, promises he will avenge her! He will tear this criminal from the lands and the titles he stole and restore her and her child's rightful place once more.

Following his verdict, Isis took off her disguise and revealed her true identity to all who stood to watch. Set had condemned himself in front of all the other gods to see.

Justice was served.

Horus became the rightful ruler. With both his mother and aunt at his side, he restored the failing lands of Egypt to their former, thriving glory.

Watching from the underworld, Osiris smiled, knowing that his bloodline lived on.

Rooted in the story of Osiris, who is frequently hailed as the deity of rebirth, the afterlife, and the underworld, was the ancient Egyptians' hope for overcoming death. This legend offered them the promise of resurrection and an unending life beyond their mortal existence. Pharaohs held the conviction that they would achieve immortality after death, emulating Osiris and continuing their existence in the underworld. This belief eventually permeated the masses, leading many to trust in their own continued existence in the afterlife.

To this day, many religions speak of a God and eternal life after death.

Chapter 13

In the present day, Aias and the other three traveled to the Temple of Edfo.

Before entering, Kesia read from her oracle, "It says here that for two hundred years, this temple was buried under almost forty feet of desert sand and silt from the Nile."

"The silt must have helped to conserve it to near perfection! Look at this place," Aias said in amazement. "Hey, look. It's Rana."

The girls looked toward where he was pointing.

"Peachy," Kesia whispered.

Aias asked, "Did you say something, Kesia."

"Crazy."

"I know. But, of course, Rana would be here since she is a historian and all," Aias said as he picked up his pace, waving at her.

"Perfect timing," Rana said as the four of them neared her. "I was just about to start the tour."

Lexi smiled at Kesia, and Luna gave her a shoulder bump with her own, signifying to cheer her up.

Rana was facing the group, with her back to the temple. "As you may already know, each temple built here in Egypt was to either honor a god or a pharaoh. This particular temple was built between 237 and 57 BC, in honor of the falcon god, Horus of Behdet, the avenging son of the goddess Isis and god Osiris."

Luna put up her hand and said, "Don't you mean 57 and 237 BC?"

Rana smiled and said, "If years start at zero, and BC implies it is before zero, then the count is the opposite. So, 237 BC is 180 years before 57 BC."

"I don't get it," Luna muttered.

"Imagine the zero is your starting point. You start to count from one in both directions."

"Oh, right. I forgot that part. Thanks for clarifying." Thinking of another question, Luna asked, "What does BC stand for?"

"BC stands for before Christ, and AD stands for anno domini, Latin for "in the year of the lord," and refers specifically to the birth of Jesus Christ."

"Jesus was born in year zero?" Luna asked.

Rana answered, "It was believed that Jesus Christ was born that year, but as historians and theologists now know, he was born in 7 or 6 BC."

Before they entered, Rana put a shawl around Luna's shoulders.

"Thanks, but I'm not cold."

"It is etiquette not to enter our sacred buildings with bare shoulders. Likewise, for that matter, shorts or any other skimpy clothing."

"Oh."

As the larger group entered the one hundred-and four-foot gateway, guarded by two granite statues of Horus, Kesia read from her oracle, "The walls are decorated with colossal reliefs of Ptolemy XII Neos Dionysos."

"That is correct," Rana said. "Here we have Ptolemy XII, a general for Alexander the Great, holding his enemies by their hair before Horus and is about to smash their skulls."

Lexi was mystified by the large inscriptions carved into the sandstone walls.

Rana said to the group, "Some call this temple Edfo Text."

"I wonder why the Egyptians felt it necessary to carve these stories into the walls?" Luna whispered to Kesia.

Hearing this, Rana answered, "All temples, statues, and pyramids in Egypt have extensive carvings that have provided valuable information to historians about Egyptian history. The exquisite reliefs give us insight into their religion, mythology, and their way of life. The Temple Edfo's stories tell us mostly about the creation of the world."

"How did it come to be?" Luna inquired.

"The carvings suggest that mighty deities shaped the Earth. They describe how two gods descended from the heavens to form a domain known as the Island of the Egg, which was positioned at the center of the everlasting lake, this island was their handiwork. Observe this section. It indicates that the wise ones, the masons, and the shebti emerged from the waters to construct the first temples. After the creator gods finished their work, the script refers to their meeting with the immense bird, often called the Great Winged Disk, before they ascended back into the sky."

"A massive bird, a winged disk?" Luna questioned.

"Most historians believe that it meant their spacecraft," Rana clarified.

"I wonder where they went?" Luna queried.

Rana answered, "The text inscribed in these temple walls of Edfo says that not all of the gods left right away. That they stayed until they had created a lineage."

"A lineage?" Luna questioned.

Kesia answered this time, "It says here that lineage means the members of a person's family who are directly related to that person and who lived a long time before him or her."

"So, they mated?" Luna said, clueing in.

"Yes," Rana nodded.

"Ah, I am starting to get your lecture the other day by the Nile," Luna said, remembering that Rana had spoken about alien gods.

Rana nodded, then explained to the whole group, "The text here tells us that there was a war of some kind between Horus, the Falcon Sky God, and an enemy represented by a snake called the Great Leaping One or Seth, also known as Set, Horus's uncle and the god of chaos, discord, envy, fire, desert, storms, and trickery. It says that when Seth arrived in the sky, the sky became dark, and floods destroyed this sacred island and all of the ancient ones."

"I wonder what miracles Horus could do?" Aias wondered out loud.

Answering, Rana elaborated, "The Eye of Horus is associated with the goddess Wadjet and is also called the all-seeing eye or the third eye. The hierographic symbol for Horus is shaped to resemble a falcon's eye, along with the distinctive teardrop on the bottom, and is usually shown as a left eye."

"What does the eye symbolize if it is the right eye," Luna asked.

"The eye of Ra, the sun god. This magical symbol of Horus is believed to provide protection, health, and rejuvenation. It depicts the secret areas of the brain that hold the potential for each human to attain enlightenment."

Aias put up his hand, "You are referring to the brow chakra?"

"The Eye of Horus depicts the secret part of the brain connected with our emotions. The third eye or brow chakra stays dormant until the soul reaches a certain spiritual level. Therefore, ancient Egyptians believed that it was essential to nurture our limbic brain so that the third eye would lead us to spiritual awakening, reach inner peace, and live a meaningful life."

"So, you say that Horus's magic or miracles are held in the third eye?" Aias repeated.

"The eye of Horus is the gateway to the limbic system," Rana answered.

"Let me get this straight," Luna said. "The text written all over this Falcon God Horus's Temple of Edfo is proof that there was an alien race of gods that came down in flying machines, created Earth, and populated it?"

"Yes. There is inscribed proof that these gods, these "fiery serpents," the seraphim." Rana paused slightly, "In Hebrew, seraphim mean "fiery angels" or "burning ones." These gods traveled across the vast distances of interstellar space and brought the tree of life to this planet."

"Lit!" Luna said, bumping Kesia's elbow with hers.

"Lit," Kesia said half-heartedly, wishing it was anyone other than the brilliant Rana giving the tour.

Chapter 14

That evening, in her modest studio apartment, Rana shed her clothes and settled into bed. As she lay there, thoughts of Luna filled her mind. Suddenly, her phone chimed with a new message notification. To her astonishment, it was from Luna.

Reading the text, it said,

Thanks for today. I find your lectures fascinating. I would love to get together and discuss more of what you have to say.

Love Luna.

Rana smiled. Her instincts were correct. Luna had been flirting with her. Rana texted back, I wish it were different for me here in Egypt, but the Egyptian government continues to target gay, lesbian, bisexual, and transgender people in a "systematic fashion" through arbitrary arrests, torture, and other forms of abuse, including forced "virginity tests."

Luna instantly texted back. You're kidding, right?

No.

That is so barbaric!

It is what it is. Rana texted back.

Is it also true what they say about female genital mutilation? Luna texted.

It was true, up until 2016, that is when it became law to stop the act of female circumcision.

Why would they ever do that in the first place?

Its primary purpose is to preserve chastity. Actually, Luna, I have to delete all of these texts for fear of my phone ever being searched. Egypt's National Security Agency police personnel and officers entrap LGBT people through social networking sites and dating applications. Would you please delete all your texts to me and call me?

After deleting her texts to Rana, she called her. "Hi."

"Hi," Rana answered back. "Sorry about the cloak and dagger, but I can't take a chance. I could lose my job."

"Not a problem. How long has circumcision been performed?" Luna's curiosity was getting the better of her.

"Dating back to 2300 BC, there are ancient Egyptian hieroglyphic wall paintings describing circumcision. Also, there have been observations of some female mummies."

"Wow. That is a long time," Luna remarked.

"I don't know why you are so surprised. Many religions perform male circumcision, so why would female circumcision be any different?"

"I know Catholic and Jewish boys are circumcised, but the female babies aren't. I have never heard of female circumcision before."

"It was very common here."

Luna had to ask, "Does that mean you are circumcised?"

"As a tradition in the Islamic religion, a Muslim girl between the ages of six to ten is circumcised as a right to passage into adulthood. It is customary for the family to prepare their daughter to be marriageable. So, yes."

"Does it affect your sexual desires?" Luna asked fascinated

"I wouldn't know."

"What? Have you never had any desires?"

"Luna, you must understand. Here in Egypt, a female does not have the rights that you are accustomed to in America. For example, there is no sex before marriage. In fact, there is no dating before marriage. The Quran actually tells women to cover themselves so that they can be appreciated for who they are as humans instead of being looked at lustfully."

"How do you meet your life partner then?"

"Luna, I should consider myself lucky. My parents allowed me to educate myself before I wed, which is going to happen in just a few days. I will be his wife, number four."

Wife number four. Luna paused. She didn't know what to say, "So, there is no way there could ever be something between us?"

"I wish it could be different, but no. Other than being friends, there could never be anything between us."

Heartbroken, Luna said, "That is too bad. I really felt a connection."

"Me too. Maybe in the afterlife," Rana said before she had to go. "Night, Luna."

Saddened, Luna said, "Night, Rana."

Chapter 15

Kesia walked into the hotel room she shared with Luna, saying, "Hi. You won't believe what we did tonight. I wish you would have come with us."

Luna didn't respond.

Looking over at Luna lying in her bed with her back to Kesia, Kesia whispered, "You awake?"

"Yep."

"What's wrong?"

Not wanting to tell a lie, Luna said, "Life isn't fair."

Kesia went over and sat on Luna's bed. "What happened?"

"I thought I found my true love."

Kesia was excited, "You never told me."

"I wasn't sure I could."

Not understanding, Kesia said, "Why?"

"I'm not like you Kesia. I am not attracted to men."

Kesia relaxed and said, "I know."

Luna turned over and looked at Kesia, "You did?"

"Yep."

"It was that obvious?"

Kesia shook her head, "No, but in high school when Bobby Martin asked you out in ninth grade, you made such a scene."

"I forgot about that," Luna said, smiling. "Poor guy. I hope I didn't hurt his feelings."

Kesia exaggerated her answer, "I am sure that is why he didn't ask another girl out in high school."

Not catching on, Luna sat up, "Ah. I should apologize to him."

Kesia chuckled, "I can picture it now. You, going up to Bobby and saying, Hey, by the way, I'm gay."

Luna laughed. "Ya, I guess."

"Anyways, most people knew in school."

"Really?"

"Ya."

"I thought I hid it well," Luna murmured. "How did people know?"

"Subtle actions."

"What did I do that you could tell?"

"How you smiled whenever Lili was around."

"Man, I had a crush on her since second grade," Luna admitted.

"So, who broke your heart this time?" Kesia asked.

"Rana."

Dumbfounded, Kesia repeated, "Rana?"

"Hey, don't judge, and besides, she's getting married in a few days."

"She is?" Kesia hadn't felt this good since she met the girl. "And here I thought Aias liked her."

"Ya, you don't hide your jealousy very well."

"That obvious, huh?"

"Yep."

At the same time, both girls got a text.

Reading it, Kesia said, "Wow, Rana invited me to her wedding."

"Me too."

A knock came at their door.

Opening it, Kesia said, "You guys too," and let Lexi and Aias into their room.

"Isn't it great?" Aias said.

"It is," Kesia said, honestly, knowing that he meant Rana's wedding.

"I love weddings," Lexi confessed. "Even though I keep having problems with my own."

As Aias walked by, he tapped Lexi's shoulder before taking a seat and remarked, "Trust me, Lexi, you'll be overjoyed with the person you end up marrying."

"Oh, tell us more. Who does she marry?" Kesia begged.

"What fun would that be if I spoiled the surprise?" Aias smiled.

Lexi grinned from ear to ear.

Wanting to know, Kesia went over and tickled Aias. "Tell me."

"No. It's a secret."

As she tickled him some more, Kesia whispered, "Tell me."

Instead, he quickly kissed her.

That shut her up.

Luna looked at the group and asked, "So, are we going?"

"Heck, ya," Aias stammered as he moved his mouth away from Kesia's. "I wouldn't miss an Egyptian wedding for all the tea in the cosmos."

Chapter 16

Months before her engagement party, her
soon-to-be husband had followed the Arabic
customs by bringing his family to meet with
Rana's family. During the meeting, the dowry
was paid to her father, and they settled on the
two gifts for the bride-to-be: gold and precious
stones.

Wearing a simple blue dress, Rana was
excited to see that her new American friends,
Aias, Kesia, Luna, and Lexi, had shown up for
her lavish engagement party. Paid by her
fiancé's family, it was held in an elaborate
banquet hall decorated with flowers of every
kind and flashing lights of every color.

Aias, Kesia, Luna, and Lexi watched as
Rana's fiancé gave his agreed-upon gifts. One
was a gold ring that he placed on her right ring
finger.

Later that evening, as Rana and her fiancé made their rounds, she showed off her ring to Luna and the others and said, "The tradition of a ring is from Ancient Egypt. It symbolizes infinity—no beginning, no end."

Kesia genuinely smiled and said, "I wish the very best for the two of you. Where will you live after the wedding?"

Looking at her fiancé, Rana said, smiling, "As Baniti already owns a house, we will be married in two days. After that, I will move in with him, his other three wives, and their children."

As Kesia tried to hold back her shock, Lexi said, "There is so much to learn about other cultures, customs, and traditions. I wish you all the best for your future. Thank you for including us in your festivities. We will remember this night forever."

"It sounds like you are not joining me tomorrow night. I thought you understood that you are all invited to the wedding?"

"Oh," Lexi said. "I thought it was just for tonight."

"No. No, you must come to my Henna party tomorrow, and Aias, you are welcome to join in with Baniti and the other men."

Aias spoke up, "I wouldn't miss it."

"Wonderful. I will have a car pick you all up at your hotel."

The rest of the evening was celebrated with a magnificent feast, dancing, and plenty of joyful howling from the womenfolk.

The next evening, Aias was dropped off at Baniti's house to celebrate with the men, and Luna, Lexi, and Kesia were dropped off at Rana's parent's house.

Rana was wearing a luxurious pink gown made of silk. She looked beautiful. When the three girls entered the room, her hands and feet were tattooed with henna.

"Look at that,' Kesia said to Luna and Lexi. "Have you ever seen such a design?"

The elaborate designs drawn on Rana's feet went up above her ankles, and on her hands, it covered the backs from fingertips to past her wrists.

"What is it made of?" Lexi asked.

Rana answered, "The reddish-brown substance is made from a flowering plant and mixed with water to form this paste. She is almost finished. She just has my palms to do."

Kesia asked, "Is this a Muslim tradition?"

"Actually, ancient mummies were found with henna tattoos," Rana said as she turned her palms up.

"Is there a reason it is applied?" Luna asked, finally getting the courage to say something after her and Rana's conversation the other night.

"Yes, it keeps evil away and is considered good luck for the wedding couple."

"Fascinating!" Lexi exclaimed.

"How long does it last?" Kesia asked.

"The longer, the better. While I have these tattoos, I don't have to do any chores. The tattoo will last anywhere from one to five weeks."

For the rest of the evening, the girls enjoyed singing and dancing.

~

The next day, entering the grand marriage hall, Rana wore a brightly colored jewel-encrusted dress and veil. The groom was wearing a ceremonial tribal costume.

Lexi loved watching the traditional ceremony.

Rana smiled as her parents signed the wedding contract according to the Egyptian marriage laws in the presence of the mazoon.

Rana looked on as Lexi and the others drank the juice made of rose water to highlight the wedding party. The fragrant drink, known for its elegant sweetness, lingered in the air, subtly binding the joy and solemnity of the union being celebrated.

As dinner plates were cleared and conversations simmered down, a melodious reverberation gently permeated through the banquet hall, teasing the arrival of a different kind of feast—one for the eyes and the soul. The lighting dimmed ever so slightly, lending the room a soft, magical glow as the first notes from the traditional oud serenaded the guests. Subtle whispers of excitement flitted through the room, punctuated by the gentle clinking of metal, harmonizing with the escalating music.

A troupe of belly dancers, adorned in resplendent costumes that mirrored the vibrant sunset hues, emerged from a curtained enclave. They moved as if they were extensions of the melody itself—each step, each undulation, a physical echo of the lilting tunes. Delicate anklets chimed with their every step, whispering tales of age-old traditions and long-lost loves.

Atop their heads, they balanced candelabras, the flickering flames casting a warm, ethereal light upon their serene faces, the delicate shadows dancing in tandem with them. Their eyes, lined with the blackest kohl, spoke of mysteries, of stories untold, as they locked gaze with the audience, inviting them into a world where the enchantment of ancient tales and the joy of the present moment converged.

Lexi, watching from afar, felt herself being gently lulled into this mystical world, her heart pulsating in rhythm with the tablas. She watched as the flames atop the candelabra danced, seemingly alive, cavorting with the tunes and the twirls of the dancers, enchanting every soul in the room. The scent of sweet and heady incense wafted through the air, entwining with the melodic tunes and leading the senses into a gentle embrace of the moment.

As the music gently navigated through rhythms and scales, the dancers maneuvered with graceful strength, their bodies telling stories of celebration, love, and a timeless tradition that has witnessed countless unions such as this. It was as if the flames they balanced were igniting the tales of the past, illuminating them for the current generation to witness, to become a part of, and to pass down to the ones to come.

Each twirl, each heartbeat of the drum, drew Lexi deeper into the narrative being woven before her eyes, where every movement was a word, every glance a sentence, and every chime punctuation in this ephemeral story of jubilation and culture. And in that transitory, spellbinding moment, Lexi found herself not merely a spectator but a participant in a tapestry that spanned generations, bound not by threads but by shared moments of joy, love, and celebration.

Lexi, amidst the vibrant wedding party, beheld the charming scene unfold as the new bride, Rana, gracefully mounted the camel, her visage glowing under the gentle caress of the moonlight. Her heart swelled with a mixture of joy and gentle melancholy as she gazed at her friend, now embarking on a poignant journey towards a new chapter of her life, nestled within the comforting arms of ancient traditions.

With the camel moving in gentle, rhythmic motions beneath the vast, starlit expanse, Lexi and the vibrant caravan of well-wishers commenced the journey to the groom's house. Her feet, adorned in soft, embellished flats, patted gently against the dusty earth, keeping time with the pulsating rhythm of the traditional drums. The melodic strains of the oud harmonized with the dulcet tones of the singers as they celebrated the union with songs of love, prosperity, and future happiness.

Each step was an echo of centuries of tradition, every beat a rhythm passed through generations, and as Lexi danced and sang, she felt an inexplicable connection to the countless others who had walked this path in times gone by. Her arms swirled above her, creating silhouettes against the star-sprinkled sky, as she became a part of a timeless tapestry woven with threads of shared joy and collective celebration.

She gazed ahead at Rana; the gentle sway of her silhouette against the horizon seemed to merge with the undulating dunes around them, forming a picturesque scene that Lexi knew would forever be etched in her memory. Her emotions danced with the twirling bodies around her, happiness for her friend intertwining with a nostalgic ache that quietly whispered of times that once were.

As the newlywed couple departed into the house, Aias patted Rana's father on the back, saying, "Thank you for allowing us to be part of such a beautiful celebration."

Never having witnessed a miracle, her father replied, "From the grace of God."

Chapter 17

Sitting at a table outside the café the following day, Luna asked Aias. "What did you do to Rana's father?"

Interested in the conversation, Kesia and Lexi looked at them.

"I merely thanked him for allowing us to be there."

"Ah, you did more than that," Luna said as she read the many texts Rana was sending.

"Why are you asking, Luna?" Kesia asked.

"Oh, he did something alright." Luna kept reading the texts.

"Let me see," Kesia said as she stood up and stood behind Luna so she could read the text.

Luna moved a bit so she could read it easier.

"Aias, did you touch him?" Kesia asked.

"I might have."

"Well, you've done it now."

"What harm did I do?"

"I don't think that is the problem."

As Luna gave her phone to Aias to read, Lexi said, "Ah, guys, we have a problem."

Luna and Kesia looked to where Lexi was staring and saw a crowd of people coming their way.

Before any of them could get up, the crowd was upon them, yelling, "From the grace of God."

Pulling at Aias's sleeves, many were speaking at once.

Rana came up through the crowd, holding onto her father's arm. "Aias, my father thanks you for using your gift on him. He has been troubled for years now with bursitis in his toe. It had almost crippled him from walking."

"What did Aias do?" Kesia asked Rana.

Looking at her, she said, "My father's right toe has completely healed. There is no evidence of bursitis."

"How do you know?" Kesia asked.

"Look." Rana showed her father's feet.

Through his sandals, you could see his toes.

"What am I looking for? They look normal to me," Kesia said.

"Exactly! His right toe used to be red with a very large bump on the side."

Kesia looked at Aias and asked, "Did you know you healed him?"

"There can always be a healing when I touch someone."

The crowd started to yell out, "Allahu Akbar."

Scared, Lexi asked, "What are they yelling?"

Rana answered, "God is the greatest."

"Aias, these people are my family and friends. I wish you would touch them as you did, my father."

Luna looked and saw at least twenty people. "Aias, do you think that is wise? Can you heal that many people?"

"I guess I am about to find out."

Rana led the way as the group followed Aias to a park near the café.

Sitting on a bench, Aias touched each person as they came up.

Tears were flowing down Rana's cheeks as she witnessed the miracles performed by Aias, touching her friends and family.

Luna was looking at the lineup. It was not becoming any shorter. As one person left, two more seemed to show up. Then, looking at Lexi and Kesia, she said, "Guys, we have to get him out of here. Look."

Lexi and Kesia looked at the end of the line. At least forty people were standing there, and many more were walking up. "She's right. We have to get him out of here," Kesia agreed.

Walking right in front of the next person in line, Luna grabbed Aias's arm and pulled him up off the bench, saying, "You're done for today."

"But I have to help these people."

"No. You don't."

Kesia and Lexi guarded him as they all started to run toward their hotel.

Luckily, the hotel would not allow the crowd to enter.

Once they were safely inside Lexi's room, she said, "Aias, are you okay? You don't look well."

"I. . . I. . ." Before he could finish his sentence, he passed out on her bed.

"Oh my God!" Lexi yelled as she tried to catch him.

Chapter 18

Like thieves in the night, Lexi and Luna carried their luggage while Kesia wheeled an unconscious Aias out the hotel's back door in a wheelchair.

"Thank God Isabella has connections," Lexi said to the others as they got into a helicopter waiting for them.

The girls looked down at the ever-growing crowd as the helicopter lifted off.

"Wow, there must be a couple of hundred people down there," Luna commented.

"At least," Kesia answered.

"Lexi, where are we going?" Luna asked, wondering where Isabella had told the pilot to fly.

"All I know is that she said she wouldn't end our vacation."

Thirty-seven minutes later, the helicopter touched down.

Aias stirred and woke up as they got out, asking, "Where are we?"

"Good question," Kesia said as she climbed out.

Lexi pointed to a sign, "The holiest city of them all, Jerusalem."

Aias and the girls looked in the direction that she was pointing.

"Awesome!" Aias said, happy to know they were at his next stop on his pilgrimage.

~

The dawn of the following day brought with it a gentle anticipation that delicately stirred the air. A taxi, punctual and subtly humming, awaited to shepherd them towards the legendary Mount of Olives. Upon their arrival at the Jaffa Gate, one of the magnificent seven portals into the ancient heartbeat of the Old City of Jerusalem, a profound sense of history enveloped them, whispering tales of millennia through the weathered stones underfoot.

Together, the quartet meandered towards Golgotha, every step saturated with the palpable resonance of joyous and tragic stories that had seeped into the very earth they trod upon. It was here, amid the gentle murmur of pilgrims and the soft rustling of ancient olive trees, that they stood where Jesus was crucified, a place of profound sorrow and boundless love interwoven through time.

Now, in its stead, the Church of the Holy Sepulchre silently keeps watch, a solemn guardian of sacred memories and eternal promises. As they entered, the cool, hallowed air gently caressed their faces, and for a moment, time seemed to stand still, suspending them between the earthly and the divine amidst a silence that spoke more profoundly than words ever could. This sacred juncture, where agony and redemption eternally dance, invited them to pause, remember, and carry forward the embers of a love that transcended time.

Aias sat down in the lotus position and said, "Does anyone want to join me in meditation?"

Kesia sat down beside him, saying, "I'm in."

Luna sat down and said, "Why not."

Lexi sat down, "Lead us in the meditation, please."

Aias smiled at her and said, "Take a deep breath and sense these ancient holy grounds. Every breath you take takes you closer and closer to your connection with Jesus and his experience here on that dreadful day."

Lexi took a few deep breaths.

A few moments later, she was back in time, and to her horror, in the body of one of the criminals hanging from the wooden cross to Jesus's right, looking at Jesus.

She awoke from her trance state in a split second, jumping up and trying to walk off what she just witnessed.

Hearing Lexi gasp as she got up, Kesia, Luna, and Aias came out of their meditation.

"Lexi, what is it?" Kesia, concerned, got up and walked over to her.

Hands on her knees, trying to catch her breath, Lexi gasped, "Oh my God, they knew."

Confused, Kesia asked, "Knew what?"

"They knew about the chakras."

"What are you talking about? Who?" Luna asked.

"The Romans under the authority of Pontius Pilate, the man who sentenced Jesus to his death. I saw them place the crown of thorns upon his head, blocking his third eye chakra and stopping his ability to connect with his people intuitively. Next, I saw the Roman soldiers drive the nails into his hands, blocking his healing abilities, and as they drove the nails through his feet, his ability to ground with the Earth was also blocked. Hanging there for hours, by the ropes tied around his wrists and ankles, Jesus fought to stay conscious. The sadists! Instead of breaking Jesus's legs for a quick death, the soldiers pierced his side, blocking his sacral chakra. With this action, they blocked his connection to his people. Luckily, his crown chakra was not blocked, and he still could connect with God. I heard him say before he took his last conscious breath, "My God, my God, why have you *forsaken me?"* Luckily, I came out of the meditation just before the earth shook and the rocks split."

Dumbfounded, Kesia repeated, "You think they knew back then about chakras?"

Lexi nodded. "They must have. It was all too real."

Aias spoke up, "I studied a book that talked about Jesus's life. He studied the "craft" and not meaning carpentry. I recently studied the unknown life of Jesus based on records preserved in the archives of ancient monasteries of the Essenes and the Rosicrucian Order. Jesus was not the first of virgin births. Horus was born to his virgin mother, Isis. The Holy Ghost was also Aesculapius's father and John the Baptist to his mother, Elizabeth, cousin to the virgin Mary."

"There were other virgin births?" Lexi questioned him.

"Yes, noted from countries worldwide, many avatars were born to virgins."

"But in the Bible, I thought Joseph was his father," Luna said, so confused.

"At Helios, Joseph was given the staff that bloomed into a leaf, and then a dove flew up to Heaven. He was the one that God had chosen to look after Mary."

"That must have been a shock," Luna said.

"Actually, he refused, confessing that as a widower, he was too old and had a couple of sons already. Not to mention that Mary was not the age to marry as to the law. She wasn't even thirteen."

"No wonder Mother Mary is known as the saint of children. She was a child herself." Lexi noted.

"I will skip through all that leads up to Jesus's education," Aias continued.

"His education?" Lexi questioned.

"Yes, you don't think that God just granted Jesus the ability to speak three languages. No, he had to learn them just as you and I would."

"So, where did he go to school?" Luna wondered out loud.

"Mount Carmel is known as the school of the prophets. It is a short distance from the village of Galilee."

Lexi asked for confirmation, "The place where Elijah and his son lived."

"Yes, the mystic mountain can be found along with the coastal mountain range in northern Israel."

Interested in this conversation, Luna asked with great curiosity, "Is the school still there now?"

Aias, doing all his homework on the life of Jesus prior to the trip, answered, "No, but all the sacred manuscripts and records were transferred to a secret monastery."

"Man, if you could read those books, you would probably find what you are searching for," Luna said as she thought of a spell that would locate the manuscripts.

Thinking about a young Jesus, Kesia asked, "Do you think that Mount Carmel is the only place Jesus studied?"

Aias knew this answer, "No. There is scripture stating that when he was thirteen, he told the doctors at the Paschal Feast in Jerusalem that he would leave Galilee early in the fall to go and study at schools in foreign lands. One of which was the Supreme Temple at Heliopolis, and that he would not return to Palestine for many years."

"What do you think he learned while he was in these foreign lands," Kesia asked.

"It is believed that he became familiar with the heathen religions, pagan beliefs, rites, and creeds of the places he visited."

"Fascinating," Luna said. "So, where are we off to next?"

Aias contemplated for a moment, "I will receive my father's inheritance soon. Soon, the world will be my oyster." Aias smiled, knowing that they would travel to many places, "For now, since we know there are various other sacred books—originally forming the library of sacred writings from which the present books of the Bible were selected, but unfortunately were rejected—I think I need to go find those not as famous scriptures."

So, where are we going?" Luna asked again.

"Back to where Jesus and I spent a year."

"And that is?" Luna said, a bit annoyed.
"To the monasteries in India and later Tibet."

Chapter 19

That night, Lexi had a dream about an Archangel. He was older, maybe in his fifties. His hair was white as fresh snow, and his wings glistened and shimmered like snowflakes. He held a hook that had a large fish and a basket filled with bread and coins.

Who are you? Lexi asked.

I am Hamied, the angel of miracles, prosperity, and abundance.

You are so bright that I can only make out your eyes.

I hold the light of Christ. I was there when Jesus turned water into wine, healed the sick, cast out evil, and fed the people. I was there when Moses performed his miracles. I am there when any mortal performs a miracle, saint, or other. I am the divine energy, power, or influence that proceeds from God, bringing life and light to all things.

Why are you here now, speaking to me?

Lexi, your soul is pure. Therefore, you have within you the power to heal.

I think you are mistaken. I have witnessed Aias's miracles, and I do not possess any elf magic.

Who do you think granted the elves to possess such ability?

I never thought about it.

Lexi, each person possesses at least one of the nine spiritual gifts granted by Spirit at birth, but they are all attainable. The manifestation of food or items is the ability to bring forth the specific atoms that make up the compound. The earth's atmosphere is filled with elements. One just needs to ask. If one had the faith of a mustard seed, one could move mountains.

I am not worthy.

And there lies the problem.

So, you agree I am not worthy?

No, you believe that you are not worthy. Let me tell you a tale of a girl who had visions of people that others could not see. Who had the power in her hands to perform miraculous healing miracles unbeknownst to her. A girl who had grown up in a religion that said that only a saint could do those things. A girl who was too scared to go to the church and ask for help because she was too scared that she would be crucified or considered a heretic. A girl who ended up studying metaphysics with others like her, people who had visions, felt things, heard things, or knew something that many others could not. To this day, she is still questioning the miracles granted by God.

I feel like that.

That is why I am telling you the story. Do you think Jesus didn't question his abilities? Do you not know that Aias is also questioning his abilities? It is natural to question what others find impossible. What others find as a threat?

A threat?

The vibration of money is not in itself heavy. But, the sin of greed weighs down the person and calls upon the demon, Mammon.

Money brings the demon Mammon.

No, greed does. In opposition to Mammon, I work with Archangel Michael and the virtue of charity. Charity is held to be the ultimate perfection of the human spirit.

How so?

As Henry Ward Beecher said, every charitable act is a stepping stone toward heaven. Charity is kindness and understanding towards other people.

I thought it was giving money to other people.

The Japanese have the correct concept. They believe it is morally their responsibility to look after the sick, the very poor, or those with a disability.

Aias told us about a lesson from Doctor Usui that there should be an equal energy exchange.

Did Doctor Usui ask the person if they needed to be healed?

I am not sure.

Charity is giving without expecting anything in exchange. Charity can be anything from gifting items—anything from time to food to sitting and reading. Charity comes from your heart and without judgment.

Aias gave the other day without asking for anything in return, and he passed out due to the need of so many sick people.

Every person needs to know their limits. One cannot give what one does not have.

Is that what you think Doctor Usui meant by equal energy exchange?

There is nothing wrong with charging for an exchange of goods or services, but charity is free with no strings attached. Charity should be gifted with no thought or feeling of any sort, even later, that you gave this, so something is deserved back. Even though prophets may have been blessed with necessities, they never asked for them. It was graciously offered. True philanthropists never expected anything in return.

Is that what happens when a miracle appears?

Miracles are believed to be extraordinary and astonishing happenings that are attributed to the presence and action of ultimate or divine power. God does not require anything more than you to believe.

I remember reading for a person to become a saint in the eyes of the Catholic church, they must be a servant of God. They must have led a virtuous, heroic life, performed verified miracles, and been dead for five years. Lastly, at least one other miracle must have been received while they were dead by a person praying to them.

There have been people from all over the world and from many religions who have performed miracles, using an item or not.

An item or not? What do you mean?

Some people can heal with their hands. Then there are items such as amulets, staffs, wands, or statues that are believed to possess magical virtues.

There are? Name a specific item.

Here are two items—the statue of the weeping Virgin Mary in Hobbs, New Mexico, and the Madonna of Syracuse, Sicily. Also, there are sacred places that are believed to have miraculous power.

There are?

Yes, there are sacred groves, temples, and places like Lourdes, Mecca, the Ka'bah in Islam, and the Buddhist stupas.

Why are you telling me this?

Lexi, your eyes have been opened, and it is time to help Aias on his journey to find out the truth behind miracles.

Chapter 20

Lexi opened her hotel door to find a sleepy-eyed Isabella. "Hi!"

Pushing past her and a bit tipsy, Isabella said, "Hiya, chicky."

"Isabella, are you okay?" Lexi said, having never seen Isabella drunk before.

Wobbling to the couch, Isabella said, "Sure, sure," right before sitting down.

Sitting down beside her, Lexi said, "Iss, is everything okay?"

Slurring her words, she answered, "Yep, why do you ask? Do you have anything to drink?" Then, eyeing the small fridge, she opened the door, saying, "Eureka, there you are, my pretties," and then grabbed a couple of miniature liquor bottles.

Knowing something was wrong, Lexi asked, "Iss, what happened?"

Downing the two bottles, one right after the other, straight up, bursting into tears, Isabella said, "They fired me. Me. Isabella Jackson." Wobbling back to the fridge, she said, "I'm a famous movie star, you know. Me. A famous movie star. They fired me."

"Ah, Iss. I am so sorry." Then, taking the bottles out of her hands, she said, "Here, come sit back down. Tell me all about it."

Following the empty liquor bottles, Isabella followed Lexi back to the couch.

"So, what happened?"

"They found out about Aias."

"What did they find out?"

"That he is an elf. Oops, half-elf."

"How did they find that out?"

"Instagram. No, wait, maybe it was Facebook. I can't remember."

"What, did someone post something?"

"Ah, there were thousands of posts, not just one. Something about using his healing powers the other day. You know, you were there."

"Someone posted Aias healing people when we were in Egypt?"

"Yep," Isabella said as she grabbed for the tiny bottles in Lexi's hands, forgetting they were empty.

"Ok, I don't get it. Why were you fired?"

"You know that director from my newest film?"

"I remember you talking about him. What of it?"

"He hates me."

"I'm sure he doesn't hate you," Lexi said, trying to hide the bottles behind her back.

Slurring, Isabella said, "Yep, he does."

"What exactly happened?"

"I don't reckon I know."

"Isabella, focus. What happened to get you fired? And what does it have to do with Aias?"

"Oh, ya. My precious baby." Getting up and wobbling to the door, Isabella said, "Where is he anyway?" Then, calling out, she yelled, "Aias." Trying to open the handle to get out, Isabella said, "Aias, where are you? Momma's here."

Taking Isabella's shoulders and turning her around to go back and sit on the couch, Lexi said, "Shh. He is sleeping. It is the middle of the night."

"It is? It was night when I left New York. I thought it would be morning by now."

"There is a time change. It is night again."

"Weird," Isabella said as she tripped and fell onto the couch.

"I'll make you some coffee."

"No. I'm good. But I will have another of those tiny bottles of wine." Then, getting up again and wobbling over to the fridge, Isabella said, holding up another bottle, "Why do you think they make these so tiny?"

Lexi moved quickly over and took the bottle out of Isabella's hands. "I think you have had enough for one night."

"It should be morning, maybe even lunch. Hey, I'm hungry. Let's order room service," Isabella said as she picked up the phone in the room. Slurring, and before Lexi could take the phone away, she said, "Room service. I'll take one of everything." Then, looking at Lexi, she said, "What room are we in?"

Taking the phone from Isabella, Lexi said, "I'm sorry, please cancel that order," and hung up.

"But I'm hungry."

Lexi pulled a package from her purse. It was the cookies from the helicopter ride over. "Here, eat these."

Taking the package, Isabella held it up close and slurred, "I can't eat these."

"Why not? They're chocolate."

"Carbs. I can't eat carbs. Who is going to hire a fat Isabella Jackson?" Then, starting to cry, she said, "They fired me. Me. Isabella Jackson."

"Please, Isabella. Tell me what happened."

"Fine. I was on set when it happened. One of the other female cast members, who was off to the side and not being filmed, shrieked. The director hollered, stop! She wrecked a perfect performance."

"I see, and then what happened?"

"Well, then I had to stop."

"I get that. I mean, about what happened leading up to you getting fired."

"Oh, that, alright, I'll tell you."

"Please do."

"Well, you don't have to say it like that. Really, Lexi. I thought you, of all people, would have some sympathy for me."

"Isabella, I love you, but you woke me from a dream, and I am tired. It is the middle of the night here. Please, I am sorry, continue."

Getting up and going to lie down on Lexi's bed, Isabella said, "I. . ." but she didn't finish. Instead, she passed out.

"Good gracious." Getting up and shaking Isabella's shoulder, Lexi said, "Iss? Wake up. Ah, what's the use?"

Not able to move Isabella, Lexi grabbed an extra blanket from the shelf, laid down on the couch, and fell back to sleep.

Chapter 21

"I thought I heard voices last night," Luna said as she came through the adjoining door to Lexi's room.

"Isabella," Kesia said excitedly.

"Shh, she's still sleeping, Lexi whispered.

"The famous actress? Aias's mom?" Luna said, shocked, just as Aias walked in using an extra key that Lexi had given him.

"Mom! How did I not know you were here?" Aias said, surprised. "I can always sense you."

"She had a lot to drink, Aias. Maybe alcohol disguises a person's energy frequency?" Lexi said, trying to think of a logical answer.

"Fascinating," Aias said as he went over and touched his mom.

Instantly, Isabella was sober and awake. Then, sitting up, she said, "Aias, oh my baby, how I've missed you," then kissed him.

Sweeping her many kisses away, he said, "Mom, enough, not in front of everyone."

"What? A mom can't kiss her baby?"

Kesia saved Aias from any further embarrassment by coming up and hugging Isabella, saying, "It is so nice to see you. I am glad you got time off from filming to come and see us."

"Ya, about that," Isabella said. Then, shifting her emotions and smiling, she said, "I will be joining you all on your adventure."

"But aren't you filming a movie right now?" Luna said bluntly.

Isabella looked at her and said, "And you are?"

All at the same time, Lexi said, "Iss, this is Luna." Aias said, "Mom. This is Luna. I told you about her." And Kesia said, "This is my friend from high school, Luna."

"I know, I was just kidding. Hi, Luna. Nice to meet you."

Luna smiled and said to Aias, "I like your mom."

"Why are you really here, mom?"

Lexi couldn't wait to hear the answer. She had been wondering that since last night.

Touching Aias lovingly with her fingers and slightly moving his hair, she said, "They said I was lying."

"Who said you were lying?" Aias asked, then saw what had happened as his mom touched him.

Many were standing in line as he was healing. The others took videos of what he was doing and posted them on the internet. His performance went viral, with millions of hits on many sites. One of his mother's co-actors was looking at her phone when she screamed in disbelief at what she was watching. Not only once, but with each person being videoed, there was a spark of light, one so slight you might have missed it. Then, instantly, you could hear the person say something in another language but also written in English subtitles, what the person proclaimed after they were healed.

"I don't get it, mom. What did I do that would make them say you were lying?"

"It wasn't exactly what I said. It was what the girl said."

Aias shook his head, not getting it, and then suddenly, he knew what happened. The girl on the set had seen him bilocate when he visited his mom, and that was what she was shrieking about. She recognized him in the video and was yelling about it to everyone on the set, claiming that it was Isabella's son and that he was a demon. Only a demon could have the ability to age that quickly and to create hallucinations of appearing and disappearing. That only a demon would be cocky enough to want to show off to the world. That Isabella's son was a false prophet and that she should be ashamed of what her son was proclaiming.

"I am so sorry, mom."

"You have nothing to be sorry for. You don't have control over what other people think."

Lexi came up and said, "Isabella, I am so sorry," and hugged her.

Not being able to hold back the tears, a sobbing Isabella said, "They called you the Devil. They said that only Jesus has the power to heal, and it must be a trick to make money that you paid all those people to act like they were healed. That you were doing it to get famous."

Lexi patted Isabella's back.

"I told them that you were a gift from God and that he bestowed on you the power to heal by touch, that he bestowed on you the ability to bilocate, that it was a gift that you were born with. She called me a liar and said that I was a witch. She said this film was cursed because a witch cast a spell on the producer and director. Also, her demon son corrupted innocent viewers, people who looked up to Isabella Jackson and would believe such a lie about her son."

"Then what happened," Luna asked.

"I came off the set and punched her in the face, giving her a split lip."

"Is that when you were fired?" Luna asked.

"No, it was when the security guard came over and pulled me off the director."

"What? The director? What did he do?" Luna asked in shock.

"He said that he knew something weird about my son and that it all made sense now. That I bewitch people and that I was a has-been."

"He said you were a has-been?" Luna repeated.

"Yes, that I was all washed up, That I wasn't a good actress anymore. That this film would be a dud and that they would be wasting their money on me."

"Is that when he fired you?" Lexi asked.

"No, it was when I said that the film wouldn't be anything without me and then stormed off the set. He yelled at me as I walked away and said that I was fired if I stepped out of the building."

"Ah, so I gather you stepped out of the building," Luna said.

"Only after he yelled out that I bore a demon. Then I left, showing him a middle finger, and yelled back. He's not a demon. He's a half-elf."

Aias hugged his mom and said jokingly, "Well, good thing that I can claim my inheritance then, isn't it? 'Cause somebody is going to have to pay for your lifestyle."

Chapter 22

The next morning, the five of them got into a shuttle that took them to the airport. Isabella still had the airplane she had chartered to fly her to Israel.

As they got on and into their seats, Luna said, "This has been such an awesome summer. I can't wait to see what these last four weeks will reveal."

Kesia nodded in agreement.

Sitting across from Kesia, Luna chanted, "Want to do a spell with me?"

Aias said, "Yes," even though she wasn't talking to him.

Kesia smiled, looped her arm through his, kissed him on the cheek, then nodded at Luna.

"So, what kind of an adventure do we want?" Luna asked the other two.

"Well, it has to be something to do with learning how to activate the power that grants me the gift of healing," Aias said.

Kesia added, "It has been pretty lit so far. I can't imagine anything better than what we already have experienced. So, let's ask for more of what we have had already."

"Good idea."

Luna took out a notepad and started jotting some ideas while Kesia and Aias talked. Lexi and Isabella were busy talking about anything and everything, catching up on what the four of them had been doing.

After about ten minutes of writing, as she pulled out five stones from her pocket and held on to them, Luna said, "Okay, how about this? Spirits of the earth, fire, air, and water. I ask you, mother goddess, as we venture out, regardless of our route, to protect and guard, be it visible or unseen. With no mishaps, please intervene. Keep our journey from evil and harm. And allow the miracles of each day to unfold and be the charm. So mote it be."

"Yep, I like that one," Kesia said.

"If she likes it, then I like it," Aias said, trusting Kesia's judgment.

"Awesome," Luna said, passing a stone to the other four.

As Lexi and Isabella went to take their stone, Lexi said, "What is this for?"

"Carry it with you. It is a stone to protect and bless us on our next adventure."

"How cute," Isabella said. "Thank you."

Before Lexi took her stone, she said, "Luna, I warned you of this. You were supposed to ask for my permission if you included me in a spell."

Isabella looked at Lexi and said, "Come on, Lex, take the rock and let her be. She was just being nice."

Ticked off at Isabella for making her feel like she was wrong in stating her feelings, she said, "No. Actually, I am going to pass on this one."

Isabella took Lexi's stone from Luna and said, "She doesn't know what she is saying," and put the stone in Lexi's hand.

"Isabella, I said I didn't want to partake in her spell, and I meant it," and passed the stone back.

"Don't be childish, Lexi. Humor the girl."

Luna didn't know what to do, so she just stood there.

"What's going on?" Aias asked.

Isabella said, "Lexi is being a big baby and won't take the stone."

"Well, if she doesn't want to take it, she shouldn't have to," he said.

"This is getting all blown up," Isabella ranted. "Just take the stupid stone."

"No."

Luna started to cry, and it took a lot to make her cry.

"Now, look what you did," Isabella said as she got up and put an arm around Luna.

"Oh my God, alright. Give me the stupid stone."

Isabella went to pass the stone to Lexi, and Luna screamed out, "Forget it! The spell is ruined," and ran to the restroom, locking herself in.

Looking at Lexi, Isabella said, "Really, Lexi. You couldn't have just taken the stupid stone," then went and started knocking on the restroom door.

As she did, the plane shook and started to descend. The air masks came out, and the lights began to blink.

Isabella grabbed for the first thing she could hold onto, forced herself into a chair, and buckled up.

Luna screamed, "We are cursed!"

Over the intercom, one of the three pilots yelled, "Brace yourselves. We are going to crash!"

Chapter 23

"Everyone okay?" Lexi yelled.

There was a moment of silence.

Isabella grunted, "I'm okay. A little bruised, but I'll live."

Lexi got up and lightly shook Kesia's shoulder, "Are you okay?"

A bit dazed as she came to, Kesia said, "Ah, I think so. What did we hit?"

Lexi smiled as she said, "Always an inquisitive mind. But, hey, can you wake Aias up?"

As she gingerly shook Aias, Kesia said, "Hey, Aias, wake up. Aias, wake up." Her voice changed to concern as she shook him harder and said, "Aias, hey, wake up. Lexi, he's not waking up. What do I do?"

Lexi watched as Isabella got up and went over to her son.

The co-pilot came out of the cockpit dripping with blood and asked, "Is everyone all right?"

"He's not waking up," Kesia answered, pointing at Aias.

"Here, get up. Let me see."

Still watching Isabella as she quickly moved behind her son's seat and leaned closer to his head, Lexi could hear her say anxiously, "Aias, Aias, baby. Come on, wake up."

"Ma'am, please move back. Let me take a look at him," the co-pilot demanded.

The third pilot came out of the cockpit and said, "He didn't make it."

Isabella screamed.

"The captain?" the co-pilot asked him for confirmation.

"Yes," the third in command answered.

Lexi rushed over to Isabella and said, "Isabella, he's talking about the captain, not Aias."

Not hearing Lexi, Isabella went into hysterics.

The co-pilot said, "Great, that's all I need. A hysterical mother. Somebody, get her under control." Then, looking at the third pilot, he said, "Aaron, do a headcount, will ya? Make sure everyone is accounted for."

As Aaron counted, he said, "I only count four. Are there not five of them?"

Lexi counted everyone. He was right. *Who's missing?* It only took a second, and then she said, "Luna, where is Luna?"

Kesia looked around, "Didn't she go into the restroom?"

"Right!" Quickly moving to the door of the toilet, Lexi banged on it and yelled, "Luna, are you okay?" Then, banging on the door again, "Luna?"

No answer.

Alarmed, Lexi said, "She's not answering!"

Arron came over to help Lexi as he said to Kesia, "Do something." Then, pointing at Isabella, "Try to make her stop screaming, will ya?"

Kesia went over to Isabella to try to soothe her.

Arron came over to the restroom door and knocked, saying, "Miss? Tap on the door if you can hear me."

A second later, there was a very quiet tap on the door.

Lexi yelled, "Thank God! She's alive." Then asked the pilot, "How are you going to open the door? It's locked."

He looked at her as Isabella started to scream, "My baby! My baby! Somebody, save my baby!" Then, looking back at the door, he said as he walked towards the cockpit, "I'll have to find a screwdriver."

As he took a couple of steps, the plane wobbled, and the nose went up a bit. Standing still, he yelled, "Don't anyone move."

But it was too late. Isabella had sat down as she almost fainted.

The plane tilted its nose up, and everyone standing grabbed onto something as the aircraft started to slide backward.

The co-pilot yelled, "Try to get into a seat and buckle up!"

Lexi and Kesia did as instructed and grabbed a seat as fast as possible.

Lexi sat beside the screaming Isabella, buckled her in, and quickly buckled up her belt.

As the plane picked up speed, it bounced and shook like a car on a rollercoaster ride.

Everyone held on for dear life.

The crash was the scariest sound that Lexi had ever heard. It made her recent car accident seem like a bumper car ride. Too scared to move, she called out, "Is everyone okay?"

Ignoring Lexi, the co-pilot unbuckled his belt to get up and started to give Aaron orders, "Check where we are. See if any fires started or if there are any fuel leaks."

"On it."

Lexi couldn't move. Not from fear but because her seat had moved, and she was jammed up against the other seat. She couldn't feel her legs. "Trying not to panic, she said to Kesia, "Can you help me?"

Kesia didn't answer.

Lexi asked again, "Hey, Kesia, can you help me, please?"

There was blood coming from Kesia's forehead. She was unconscious.

Struggling to get free, Lexi yelled to Isabella, "Iss, can you move?"

Isabella couldn't move. She was pinned in as well.

Lexi fought for her life and used all her strength to wiggle free from her constraints. *God help me, please!*

Chapter 24

Before Aaron left to check the plane, he said, "Mike, there is a girl stuck in the restroom. She was alive before the plane slid."

The plane had luckily landed top-side up. However, the plane's tail had broken away, leaving a six-foot opening.

In case the plane slid some more, Aaron gingerly stepped through the tail end of the plane.

As he looked out, all was dark.

Knowing there would be a flashlight, he searched the cabin cabinets.

It only took a few moments before he found what he was looking for.

Maneuvering through the wreckage, Arron directed the light out of the plane.

Not sure he saw what he thought he saw. Arron moved the light to inspect the ground better. The ground seemed like an open graveyard of goats, snakes, and birds—their bones littered the limestone floor.

Stepping out, he shone the light to the sides and realized the plane had slid into a gigantic cave. He could see thousands of rather rough cave pearls and numerous high stalagmites.

Natural moonlight shone through an opening far above as he stepped out of the plane. "Man, that must be at least one hundred yards up, if not higher. Not sure how we are getting out of this place."

After walking the perimeter of the plane and checking the damage, he came back inside to tell Mike.

"Mike, you are not going to believe where we are."

Lexi looked up as Aaron came back in.

"We are in a gigantic cave." Looking around, he could see that they had gotten the girl out of the restroom. She was bleeding, but he could see her chest moving and was relieved to know that she was going to live. Looking at Lexi, he said, "How is everybody?"

She hesitated, then answered, "Everyone is alive, but Kesia and Aias are still unconscious, and the pilot gave Luna something for the pain."

Aaron looked over at Isabella. She had stopped screaming but was staring into oblivion. "Is she alright?"

Lexi answered, "She is in shock."

"Where is Mike?"

Lexi looked around, "He was here a moment ago."

Aaron walked to the front of the plane and found Mike sitting in the co-pilot seat, staring at the deceased pilot.

"Mike, are you okay?"

No answer.

"Mike?"

Coming out of a daze, he answered, "What?"

"You okay?"

"Ya. What did you find?"

"We are in some type of cave."

"That makes sense. I can't reach anyone on the radio."

"I am afraid we are stuck down here. I hope that when the sun comes up, I will be able to see better. There is a small opening in the ceiling of the cave."

"Help me get him out of here, will ya?"

"For sure," Aaron replied. "I'll get something to wrap him in."

He was only gone for a few moments, but Mike was slumped over in his chair when he came back in.

Immediately checking the pulse on Mike's neck, Aaron took a breath of relief. Mike had just fallen asleep from exhaustion.

Wrapping the pilot's body in a blanket, Aaron picked him up and placed him over his shoulder as he carried him out of the plane.

Lexi had followed Aaron out. "I am sorry for your loss."

"He was a good man. Loving husband and father to three young children. It will be heartbreaking to tell his wife the news."

"You'll have to tell them?"

"Yes, he was my second cousin. It will have to be me that tells them."

Changing the subject, Lexi asked, "What happened? Why did we crash?"

"I am not entirely sure. All I remember was seeing something coming straight for us."

Lexi was surprised, "What do you mean, like a bird?"

"No bigger."

"Like a missile?"

"No. Nothing like that." Aaron shook his head. He could have sworn that what he saw coming at them had a ghostly body.

"Do you know where we are?" Lexi asked.

"For a split second, just before we crashed, the monitors read that we were off course and were just above Oman."

"Where is that?" Lexi asked, never hearing the name before.

"On the southeastern end of the Arabian Peninsula. It borders the United Arab Emirates in the northwest."

"Weren't we supposed to be flying over Iran?" Lexi asked.

"Yes, but somehow, we ended up further south and on the other side of the Persian Gulf."

As she cautiously stepped out of the plane, she said, "I heard you say we are in a cave."

The morning light was just starting to peek through the hole in the cave's ceiling, and the beams of light moved unusually fast.

"What a bizarre sight," Lexi said as she watched the beams of light move as if time was fast-forwarding.

"I've read about this," Aaron said. "It is even stranger in person."

"Why do you think there are so many bones down here?" Lexi said, trying not to walk on any.

"My best guess is that they fall in."

"That makes sense. So, how are we getting out of here?"

Shaking his head and about to answer her that he didn't know, he saw a long rope fall from the above hole. "Look," he said as he pointed up. "Someone is descending from above."

Lexi looked up as Aaron ran over and yelled, "We are over here."

Waving his arms and shining his light as a beacon, Aaron felt a wave of relief come over his body. A tear escaped, and he was so excited that he didn't care if Lexi saw it.

Looking back at Lexi, he yelled excitedly, "We will be okay!"

Chapter 25

"Guys, you are not going to believe what the noise was caused by!" Jerome yelled up from the rope he was using to descend the entrance of the cave called Khoshilat Maqandeli.

Ever since he was a kid growing up in Harlem, Jerome has always known he wanted to be a firefighter. Climbing gave him a thrill that he couldn't explain. Ladders, mountains, it didn't matter. He loved to climb. The higher, the better.

Maybe it was because his great-grandfather was a Hellfighter, the most celebrated African-American regiment in World War I. Private Jerome Kennard the 1st. Jerome's great-great-grandmother named her son after Saint Jerome, also known as Jerome of Stridon. Maybe that is why Jerome had no fear. He had the namesake of a Saint.

He and his team had come to Oman, southeast of Muscat, to explore the Majlis al Jinn cave chambers—in Arabic, the word for "genie" is "al-Jinn"—the meeting place of the genies.

It took him a while to figure out how to get the special permit needed from the Ministry of Tourism Oman to make the descent, but he succeeded.

After months of planning, it had taken his team two hours by four-wheel-drive to climb the steep slopes of the Omani Hajar Mountains. Then, they had to walk the last five or so miles on foot, carrying all their ropes and equipment. They were informed before where they could stay and decided to camp overnight, about a mile from the cave entrance.

Jerome awoke to a horrendous loud noise. Twenty minutes later, another loud noise came from the direction of the cave. This time, the chilling sound of metal pierced the tranquil air. Like an eerie whisper through the sparse, rugged terrain, the distant, tortured symphony of metal against unyielding stone lasted a few moments and then complete silence. Still too dark to go and explore, he had no choice but to wait until dawn. *How did these guys not walk up to the sound?* Not able to go back to sleep, he got up and made coffee.

Being an expert mountain climber, he had dreamed of this moment when he could descend into the abyss instead of ascending into the clouds.

He had researched the Majlis al Jinn and knew that it represented a single, giant chamber with three holes in the ceiling. The surface of the Selma Plateau, where it is located, was 4560 feet above sea level. The cave was said to be as big as eleven football fields.

Mixed emotions of anticipation, excitement, and the unknown from entering the narrow chimney were nothing compared to the vast space he was now looking down into. It was as if he had entered the mouth of a serpent that could swallow him whole. He prayed he had enough rope to reach the bottom.

From above, his best friend Jeff yelled and said, "What aren't we going to believe?"

"I think it is a plane. But wait. Hey, there are people down there."

"There are what?" Jeff yelled for confirmation.

"People," Jerome said. "Hurry, get me down there. Faster. They're in trouble."

Jerome yelled to the people as he approached the cave floor, "Are any of you hurt?"

"Yes," Aaron yelled back up. "We need an air ambulance. There are eight of us. Three are unconscious, and one is dead."

"Dead?" Jerome yelled.

"Unfortunately, yes," Aaron whispered but nodded.

As Jerome's feet touched the ground, he called on a walkie-talkie-type device to Jeff.

"We need one of our team members to return to Muscat and get help. There are seven survivors and one deceased from a plane crash. Three of them are unconscious."

"Shit!" is all Jerome heard before Jeff ended the conversation.

"My guys are going for help, but it will take many hours before help arrives. How can I help?"

"Anyway, to pull us up?" Aaron said honestly.

"Do you have a board that we can use to lift the unconscious people?"

"Yes, I can make that happen," Aaron said as he returned to the plane.

Jerome and Lexi followed Aaron into the plane.

Jerome's firefighting instincts went into action as soon as he entered the plane. "We have to get all of you out of here. It is not safe. The plane could blow."

Lexi turned to Aaron and said, "I thought you said there were no fires?"

"There aren't," he answered.

Jerome cut in and said, "In a crash, sparks could be happening in areas of the plane that you cannot see. So, it is better to be on the safe side."

Too tired to care that Lexi seemed to blame him for an unsafe procedure, Aaron pulled a foldable scoop stretcher from a hidden compartment and gave it to Jerome.

"Perfect," Jerome said as he took it and went over to the first unconscious person.

Mike came over and asked, "Who are you, and what do you think you are doing?"

Barely looking up as he searched for a pulse, Jerome said, "Lieutenant Jerome Kennard the 4th. NYFD at your service."

Jerome didn't have to look up to know that the pilot was speechless. His silence said everything. "Help me get this guy onto the stretcher, will ya?"

Aaron and Mike helped Jerome move Aias safely onto the stretcher.

Jerome took the lead and took hold of the stretcher, guiding the others to move Aias out of the plane. Then, yelling back, he said, "Bring some blankets."

Lexi started opening compartments until she found the blankets.

Jerome didn't stop until everyone was safely out of the plane and at the base of the rope.

Jeff had descended in the meantime and was waiting with the proper equipment to lift everyone out.

It took most of the day, but by the time the last person was out of the cave, an army helicopter was approaching the plateau.

There wasn't enough room for everyone from the plane crash, so Lexi volunteered, "That's okay. I'll catch a ride back with you guys if that works?"

Jerome didn't really have a choice and just smiled.

Chapter 26

After the helicopter left with Aias, Luna, Kesia, Isabella, Mike, and Aaron, Lexi sat next to a fire that had been burning since this morning. "It is a miracle that of all the hikers. God would send a group of firefighters, and not just that, but from New York City."

Jerome sat down next to her and said as he passed her some fire-cooked wieners and beans with cornbread, "You believe in God?"

Startled, Lexi turned to him and said, "You don't?"

"I didn't say that."

"It sounded like it," Lexi replied as she took the plate he held out to her. "Thank you."

"You're welcome. There is nothing like wood fire cooking."

"You would think you would hate the smell of a fire," Lexi said.

"You would think."

After a few moments of silence, Jeff approached Jerome and said, "There are a good few hours left of daylight. Are you coming down with us to explore the cave?"

Jerome looked at Lexi and said, "If she goes, I will."

"Jerome, our permit only allows for today's descent."

Lexi was shocked that they thought she would return to the pit. "Ah, really, back down there?"

As Jerome got up, he said, "Come on. You won't get to have an opportunity to see the sights of this cave ever again."

Looking at Jerome's friends, Lexi knew she was holding back Jerome from an experience that he had come all this way for. Taking his outstretched hand, she shook her head and said, "I must be crazy."

Jerome's team consisted of five other guys. Lexi met them all—Jeff, Pete, Sal, Harold, and Langston.

Being lowered into what she found out was called the chimney, Lexi was in awe. Jerome said as he descended right beside Lexi to make sure she was safe, "Majlis Al Jinn is considered one of the largest underground caves in the world."

"Why do they call it the meeting place of the genies?" Lexi asked.

Jerome smiled.

Lexi couldn't help but notice how white his teeth were. Down here, his skin blended into the darkness, and when he smiled, his teeth became the light. He had an amazing smile.

Jerome answered by saying, "In the hinterlands of Oman's mountains, legends tell of jinn, or genies, who possess the landscape, haunting craggy mountains, majestic forts, and colorful mosques. Well, anyways, that is what one of the websites I researched said."

"Genies, really? You mean like rub the lamp, and a genie appears type of genie?" Lexi asked.

Helping her untie from the ropes, he said, "You haven't done your homework now, have you?"

"Homework? I was supposed to be in India right now."

"Oh right, the plane crashed," Jerome said as they walked past it.

Trying to get her mind off the life-changing experience, turning her eyes away from the plane as she passed, she said, "No, really, what do they mean, genies?"

"You have heard of Sinbad the Sailor and the Queen of Sheba?"

"Of course, they are kids' stories," Lexi said as she moved carefully through the cave.

"Well, then you know that genies are not all cute and cuddly as Walt Disney makes them out to be. Here in Oman, genies are shape-shifting spirits made of fire and air. Did you know that there is mention of jinn in the Quran?"

"No," Lexi answered honestly.

"I read that pagan Arabs worshipped jinn long before Islam was introduced in the seventh century. They believed that these shape-shifting spirits were masters of certain crafts and elements of nature. For example, they had the power to turn plots of land fertile."

"That's kind of scary," Lexi said as she watched her footing.

"From what I have read, jinn can possess a human."

"I thought they just granted wishes," Lexi smiled.

Jeff joined the conversation, "These smoke-like spirits are said to be good or bad but can control the elements."

"So, the Arab people believe the jinn controls the weather?" Lexi asked innocently.

"Seems that way," Jeff answered.

Following behind the others, Langston said, "There is a relief on the north wall of the Palace of King Sargon II at Khorsabad in Iraq that depicts a winged genie approaching the Tree of Life."

"I read that the Arabs of pre-Islam invented a whole set of exorcism procedures to protect themselves from the evil actions of the jinn on their bodies and minds, such as the use of beads, incense, bones, salt, and charms written in Arabic, Hebrew, and Syriac, or the hanging around their necks of a dead animal's teeth such as a fox or a cat to frighten the jinn, and keep them away," Sal added.

Pete wanted to join the conversation and said, "In Bahla, a remote Arabian outpost, residents claim to experience jinn sightings regularly."

Harold cleared his throat, "Islamic tradition tells us that Allah created the angels on Wednesday. On Thursday, however, the jinn came into being. According to Muslim tradition, the jinn is one of the three intelligent beings created by God."

"What are the other two?" Lexi asked him.

"Angels and humans."

A weird thought came to Lexi, "Are all genies male?"

The guys looked at each other. "Good question," Jerome said. "I don't know."

Harold piped up and said, "No. A female jinn is called Sila, which means Hag. These spirits are classified as one of the most malicious classes of jinn."

Jerome laughed, "Of course, you would think that." Then, leaning over to Lexi, he whispered, "His woman just left him and took everything."

"Ah, I see," Lexi whispered back.

The next day turned out to be a marvel. Lexi was grateful that she stayed behind and returned with these fine men.

On the drive back through Wadi Ash, she saw the Bronze Age Tombs—approximately 4,000-5,000-year-old beehive tombs built with local flat stones stacked in the shape of a beehive.

She also saw fantastic vertical drop-offs and narrow shelves riskily perched beneath the soaring cliffs that sit mightily above the Grand Canyon of Oman, where turquoise swimming holes and actual ghost towns are rarely seen by outsiders because of their randomly remote locations.

The guys camped on one of Oman's pristine beaches to finish their trip. That is where Lexi saw endangered sea turtles and endless fields of sand dunes.

Camped beneath the stars, Lexi said a silent prayer. *Dear Archangel Hamied, thank you for your presence. I know we are alive because of your team of angels performing these miracles. I am forever in your debt. Amen.*

Chapter 27

Back in New York City, the first thing that Lexi did was go to the hospital. "How is he?" she asked Isabella.

Isabella answered with tears in her eyes, "The doctors don't know why he isn't waking up. They say that he doesn't have any unusual organ damage other than bruising. They figure he must have a serious concussion."

"I am so sorry, Isabella. Is there anything I can do?"

"You could pray for him. You seem good at that, and maybe ask Susannah for help?"

"Sure, I can do that." Lexi bowed her head and closed her eyes—*Dear God and anyone else up there who can help me. Susannah, if you are listening, you too, please. My dear friend's son, Aias, requires a miracle. He is a sweet boy with many gifts still needed in this world. Please cure him. Amen.*

Hi, little sister.

Susannah?

I am here.

Oh, thank God. Aias is in trouble.

Yes, he is visiting us in the angel world right now.

Please tell him to wake up. His mom is worried sick.

Lexi, you know I don't have powers like that. I can only help you.

Oh. Lexi thought for a moment. *Can you help me to help him?*

You know I can't answer that question.

Why?

You know you have to be specific.

Oh, right. Lexi thought for a moment. Then she had a great idea. *Okay, Susannah, I got it. I will try to do that hands-on healing stuff that I learned in Japan.*

Susannah didn't answer.

Don't you think that is a good idea? Susannah?

I'm here. You know I can't think for you.

Oh, right.

Well, that is what I am going to do.

Lexi opened her eyes, placed her hands above Aias's body, and waited.

Nothing seemed to be happening.

Isabella looked over at Lexi and asked. "What are you doing?"

"I think it is called Reiki."

"What is supposed to happen?" Isabella asked curiously.

Lexi shrugged her shoulders.

"Aias just touched people, and they healed instantly. Can't you do that?" Isabella asked.

Lexi lowered her hands and touched Aias.

Nothing happened.

"No, apparently not."

"Well, try harder, "Isabella said, not meaning to be hurtful, just desperately wanting her son to wake up.

Lexi shut her eyes. *Susannah, what am I doing wrong?*

No answer.

Oh, right. Susannah, please find a spirit who can help me do this hands-on healing.

A moment later, a spirit with a male voice and a thick Japanese accent said, *you forgot to bring down the power.*

I did? How do I do that again? Lexi asked.

Bring the heavenly healing power down through your crown chakra. This invisible channel runs through the top of your head—where a baby's soft spot is.

Lexi did as he said and imagined the power coming down from the heavens and entering her head.

She could feel a tingle as it touched her crown. She imagined that the energy touched her heart for love and then ran out through her palms to Aias's body. *How long do I wait?*

As long as it takes.

Is there a way that I can do this but not have to hold this position?

Not with Reiki.

Is there another modality that does?

Not that I know of.

Susannah, please find a spirit that can teach me the modality similar to Reiki that heals, but I don't have to hold the hand positions.

Moments later, Lexi heard Tamara's voice. *It is called the healing pool.*

Tamara? Is that you?

I am called Sophea now.

Oh, my God, I have missed you so much. Hey, wait. Are you dead?

No.

How are you talking to me then?

It is something I learned here in Nepal.

Wow, so cool.

Isabella asked, "Lexi, are you okay? You're breathing funny."

Lexi opened her eyes and said, "You're not going to believe who is here talking to me."

"Who?"

"Tamara, but she is now called Sophea."

"Is she here to help?"

"I think so. I'll tell you in a moment." Lexi shut her eyes and focused back on Tamara.

Sophea, are you here to help me?

Yes.

Opening an eye, Lexi peeked out for an instant to tell Isabella yes. Then she closed her eyes again and asked, *Sophea, what do I need to do to help Aias wake up?*

It is called the healing pool.

What do you want me to do?

Do as I say. First, let go of the Reiki energy.

Lexi released her hands and lightly shook them. *Now what?*

Isabella watched Lexi and asked, "What are you doing?"

Lexi opened her eyes and said, "Sophea is guiding me on something called a healing pool."

"Oh."

Lexi shut her eyes and asked Sophea, *What's next?*

Relax by taking three deep breaths.

She remembered Tamara teaching her this years ago and took three deep breaths. *Now what?*

Imagine that you are walking on a pathway that leads to a building.

Lexi imagined doing what Sophea told her. A moment later, a building appeared in Lexi's mind. *I see it. Now what?*

Enter the building and go to the backdoor.

Lexi imagined what Sophea instructed. *Okay, I am at the back door. Now what?*

Go out through the backdoor and enter the garden. This garden has a healing pool with a flowing waterfall. Walk over to it.

Lexi imagined opening the door, walking to the pool, and looking at the water. *How is that going to heal Aias?*

This water is magical and will heal anything that enters it.

Are you sure?

Go ahead and enter the water.

Do you want me to go into the pool?

Yes. The water is a perfect temperature.

Do I need to take my clothes off?

You can be clothed, naked, or wear a swimsuit. You decide what you are wearing.

Lexi imagined she was in a swimsuit, and instantly she was. Then she bent down to touch the water. It felt warm and soothing. She stood up and entered the water. It felt nice. *What do I do now?*

You can swim if you like. You can even breathe underwater.

Cool. Lexi was too scared to try, so she just swam. *Now what?*

Your body can become completely buoyant if you want to float. There is no way of drowning.

Good to know. What if I don't want to swim?

You may sit at the edge and have your feet or hands touch the water if you would rather.

Great, I would like that. Lexi came out of the water and sat on the edge with her feet dangling in. *Now what?*

You may stay as long as you like.

But I want to help Aias.

With those words, you are going to keep wanting.

What?

You said wanting. Careful Lexi. Remember, Spirit is literal.

Oh, right. Using the word wanting is what I will manifest, wanting.

Correct.

How long do I need to stay in the water? Lexi asked Sophea.

You can stay a few moments, hours, days, or even years.

Years! We don't have years. And shouldn't Aias be in the water, not me?

The soul must want to be in the water. He is not here, so we can't force him into the water.

Then why did I learn this if it won't help Aias?

To help Isabella. She needs healing too, Sophea replied.

True, but what about Aias?

He is having a time-out right now. This time is for you to learn what you need to know. He is on a different path.

Will he awake?

In time.

Isabella was getting impatient. "What is happening?"

Before answering Isabella, Lexi asked Sophea, *is there anything else I need to know about the healing pool?*

Only everyone can have their own, and you can bring as many people to the healing pool as you want. But Lexi, only with their permission.

Got it. Thanks, Tamara. I mean Sophea. I miss you. Will I see you again?

In time.

Opening her eyes, Lexi said to Isabella, "I can't heal him. He has to ask me for help."

"But he is in a coma. How can he ask you for help?" Isabella said, frustrated.

"I don't know," Lexi answered honestly.

Chapter 28

While Isabella cried after hearing that, Lexi went out into the hallway to give her a few moments of peace.

"Jerome?" Lexi said as she almost bumped into him.

Looking down at her, he said, "Lexi, what are you doing here?"

She said, pointing to the room, "Aias is still unconscious."

"I am sorry to hear that," he said sincerely.

"Thanks. Hey, do you have time for a coffee? My treat."

"I wish I did, but I am here to visit a friend."

Embarrassed as she turned back to enter the hospital room, Lexi said, "Some other time then."

Grabbing her arm lightly, Jerome said, "Lexi, I would love to have coffee with you. Could we meet sometime tomorrow? I have the day off."

Stopping in her tracks, she turned around slowly and said, "I would like that."

"Great. I can pick you up here around three?"

"That would be perfect. That way, I can spend time with Aias and Isabella."

Before he turned to walk down the hallway to his friend's room, he smiled at her and said in his sexy, deep voice, "Looking forward to it."

Noticing the smile on Lexi's face as she entered Aias's room, Isabella said, "What pills did they give you out there? I want some."

Lexi's smile went even bigger as she said, "I ran into Jerome."

"Fireman Jerome?"

Lexi nodded as she sat down and touched Aias's hand.

He flinched.

Shocked, Lexi said to Isabella, "Did you see that?"

Just as shocked, Isabella answered, "I did. Do it again."

"Do what again?"

"Whatever you did to make him flinch."

Lexi shook her head and said, "I didn't do anything."

"Lexi, you must have. Do it again."

Lexi touched Aias.

Nothing.

"You're not doing it right. Come on, Lexi, do it again."

Lexi tried again.

Nothing.

A tear escaped down Isabella's already tearful cheek.

"Isabella, I am sorry. I really don't know why he flinched."

Interrupting the girls, Jerome peeked his head in and said, "Lexi, can we make it three-thirty? My friend won't be out of surgery until three."

Surprised at his voice, she smiled and said, "Sure."

He gave her another one of his amazing smiles and said, "Great. See you then." Then he left as fast as he had entered.

Aias flinched.

Lexi was still holding his hand. "Oh my God. He slightly moved again."

"Lexi, he moves when you are around Jerome."

"Why?" Lexi asked, confused.

"Think about him again. Think about seeing him tomorrow."

Aias flinched.

"What were you thinking?" Isabella asked excitedly.

"I love his smile."

Aias flinched again.

"Oh my God, Isabella. You're right. Aias does flinch when I think about Jerome."

Having an idea, Isabella said, "Think about Edward."

Nothing. No movement from Aias.

"Hmm, think about Redington."

Aias's eyes twitched and opened for an instant.

"Oh my God."

"Lexi, think about Jerome's smile."

Aias's hand flinched.

"Think about Edward."

Nothing.

"Think about Redington."

Aias's eyes twitched open again for a moment.

"Why do you think this is happening, "Lexi asked Isabella.

"The power of love is pretty amazing. Here, let me try."

As Lexi let go, Isabella took hold of her son's hand. Shutting her eyes, she thought about Hans—Erland.

Nothing.

"Why isn't it working? I love Aias's father."

"Isabella, think about the first day you met him," Lexi said, thinking there was a difference between love and new love.

Isabella shut her eyes and imagined the first time she saw Hans during a short, impromptu mid-January vacation on Red Mountain in Aspen, Colorado. When she entered the room, he was drinking in the hotel's bar with a couple of guys.

As he looked her way and smiled, their chemistry was instant. She felt a surge of energy that exploded from her heart.

He was gorgeous, even with his dirty blond hair messed up from taking off his toque.

Sitting at the only available table left, she ended up beside the three men.

Within moments of her sitting down, the men introduced themselves in broken English and asked her to join them.

They were from Switzerland and on a corporate business trip. They were lawyers.

"Your accent doesn't sound Swiss," she said to Hans."

"I am originally from Sweden," he replied.

Later that evening, she boldly asked him out on a date.

Since Han's co-workers left the next morning, she enjoyed skiing with her newfound friend for the next few days.

Lucky for her, Han's English was limited, and with his busy schedule back home, he didn't have time to follow the media and rarely went out to the movies. He didn't know how famous she was.

It only took a few days of being in his company that she knew that he was the one.

Thinking back to that weekend made Isabella's heart sing. She had fallen madly in love with Hans and loved every moment they had spent together.

"I didn't know that was how you met my father," Aias said quietly.

Isabella and Lexi squealed at the same time.

This time, Isabella's tears were joyous ones!

Chapter 29

Lexi had spent an extra few minutes, actually an hour, getting ready for her coffee date with Jerome. She didn't look quite as good as the runway models that she used to design for, but nonetheless, she could win a few beauty pageants.

"You look pretty fancy for a hospital visit," Isabella teased.

Lexi smiled at them both and asked Aias, "How are you doing?"

"Better now that you are here."

"Aw, that is sweet of you to say," Lexi said with an even bigger smile.

"Good thing you came now because he is being released. The doctor gave him a clean bill of health," Isabella said as she stroked his hair.

Before Lexi could answer, Jerome knocked on the door and asked, "May I come in?"

Looking over, Isabella said quietly to Lexi, "Now I understand why you look so pretty." Then, to Jerome, she said, "Yes, please come in, Jerome. How are you doing?"

"Good, thank you." Looking at Aias, he said, "So this is the son we rescued from the cave." Putting out his hand, he said, "I am Lieutenant Jerome Kennard, one of New York's Bravest, at your service."

Aias smiled and asked, "Is it true that the City of New York fire department is the largest fire department in the United States and universally is recognized as the world's busiest and most highly skilled emergency response agency?"

Jerome looked at the two women and then back to Aias, "That is what the internet says, but yes, I believe so."

Excited to learn something new, Aias asked, "How many fires do you go to?"

"FDNY not only responds to more than a million emergencies every year, but its personnel also strive to prevent them by continually educating the public in fire, life safety, and disaster preparedness, along with enforcing public safety codes. But just between you and me, as many as I can."

Aias asked another question, "What district are you with?"

"FDNY Engine 59, Ladder 30, in Manhattan, Central Harlem."

Aias asked him, "What is your Fire House nickname?"

Jerome chuckled, "The Harlem Zoo."

Lexi laughed, "How did you guys get that name?"

"Your guess is as good as mine. Our guys don't even know. My best guess is because of having to fight fires in the always-changing neighborhood over the last 100 years."

Aias went to ask another question.

Lexi smiled as she took hold of Jerome's arm and said, "We better get going. These two have to get ready to be discharged."

Jerome nodded and said, "I look forward to seeing you all again."

Aias said quickly, "Come for dinner tonight. I am sure Lexi would love that."

Blushing, Lexi said, "I am sure he is busy."

"Actually, I'm not. I would love to come for dinner."

Isabella added, "It would be our pleasure to show you our gratitude. See you two around six."

Lexi's smile was slightly sarcastic to Aias as she followed Jerome out into the hallway. "I am sorry that he put you on the spot. You don't have to come if you have other plans."

"No, it is okay. I want to come if that is okay with you."

Lexi smiled, "Of course it is."

After a wonderful afternoon together, Lexi and Jerome arrived at Aias's condo just before six.

Lexi used her key to get in.

"You have a key?" Jerome asked.

"Actually, I live here with Aias. It is a bit of a long story."

"I see."

Entering the condo, the aroma of Italian spaghetti sauce lingered in the air.

"Mmm, smells good," Jerome said, following Lexi into the kitchen.

Aias smiled, "Lexi taught me how to cook it."

Jerome smiled at Lexi.

Isabella came into the room with two glasses of red wine and passed them to Lexi and Jerome. "I hope you two had a wonderful afternoon?"

"They did," Aias said before either could answer.

Jerome looked at Lexi to see if Aias was correct.

Lexi blushed in confirmation.

"Told you," Aias said.

"Aias, behave," Isabella chuckled.

Trying to change the subject, Lexi said, "How are you feeling, Aias?"

"Good as new."

"That is wonderful to hear," Lexi said as she came over and kissed him on the cheek. "You had me worried."

As they sat down for supper, Jerome spoke up and said, "It is a miracle that any of you survived that crash."

Lexi looked at him and said, "It was a miracle you were there to save us."

"That too," he said in agreement.

Isabella asked the group, "Don't you ever wonder why?"

"Why what?" Lexi asked, confused.

As she took a bite of the delicious spaghetti, Isabella answered, "Why did we survive such an ordeal? Not just that, but why did we have to go through it?"

"Interesting question," Lexi said as she thought more about it.

"I have wondered that same question since my first witness of a miracle," Jerome added.

With a fork full of spaghetti, Aias looked up and asked him, "Tell us more. I would love to hear about your experiences."

Chapter 30

"Are you sure you want to hear about it? My job is not really a supper-time conversation."

Aias said, "Good. It would be boring if it were."

"Might as well entertain him," Lexi said to Jerome.

"As long as y'all have the stomach for it."

Isabella took a sip of her wine and said, "I played an actress in a fire once."

Jerome had forgotten she was a famous actress and said, "It was quite a few years back. I had passed the entrance requirements, written exam, physical exam, and candidate review. I had graduated from the five-month extensive in-class and on-field firefighting and prevention training. But nothing could have prepared me for what came next."

Aias was finished eating and sat up straighter, interested in Jerome's story.

Lexi moved the plates off the table as Isabella poured them more wine.

"It was an apartment fire, and the blaze could be seen for miles. I tried to swallow my fear, but my anticipation had turned my gut upside down."

Lexi quietly sat back down.

"I still remember the sound of the sirens as we raced to the fire. My heart felt as if it would jump out of my chest. It was beating so fast." Taking a sip of his wine, Jerome continued. "At first, my mind went blank. All the weeks of training seemed to have disappeared. However, my Captain was very aware, and even though he was barking out commands, he patted my back and said kindly, "Kennard, you've got this. Just do exactly as I tell you."

Aias adjusted his seating.

"It still feels so real." Jerome blinked as if he had just come out of a dream and said, "That is all it took, a pat on my back. Suddenly, I had the courage of a veteran firefighter. From that moment on, I seemed to know what to do intuitively."

"So, what happened to the fire?" Lexi asked.

"The Ladder Crew were tackling the situation from above. But my team entered the building from the main door. I had followed one of the other firefighters into the building. I remember there were flames everywhere. I can still smell the smoke. We could hear screams. As we hurried in the direction of the yelling, I stepped, and the floor below me caved in."

Lexi gasped, "Oh, my God."

The story transfixed Aias.

Isabella put down her glass of wine in case she dropped it.

Jerome continued, "I fell fifteen feet, but that wasn't the miracle."

"But it was a miracle. You survived the fall," Lexi said.

Jerome nodded and continued, "I remember looking around. I was trapped. There was no way out. The fire was an inferno."

"How did you survive?" Isabella asked.

"I prayed. I prayed for a miracle. I prayed that this would not be my last day on earth."

Aias nodded and said, "Prayer is amazing."

"But how did you get out?" Isabella asked again.

"One of the firefighters threw down a fire hose, and I remember the water instantly cooling down my suit. A second hose was thrown down, and I tied it around my waist. Then, both hoses were pulled up at the same time. I remember that I held the hose that had the water blasting out directly below me so that the water kept the fire at bay as they pulled me up."

"Was that the miracle?" Aias asked.

"No."

Lexi said, "It is in my eyes."

"So, what was the miracle then?" Aias asked.

"After I had been given the okay that I wasn't injured in any way, I snuck back in to help."

"You didn't," Lexi gasped again.

Jerome nodded and said, "I was young and foolish. All I could think about were the people screaming and to get back in there to help my team save them."

Aias couldn't help himself, "So, what was the miracle?"

Jerome looked at him, saying, "It was as if an invisible force was driving me. I seemed to know where to go, even though I could barely see through the smoke."

"Where did you end up?" Aias asked.

"On the third floor. I just followed my instincts and headed towards a door at the end of the hall."

"What was there? What did you find?" Aias asked with anticipation.

"I kicked the door down and entered the apartment. At first, I couldn't find anything other than more flames. But suddenly, I thought I heard a whimper."

Lexi and Isabella were on the edge of their seats, holding their breath.

"I used a chair and climbed up and opened a cupboard door, and there staring at me was a kitten."

Lexi let out her breath, "A kitten. All that for a kitten?"

"I don't think he is done. Let him finish his story, "Aias said to Lexi.

Jerome nodded to Aias, "I took the kitten out, but it got away from me. So, following it, I ended up in the bathroom. It took a moment, but I found the kitten."

Aias was holding his breath now.

"Where?" Lexi couldn't wait any longer.

Jerome looked at her and said, "Snuggled up to an unconscious two-year-old and his mother."

"Wow," Isabella said. "What a story."

"Was that the miracle?" Aias asked.

"The miracle was that no one died in the fire. My team got everyone out safely, including me."

"That is an amazing story," Lexi said.

"I bet you have all kinds of stories about miracles," Aias told Jerome. "What does it feel like to be in a fire?"

"I do, but I think that is enough stories for one night. Did I see a cake in the kitchen?"

Isabella quickly got up to get the cake.

"I don't know how you do it?" Lexi said to Jerome.

"Do what?"

"Act as if everything is normal."

"It is all in a day's work as a firefighter."

Chapter 31

"Who was that?" Pete asked Jerome.

Jerome smiled and said, "Lexi."

"The skinny girl from the plane crash? I thought you liked blonds with big butts?"

Jerome didn't answer Pete because he was right. He did, but he couldn't get Lexi out of his head. She wasn't anything like the other women that he had dated.

His curiosity was getting the best of him, so Pete asked, "What did she want?"

But before Jerome could answer, the clanging sound of the fire bell went off, and within moments, Jerome's crew of firefighters were headed towards a blazing fire in a deserted commercial building.

As they arrived, the brilliant blue and red lights of many police cars' flashed. Jerome was thankful that the NYPD had set up a protective perimeter for his team.

Don't these looky-loos know that curiosity killed the cat? Thank God for the police barricade. They make my job safer. If it weren't for them, I am sure I would have died a few times over trying to save these inquisitive souls from getting too close to the fire. Shaking his head, Jerome went to the nearest police officer and asked, "What do you know so far?"

"Not much. All I know is that we got an anonymous 911 call."

Heading towards the fire before his crew, Jerome called out, "Follow my lead."

Not knowing what was in front of him, Jerome thought back to Aias's question *of how it felt to be caught in a fire.*

As Jerome thought about it, Aias appeared.

Almost jumping out of his skin, Jerome yelled, "Aias, what are you doing here?"

Aias telepathically told Jerome, *don't worry, I am not really here. I am bilocating.*

"What are you talking about?"

Pete looked over to Jerome and asked, "Are you okay? Who are you talking to?"

Before Jerome could answer, Aias said, *you don't have to talk to me. I can hear your thoughts.*

Jerome looked at Pete and said, "I thought I heard something."

"I didn't hear anything," Pete answered.

A few of the other guys said they didn't hear anything, either.

Inside the building, it was pitch black and quiet. Jerome could only hear the sound of crackling wood until Aias asked him, *tell me what you are feeling while fighting this fire.*

Jerome tried to shake the thought that he might be losing his mind. But, as he moved his head from side to side, his protective mask shook.

You're not going crazy, Aias said. *I'll explain this all to you later. Focus your attention on the fire, not me.*

It wasn't that hard to do since Jerome and his team had to get down on their knees.

Why are you doing that? Aias asked.

Jerome thought the answer, *depending on where the fire was, was that there might be smoke above your head or around your waist, so you have to get down on your knees.*

Aias got down on his knees and followed Jerome.

It's quite an eerie place, Aias said.

Jerome answered as he squinted his eyes to see better through the smoke and darkness. *I guess it is. I've been doing this for so long that I forgot how it makes me feel.*

As the team started making their way toward the primary fire, Aias said, *it's starting to get pretty hot.*

Wait, how can you feel if you are only an illusion? Jerome asked.

That is a long story. But then, Aias changed the subject and said, *fascinating how the visibility becomes less and less.*

Jerome answered, *depending on the severity of the fire, you could be entering a room that's completely separate from the actual fire, and there's not a lot of heat, but you cannot see your hand in front of your face."*

When do you guys decide the heat is too hot and it's time to get out? Aias asked.

When your ears get even hotter, but if there are people in here who need saving, your ears might get singed.

Aias was even more curious and asked, *what do you do if there is a person inside?*

We move quicker. Jerome said, playing along with his hallucination of Aias being there. *In a fire situation, people do strange things. They might be in the cupboard or the bathroom just because they think that's the best place to be. But most of the time, people are lying in their beds.*

Really? Still in their bed.

Yes, it is with mixed feelings when you're searching a room, and suddenly you feel someone's leg or hand. It's a relief, but it's not a nice feeling because chances are they're dead. It is a miracle if they are alive.

Gross. Trying to get the thought out of his head, Aias said, w*hat is the most common cause of a fire?*

The majority of fires are cooking-related. I wish more people would clean their ovens and stove tops from grease splatter. Also, I wish more people wouldn't cook a meal while under the influence of drugs or alcohol.

I have never thought of that.

Yeah, they do stupid things like falling asleep while cooking a pizza. A fire can start in a moment, a lapse in concentration or just not thinking, and before you know it, you've got three to four-foot flames, and you panic and make a wrong decision about how to put it out.

What is the second most common cause of the fire?

Cheap mobile phone chargers that aren't authentic.

Really?

Yep.

As a door opened and the flames lit up the room, Pete yelled, "I see someone."

Jerome shook his head again and said to Aias, get out of here, crawling over to Pete's voice. *I have to do my job, and you are distracting me.*

Aias turned invisible but didn't leave. Instead, he jumped into Jerome's body.

The fire was blazing hot, and as Jerome hurried to where Pete was, Aias could feel

Jerome's ears getting even hotter and how fast Jerome's heart was pounding.

Once outside and still in Jerome's body, Aias was standing by the ambulance, watching as the attendants focused their medical attention on the man from the fire.

What was he doing there? Aias asked Jerome as he left Jerome's body.

Grabbing his chest, Jerome said, *you have to stop doing that. You are going to give me a heart attack.*

Sorry, but really, he looks like a homeless person.

Jerome looked at the man on the gurney. Unfortunately, he was running into this situation more and more. *There are many reasons why someone becomes homeless and finds shelter in an abandoned building. Poverty is the common thread among nearly everyone who experiences homelessness. Many are veterans who were injured in the war and now cannot find jobs. Some are women or children running from domestic violence. Some are people trying to survive just to meet medical care, food, or housing needs, and others are homeless because of physical or mental illnesses.*

I thought most people were homeless because of a drug issue.

True, over sixty percent of homeless people are from drug and alcohol abuse. But no matter the reason, this poor fellow died because of the fire that he started to keep warm.

Aias looked over to the paramedics doing CPR on the homeless guy. *Why are they still working on him? He's dead.*

Because EMTs can't pronounce a person dead, they have to follow protocol until they get to the hospital.

Why are they not using the sirens?

As the ambulance drove away, Jerome answered Aias. *The general rule is to have the lights and sirens on when going to an accident or call out. It is usually an unknown and potentially life-threatening situation, and every second counts. However, on the way to the hospital, the usual rule is not to have lights and sirens during the return journey unless the patient is in critical condition or to get past congested intersections, traffic lights, etc. This is because traveling fast and turning fast can kill a patient. A friend told me that his father taught EMTs to drive with a three-quarter full glass of water on the dashboard or central console— if the glass fell over, the patient died, and the driver failed.*

Aias turned and looked at the building. *Why aren't you guys putting out the flames?*

Jerome turned and looked at his team. *Sometimes, all a firefighter can do when a fire gets too big is try to contain it—keeping any of the other buildings around it from igniting. But...*

Jerome cut in and said as he walked away from Aias. *Aias, I am tired.*

Chapter 32

"*A*ias!" Kesia yelled as she entered his condo and gave him a huge hug.

As Luna entered, she said, "What's up?"

Lexi hugged Luna and smiled at the still-hugging couple, saying, "It is so nice to see you guys again. How have you two been?"

Luna answered since Kesia was too busy still hugging Aias. "It was nice visiting our moms back in Jersey Shore, but I am happy to be back in New York City. I've missed the Big Apple."

"How is Florence? I haven't spoken to her since we all got back from the plane crash."

Luna looked at Kesia and whispered to Lexi, "We don't talk about it. It makes Kesia's mom crazy thinking that her baby girl almost died again."

"Again?" Lexi asked.

"Well, you know. Her mom thinks it was supposed to be Kesia, not Trina, who died that day. And now that Kesia almost died a second time, her mom is even more overprotective."

"Ah, oh. Poor Kesia," Lexi answered just as Isabella came in.

"Look who I found," Isabella said as she opened the door.

Expecting to see Florence, Lexi was surprised it was Jerome.

"Hi, what are you doing here?" Lexi asked him.

Walking in with some attitude, Jerome passed her by and stood in front of Aias, "You better start explaining."

Kesia slowly let go of Aias and turned to look at the angry man. "Aren't you the man who saved us from the plane crash?" Not giving him a chance to answer, she jumped up and down in excitement as she hugged him. "Thank you! Thank you!" And as she started kissing his chest—because he was too tall to reach his cheek—she said, "I owe my life to you. You are an angel."

Jerome was dumbfounded by the girl's reaction and didn't know what to say. He was so mad at Aias for making him think he was going insane, but the girl's hugs and kisses distracted him from why he came over.

"Jerome, what's going on? Why are you mad at Aias?" Lexi asked.

"I can answer that," Aias said.

"What did you do this time, young man?" Isabella said as she stepped between Aias and Jerome.

"Well, actually, it's Jerome's fault for inviting me in."

Jerome shrugged and said, "What! My fault."

"Yes. You let me in when you thought about me asking you what it felt like to fight a fire."

Staring at Aias, Jerome said, "Somebody better start talking, and fast."

Lexi came over to Aias and touched his arm, "Aias, what did you do?"

Aias took a deep breath of confidence and answered, "Well, I was curious."

Lexi nodded and said, "About what?"

"What it felt like to be in a burning building."

"You went into a burning building," Isabella screamed as she shook him. "What were you thinking?"

"Mom, I didn't actually go into the building. I bilocated."

"Oh."

"Oh? Is that all you have to say?" Jerome said, shaking his head. "And that is something normal for you guys?"

Looking at each person in the room, Jerome said, "Really? None of you are freaking out right now?"

Nobody moved.

Jerome went white as a ghost.

Lexi took his arm and led him to the couch, "You better sit down."

Luna said as she sat on the arm of a chair in the living room, "There is nothing like being around you folks; there is always drama."

"Jerome, I am sure Aias didn't mean to freak you out. Right, Aias," Lexi said.

"Come on. I am not the bad guy here. I just wanted to see the miracles that firefighters perform," Aias said, shaking his head. "I don't know what the big deal is."

"Big deal?" Jerome spoke up. "Aias, people's lives count on me to be focused while trying to save them."

"The guy was dead. You couldn't have saved him anyway."

"Aias!" Isabella yelled.

Jerome said to Aias, "No, I couldn't have. I was not there fast enough to save a homeless man's life."

Luna shrugged and said, "All this fuss over a homeless guy. Lighten up, Jerome. If the guy were alive, Aias wouldn't have done what he did."

Jerome turned to Luna. "There was no way that anyone knew that he was in the building. So, are you trying to tell me that Aias has special powers, like x-ray vision?"

Luna looked at Aias.

Aias answered her look by saying, "It doesn't work like that, but yes, I knew the guy was dead."

Jerome got up and said, "I have heard enough." Then, turning to Isabella, "If I didn't think that I would be put into a straight jacket, I would have Aias arrested for what he did."

Lexi stepped in to defend Aias. "I know that this seems crazy, but there is an explanation."

Getting up and walking towards the exit, Jerome said, "Lexi, I really liked you, but y'all are too crazy."

"Lexi, let him go. He isn't good enough for you. He will never understand," Aias said.

Turning as he heard what Aias said, Jerome spoke with anger in his voice, "Young man, you have no right entering my mind or body without my consent. And by the way, the homeless guy was a father of three who had just lost his job, their house, and the ability to feed his family. And if that weren't enough, when he walked home one night from his second job, some kids messed around with an aerosol can, and he lost his sight. Because of it, he gave up and decided that his family were better off without him."

Feeling bad for the man's family, Aias said, "I am sorry, Jerome. I had no idea about that. But all I was trying to do was witness a miracle."

Lexi tried to help by saying, "I am sure he is sorry, Jerome, but he is telling the truth. He is trying to figure out how miracles work."

Frustrated, Jerome said, "Why?"

"It is a long story, but maybe if you let Aias touch you, you'll understand."

"Touch me? Now, why would I do that?"

Aias stepped towards Jerome and said as he touched his arm, "Because I can do this."

Jerome stood transfixed.

A flicker of light flashed like electricity, and at the speed of light right before, Jerome's body swayed.

"What the?" Jerome said as he grabbed the back of his left bicep. "What did you do? How did you do that?"

Jerome pulled up his sleeve and tugged at his arm to get a better look. "What the?"

Running to the bathroom and looking in the mirror, "What is going on? That is not possible!"

Returning to the living room, Jerome said as he sat on the couch, "He can perform miracles?"

Lexi, Isabella, Kesia, and Luna all nodded since they had witnessed more than Aias removing a large scar caused by a third-degree burn.

Chapter 33

"Jerome, are you going to be okay?" Aias asked.

"It is true," Jerome said.

"What is true?" Aias asked Jerome.

"The Señor de los Milagros."

"Who is that?" Aias questioned.

"The Lord of Miracles," Jerome answered in bewilderment.

"I have not heard of him. Tell me more about him."

Lexi, Isabella, Kesia, and Luna made themselves comfortable while listening.

Jerome was in a daze as he said, "I went to see a famous mural when I visited Lima, Peru."

Waiting patiently for Jerome to go on, and when he didn't, Aias asked, "What was the mural of?"

"They said the image was painted during the 17th century."

Trying to be polite but at the same time trying to get Jerome out of his funk, Aias asked, "Who painted it?"

Jerome looked over to Aias and blinked as if he had come out of a spell. "What? What did you ask?"

"You were telling us about a painting in Peru."

"I was?"

"Yes," Aias said, wanting to hear why he talked about the painting.

"Maybe this is too much for him, Aias. Maybe we should let him rest," Lexi said, concerned.

"No, I'm okay," Jerome said to Lexi. Then he looked at Aias. "An enslaved Black African painted it. I think his name was Benito, or maybe it was Pedro Dalcon. No matter, the man painted the image on the walls of a hut in the plantation of Pachacamila."

"What did he paint? This enslaved person, what did he paint?" Aias asked.

Staring at Aias and then at his arm, Jerome answered, "A black Jesus Christ on the cross. Above him were the Holy Spirit and God the Father. On the left was the Virgin Mary, and on the right was Mary Magdalene."

"Why are you mentioning this mural?" Aias asked, a bit confused.

Jerome looked at Aias again, "Because it was a miracle."

"Because Jesus was black?" Aias asked, confused about why it was a miracle.

"No, because the only thing left standing after an earthquake in the late 1600s was the mural."

"The wall left standing was the miracle?" Aias asked.

"That was the first miracle," Jerome said.

"Don't leave me in suspense. Tell me the other miracles," Aias pleaded.

"The story goes something like this. The sacred image had been neglected after the earthquake. About fifteen years had passed before a man named Antonio León saw the image of Christ on the cross painted on this wall. It was in the same perfect condition as the first day it was done."

"That is the miracle that the painting still looked fresh?" Aias asked.

"The miracles started to happen after Antonio tidied up the place. He had built an altar but was forced to stop work due to a strange pain that affected him."

"I don't understand. What was the miracle?"

"Miraculously, the pain Antonio was experiencing disappeared after some days. And as a sign of gratitude, he returned with harps and musicians."

"So, the miracle was him healing?"

Jerome continued without answering Aias's question. "The devotion began to grow. Others came and joined Antonio each Friday night to sing prayers to the Christ."

"Is that the miracle?"

"As more and more people attended the meetings and because no official Catholic religious practices were being followed, the civil authorities forbade the gatherings and ordered that the image of the Christ on the wall be erased."

Aias went to say something, but Jerome continued his story. "When a painter climbed up a ladder to paint over the mural, he immediately started to experience tremors in his entire body and was forced to climb down. He tried again but became so fearful that he ran away." Before Aias could say anything, Jerome continued. "Another soldier climbed up the ladder but immediately climbed down, saying that he saw the image become more and more beautiful while the crown turned green."

Quickly, Aias asked before Jerome said another word, "Was that the miracle?"

"Aias, this mural survived two earthquakes and a seaquake. That should be proof of a miracle in itself. But people were also healed when they prayed in front of it. The mural of the dark-skinned Christ is a miracle in itself but also produces miracles!"

Lexi said to the group, "A few years back, I watched the largest procession of men, dressed in purple, slowly walking across Lincoln Center, here in New York City." Then she added, "I still remember the smell of incense burning and the sounds of drums playing—the four-hundred-year-old celebration of the Lord of Miracles in Peru—is a marvelous reminder that miracles still happen."

"Let me get this straight," Aias said. "There is a replica of the mural that survived many earth destructions and has the power to heal people here in New York City?"

"Well, in late October, anyways. I am not sure the rest of the year," Lexi said.

Aias clapped his hands and said, "Well! I knew it."

"Knew what?" Jerome asked.

"That I was on the right track."

Confused, Jerome said, "What does that mean?"

"It means that the plane crashed because I was not supposed to stop investigating Jesus's ability to heal and perform miracles."

Jerome shook his head. "Now I am really confused."

Lexi got up and pulled on Jerome's arm. "Let me take you home. I'll explain on the way."

Chapter 34

"After Lexi and Jerome left, Aias said to the girls, "Get ready because we are going back to find out more about how Jesus performed his miracles."

"Aias, I can't," Kesia said. "My mom won't let me go anywhere."

"Mine won't either," Luna said. "It is too close to college starting, and she doesn't want any other disaster to happen before I start."

Aias looked at the girls and pouted. "That sucks! I am determined to find out how I can perform miracles. I didn't want to go alone."

Luna said, "I find it interesting that the opposite of a miracle is a disaster."

"What do you mean?" Kesia asked, tilting her head.

"Well, think about it. A miracle is…"

Kesia answered since she looked it up on her almighty oracle, her cell phone. "An extraordinary and astonishing happening that is attributed to the presence and action of an ultimate or divine power."

Luna smiled as she said, "And a disaster is…"

But again, before she could answer, Kesia read from the internet dictionary website, "A calamitous event, especially one occurring suddenly and causing great loss of life, damage, or hardship, like a flood, airplane crash, or business failure."

"Interesting," Aias said as he rubbed his chin.

Both girls looked at him and said simultaneously, "What is interesting?"

"We were on a journey to discover how Jesus learned how to heal. We first went to Japan to discover how Mikao Usui learned the secrets of Jesus's abilities to heal with his hands. Then, we went to Israel to search for more evidence of how Jesus learned the craft, finding out that he went to foreign lands. We were about to go to India to learn more of what Jesus learned as a boy from gurus such as Sai Baba, but somehow, our plane went off course and crashed in Oman. That counts as a disaster."

"Are you trying to say that the forces of evil created a disaster to stop you from finding out how Jesus learned the craft of performing miracles?" Luna asked him.

"What demonic entity could create a disaster?" Kesia said as she looked it up on her oracle.

Luna thought about it and then said, "Archangel Hamied is the angel of miracles, so who is his opposite? Who is the Archdemon of disaster?"

Kesia looked up from her phone and said, "Abaddon, also known as Apollyon or Asmodeus. He is a fallen angel and is the angel of death."

"Death?" Luna queried, her voice imbued with a mingling of disbelief and captivation.

"Yes, and listen to this intriguing detail," responded Kesia, an excited tremble caressing each word. "The Gospel of Bartholomew unfolds a captivating tale where Abaddon, a formidable entity, confronts Jesus in the underworld subsequent to his demise. However, Jesus, unshaken, meets Abaddon's presence with laughter, a sound that casts terrifying shivers through Abaddon and his progeny. When the moment of resurrection draws Jesus away from the abyss of death, Abaddon and his son, Pestilence, maneuver to safeguard the infernal realms. Yet, Jesus, having vacated the netherworld, left behind merely three souls to wander its desolation: Herod, Cain, and Judas.

"Aias, his eyes reflecting the flicker of deep pondering, replied simply yet thoughtfully, "Fascinating."

"It is?" Kesia asked him.

"Yes. For now, we know who caused our plane to crash."

"But why would God allow a demon to perform disasters?" Kesia said aloud, not really expecting an answer.

Aias answered, "Many fallen angels were in heaven with God and chose to follow Lucifer into another realm that we call Hell. God can't stop evil. He can only offer human souls the power of miracles to help them during their life on Earth."

"No. There is no way that anything has more power than God," Lexi said, not wanting to believe that a demon has the power to overrule good.

Kesia turned to Luna and asked, "What do Wiccans believe about demons?"

"Wicca is based on nature and the laws of nature," Luna answered. "Most Wiccans try to prevent dark energy from happening."

"I can't believe that evil can overpower God," Lexi said, shaking her head.

Aias spoke up, "Ladies. When I was studying in India, I was taught the Laws of the Universe."

Kesia and Luna looked at him and said simultaneously, "And what are they?"

"The universal laws are the law of divine oneness, vibration, correspondence, attraction, inspired action, perpetual transmutation of energy, cause and effect, compensation, relativity, polarity, rhythm, gender or gestation, and the law of giving and receiving."

"There are laws to the universe?" Kesia asked more as a statement than a question.

"Of course," Aias said. "You don't think everything is left to chance, do you?"

"Well, I thought that maybe it was a coincidence or that God controlled everything we do."

Aias remembered his time studying in the Gurukul and said, "There is no place in scripture that says the precise words that God is in control, but the Bible demonstrates the truth of God's omnipotence, his divine abilities, and powers. But even God can't overpower the universal laws set forth."

"I think I need to understand these laws if I am going to master my Wiccan powers," Luna said.

"Actually, that is a marvelous idea," Aias agreed. "That is what we will do."

"What are we going to do?" Kesia asked, confused.

Chapter 35

"So, let me get this straight. Jerome said as he stared out his truck's passenger side window.

Lexi had insisted on driving while she told him the story. "Half-elf."

"I beg your pardon, half-elf," Jerome said as he rolled his eyes. *As if half makes a difference.* "He can bilocate, heal, teleport, manifest, and possess another person's body."

"I think he considers it was browsing," Lexi smiled.

Frustrated with this far-fetched story, Jerome said, "Next, I guess you will tell me that he can also resurrect a person from the dead."

Lexi lifted an eyebrow, "Interesting question. I don't know if he can do that. I'll have to ask him."

Trying to make sense of all this, Jerome turned to Lexi and said, "Lexi, people aren't able to do the things Jesus could. He was the son of God."

"Actually, the Holy Ghost impregnated the Virgin Mary," Lexi corrected.

If I hadn't witnessed Aias healing my burn, I wouldn't even be having this conversation with her. "Lexi, this will take me a bit to comprehend."

Just as she was going to answer him, she thought she saw Redington's car and turned her head to get a better look.

Jerome quickly took control of the wheel, barely missing an oncoming car. "What the?"

"Oh, my God. I am so sorry. I thought I saw," but she didn't finish her sentence. Quickly gaining control of the truck, she stole another look through the rear-view mirror, but Redington's car was gone.

After she slightly swerved again, Jerome said with authority in his voice, "Pull over. Now!"

After a moment or two, she found a spot that she could pull over and stopped. She said, "Jerome, I am going to catch a taxi from here. I'll call you tomorrow, and we can go for coffee."

"I think that would be best. But Lexi, I'll call you when I am ready to talk about this again. For now, I need some space to process all this miracle stuff."

"Oh. Okay."

Jerome pulled off, squealing his tires. *Elf.
Who does she think I am? Why do I always pick
the crazy ones?*

~

Lexi pulled out her cell phone and called
Redington.

It went to voice mail.

"Red, I know you are in town." Pausing
before, she added, "I am not with Neo."

Before hailing a cab, Lexi sat on a ledge of a
short rock fence that marked the entrance to a
townhouse. *Why is he not answering my calls?
What is he doing these days? He said he loved
me, so why is he ignoring me?*

As she sat there daydreaming about
Redington, when a black SUV pulled up, and
two men in masks jumped out and ran toward
her.

Chapter 36

"*I* am confused," Kesia repeated. "What are we going to do?"

Aias pointed an index finger to insinuate for her to wait, then went and made the girl's hot chocolate, saying to his mom, who was in the kitchen, "We might be up late. I will explain the laws of the universe to the girls."

Isabella replied as she tried to kiss Aias on the forehead, "To be young. Okay, but be quiet. And when Lexi gets home, tell her to come into my room."

"Will do," he said and kissed her on top of her head. "Mom, I don't know why you keep trying to kiss my forehead. I have been taller than you for months now."

Walking into the living room with a tray of hot chocolate, he said as he put the tray down on the coffee table, "Where do I start?"

Luna smirked, "Maybe with the basics."

"Hmm," Aias said as he thought for a moment. "Okay, I got it. I know where to start."

"Thank goodness!" Luna laughed. "I was worried we would be up all night."

"Funny," Aias said, with a bit of attitude. "A Universal law happens regardless of a person's age, nationality, or religious belief. Every living creature is susceptible to the laws which govern the Universe."

"Even an ant?" Kesia joked.

Aias nodded, knowing that Kesia was just kidding, for Luna's sake. "A Universal law also works whether you believe in it or not."

"Give me an example," Kesia said with a smile.

"Okay, take the law of gravity. It works anywhere on Earth, and it does not rely on your beliefs to function."

"Touché," Luna laughed. "He got you on that one, Kesia."

Kesia smiled.

"The best law to start explaining is the *law of divine oneness*. It precedes all other laws and is the foundation for all other laws. All life laws are built on the knowledge within this law. The law of divine oneness means that the whole universe is interconnected. It is in our best interest to become more aware of how our actions and thoughts affect others. Being aware of the universal law of divine oneness enables us to be mindful of our connection with everyone and everything."

Kesia leaned forward, "But there are billions of people in this world. Are you saying that all people's thoughts and actions can affect me?"

Luna added, "Or that I can affect them?"

Aias nodded, "That is what this law states, that everything and everyone is cosmically connected. The law of divine oneness teaches that you are a part of the whole, made up of everything else around you. Therefore, what you do, say, and think affects everyone around you. There is a reason it says in the Bible to do unto others as you want to be done unto you. Your actions and thoughts create a reaction."

"Wow, that is deep," Luna said.

Kesia nodded and then leaned back into the couch.

"What is the next law?" Luna asked.

"There are twelve universal laws," Aias said. "But I have a better idea. I am going to show you how these laws affect your life." Aias got up and ran to his bedroom. Grabbing some paper and a pen, he headed back into the living room.

He placed the paper on the coffee table and said, "People believe that to manifest something in an instant is a miracle."

"Well, maybe not for a half-elf, but for normal humans, without powers, it is," Luna said matter-of-factly.

"What if I told you that even a mortal can perform miracles, like manifest their wishes, wants, dreams, and desires instantly?"

"I'd say prove it," Luna said as she sat forward to see what he was drawing.

"Oh, this will be good," Kesia said as she patted Aias.

To prove what he was saying, Aias drew a stick man and five circles around him. "Manifesting your dreams, wishes, wants, and desires is as easy as learning the twelve universal laws." Aias wrote the word subconscious mind in the first circle. "The thoughts that you think without consciously being aware are part of the law of divine oneness. Also, the law of vibration and correspondence is in this first circle."

He wrote on the paper the laws affiliated with the subconscious mind.

"What do the other two laws mean?" Kesia asked.

"The *law of vibration* means that everything in the universe, rocks, plants, and even the stars, have a unique vibrational frequency. The cells that make up your body are made up of vibrating molecules. Even your wishes, wants, dreams, and desires have a unique energy vibration. As well as your thoughts, will, actions, and feelings."

"I never thought about my thoughts as a vibration," Kesia said.

"The *law of correspondence*, also known as the universal law of communication, means that all living beings, whether plants, animals, or human beings, communicate through sound, speech, visible changes, movements, and gestures. Your subconscious thoughts and emotions will speak louder than your conscious ones. Your subconscious mind controls everything about you.

"I better get working on mindful exercises to shift the negative beliefs that might be holding me back without consciously realizing it," Luna said, thinking about what she could work on next for her Wiccan homework.

Next, Aias wrote the word 'conscious mind' in the second circle. "This is all about what you think and to be aware that you are thinking it. The laws of cause and effect and attraction are connected to your conscious thoughts."

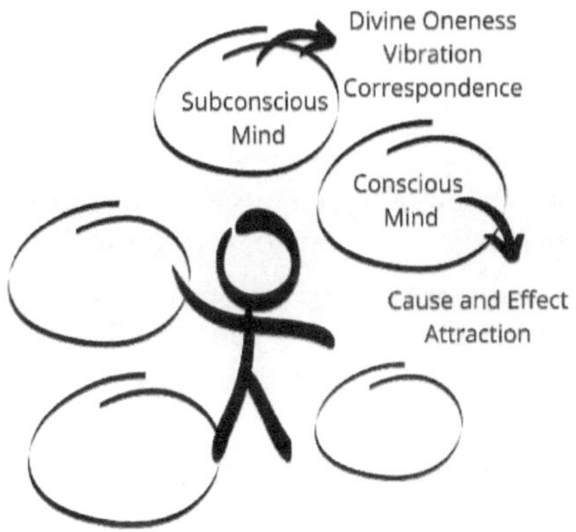

"What do these laws mean?" Luna asked for clarification.

"The *law of cause and effect* means that all actions have a reaction. This law is also considered your Karma from a past life, and that nothing in your life happens by chance or coincidence."

"So, what you are saying is that what I think, I create, but my past life can also play a major role in my manifestation ability," Luna added.

Aias nodded, "Yep. Now, I am sure you have heard of the *law of attraction*."

"I think everyone and their dog has heard of the Secret," Luna said.

"I haven't," Kesia responded. "What is the Secret?"

Luna looked at her in shock, "What, you haven't seen the movie or read the book?"

"There is a movie about it?" Kesia questioned.

Aias interrupted Luna before she could answer Kesia, "The law of attraction is the ability, skill, power, or gift to attract whatever you are focusing on into your life."

Curious, Kesia asked. "What is the opposite of the law of attraction?"

Aias thought about it, "I believe it would be repelled."

"Give me an example," Kesia asked because she wanted to fully understand the law of attraction.

Aias thought, then said, "There are three key laws of attraction—like attracts like, nature abhors a vacuum, and the present is always perfect."

"Can't you keep it simple? Give me something that I can understand," Kesia said, trying not to get frustrated.

Aias thought again, "Take a magnet. It has a positive and a negative side. If you take two magnets and put the same sides together, they repel, not attract."

"That is a great example," Kesia said, smiling.

Aias added, "To attract or manifest your wishes, wants, dreams, and desires, you need to create the energy that brings it to you, not repel it. What you think consciously and subconsciously can attract or repel your desired outcomes."

"Holy Hannah, I never thought about it like that. I just realized how important it is to think positive thoughts about what you do want," Kesia said to the other two.

Aias added, "You need to focus on the outcome plus be thankful for what you already have."

"English, please," Kesia joked.

"Okay, as you know, I am searching for the answer to how Jesus performed his miracles."

"Yep," Kesia agreed.

"As I focus my attention on finding the answers, I will keep searching?"

Luna interjected, "I think I get what you are saying. Lexi talked about when Tamara taught her that Spirit is literal and if you use the word searching, then that is what you will attract, to be searching."

"Exactly. I should have thought about this sooner," Aias said as he tapped the side of his head. "I have been focusing on finding the answer when I should have been focusing on the answer finding me."

"By thinking on the answer finding you, will you manifest your dreams?" Kesia asked Aias.

"Not quite. There is a bit more to it. Here, let me tell you about the next universal laws." Aias wrote in the next circle, action. "The laws of action, perpetual transmutation of energy, and gender and gestation are all part of this next step in creating your dreams into reality."

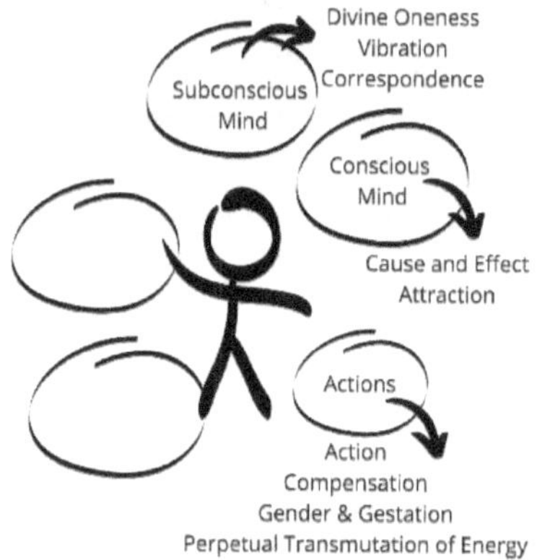

Aias started to tell the girls about each law. "The *law of inspired action* is the steps you take towards your goals that the divine has inspired. The *law of compensation*, also known as the law of sowing and reaping, states that a person will always be compensated for their efforts and contributions. The law of *perpetual transmutation of energy* is the law that states that energy can neither be created nor destroyed."

"You forgot the law of gender and gestation," Luna noticed.

"Right. The *law of gender and gestation*, Gender is Yin and Yang. Meaning that everything is made up of both masculine and feminine energy. It also decrees that all seeds have a gestation or incubation period before they can manifest and grow. Your thoughts and ideas are spiritual seeds and also have a gestation or incubation period before they can grow."

"So, you are saying that we have no control over how fast we can manifest an outcome," Luna said disappointedly.

Aias wrote manifestation in the next circle.

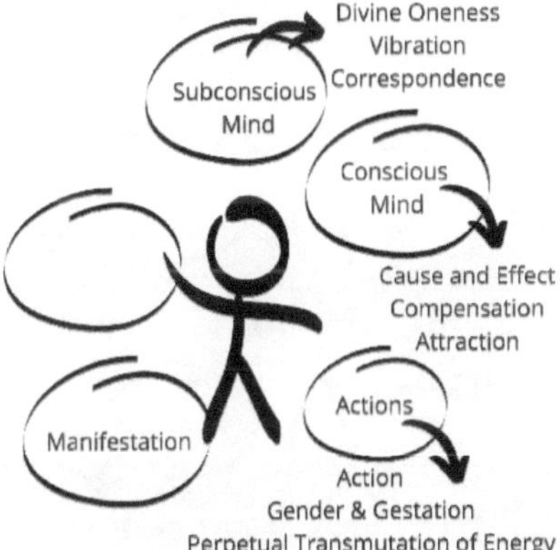

Then he answered, "Your subconscious thoughts control everything you manifest in your life. Your conscious thoughts add fuel to the power of your ability to manifest, but your actions speak the loudest. These three aspects of your being, subconscious, conscious, and actions, are all you need to manifest your reality."

"Then why do you have another circle?" Kesia asked.

Aias wrote emotions and drew a plus and minus sign in the same circle. Then he said, "These last three laws control if you get to keep what you manifested. The law of rhythm, polarity, and relativity."

Kesia looked at the drawing on the coffee table.

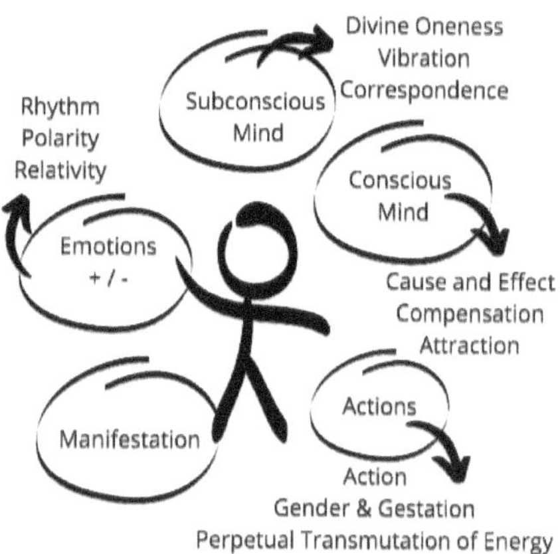

"You wrote down the word emotions," Kesia noticed.

"I did," Aias answered. "How you feel after manifesting your wish, want, dream, or desire matters.

"How do the laws affect this part of the manifestation procedure?" Kesia asked.

"The *law of relativity*, Einstein's law of relativity, is that the laws of physics are the same for all observers, regardless of their state of motion, which means that people's emotions control the ability to keep what they manifest in their life. The *law of rhythm* is explained best by a paragraph in an ancient book known as the Kybalion—everything flows, out and in; everything has its tides; all things rise and fall; the swing of the pendulum manifests in everything; the measure of the swing to the right is the same measure of the swing to the left; rhythm compensates. And the *law of polarity* is the theory that everything in the universe has a dual nature. The seemingly opposite things, such as love and hate, are actually two sides of the same coin. You can't have one without the other," Aias answered.

"Am I to understand that this is a cycle?" Kesia asked, looking at the drawing.

"It is," Aias answered. Some people believe that your emotions come even before your subconscious thoughts. A baby cries when hungry or needs change, but can a newborn baby think? Who knows?

"So, how come you can manifest in an instant?" Luna asked Aias.

"I guess because, just like Jesus, I do it with demand and command when I manifest. There is no wishy-washy emotion tied to the request. My subconscious emotions are not controlling the outcome. I expect it to happen instantly. I don't question if it can."

Chapter 37

$\mathcal{I}$sabella entered the living room and found Aias, Kesia, and Luna sleeping. *Crazy kids. They must be so uncomfortable.*

As she covered Aias with a blanket, he woke. "Mom, were we too loud?"

"No, baby, I was just covering you with a blanket."

"What time is it?"

"It is almost eight-thirty in the morning. Hey, Lexi never came into my room. What time did she get home last night?"

"Lexi," Aias whispered, trying not to wake the girls. He replied, "She didn't come home last night," Rubbing his eyes from sleep."

"That vixen. I guess she made up with Jerome."

Groggily, Kesia inquired, "Are you implying what I think you are?"

Isabella laughed and said, "Well, they are adults."

"Who's an adult?" Then, as she stretched, Luna quickly mentioned, "Mmm, I smell coffee."

"Come help yourself." As she walked back into the kitchen, Isabella announced, "I just made a pot."

"That is so old-fashioned, mom. You could have just used the Keurig machine."

"I know, but sometimes I like the old ways. Hey, I noticed the drawing on the coffee table. You guys got into some deep stuff last night."

Kesia nodded as she took a sip of coffee. "I am still trying to wrap my head around it."

Isabella told the three, "Tamara taught a class about manifestation. I remember Edward really getting into it."

"Lexi's old boyfriend, the minister?" Aias asked.

"Ya, anyways, that isn't the point. The point is that Tamara told us that Spirit or God notices everything. Even though Spirit notices when a soul is feeling, seeing, hearing, and thinking, Spirit will only help when asked, but not until enough action has happened to manifest the desired outcome."

"Can you draw that for me?" Luna asked as she grabbed a blank piece of paper off the coffee table.

"Sure. Let me remember how it went." Isabella took the pen and wrote subconscious, conscious, action, manifestation, and the plus and minus signs.

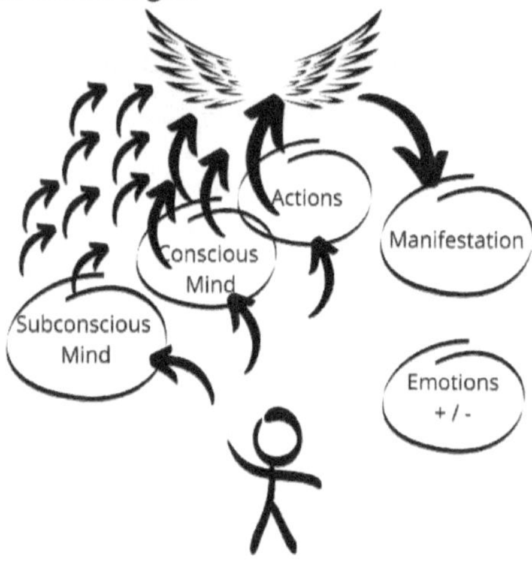

Then she said, "A person has millions of subconscious thoughts, and Spirit receives billions every second from people, plants, animals, and probably even aliens from all over the universe. Spirit pays no attention to subconscious thoughts. Spirit doesn't even pay much attention to your conscious thoughts. It isn't until you have proved to them with your actions that you are serious that they take notice to help you manifest your wishes, wants, dreams, and desires."

"Holy Hannah!" Kesia said. "I get it. If my emotions and subconscious thoughts are negative, and my conscious thoughts also predict my behavior and actions, then Spirit helps me create the bad manifestations just as they would have helped me create the good ones."

Luna excitedly said, "I get it. Spirit is just granting me what I am sharing with them. Everything I think, see, hear, and feel creates an emotion that I am transmitting to the law of divine oneness. As I activate all the universal laws, Spirit has no choice but to grant me my most vivid thought."

"I couldn't have said it better," Isabella answered. "Tamara would have been so proud."

"I miss her," Kesia said.

Isabella looked at the clock on her phone and said, "You would think that she would at least call."

"Tamara?" Kesia asked.

Isabella looked up and said, "Oh, no. I meant Lexi. Where is that girl? We had plans for today."

Chapter 38

Aias booked a flight to Egypt, Nag Hammadi, to be precise. He wasn't ready to give up on figuring out how Jesus healed. He wanted to know what all Jesus learned before he started to preach the word of God. It must have been a lot since there was missing eighteen years of young Jesus's life, and it wasn't until he was thirty when scripture spoke about him again. At this moment in Aias's life, his purpose was to fulfill his quest for spiritual enlightenment.

Kesia asked, "Why are you going to Egypt again?"

"Because I recently found out that some early Christian gnostic texts were discovered near the Egyptian town of Nag Hammadi in 1945."

"How long will you be gone? You are supposed to start University in a couple of weeks."

"I don't know. I guess as long as it takes to find out more about the miracles Jesus learned and performed as a teenager."

Kesia kissed Aias on the lips. "I am going to miss you."

Aias lifted Kesia and gave her a big hug. "Do you forget that I can bilocate? I am never too far away from you."

Kesia smiled. She had forgotten about that gift of his.

Putting her down, "Okay, I've got to get to the airport. My flight leaves in a few hours."

"You're not taking a private jet?"

"Not this time. I need to speak to someone on the flight I am taking."

"You're kidding, right?" Kesia said in disbelief. "You already know who is on the flight you are taking?"

"Kesia, why do you think I am taking a long flight just to save money? No. When I focus on a question, I get answers from my spiritual team."

"And they said to take this particular flight?"

"It was more like they showed me a flight number and a date."

"Holy Hannah! I wish I had that ability."

Aias kissed Kesia and then his mom and said, "See you, ladies, soon."

The ride to the airport was quick. Traffic flowed as if a path was laid out just for his Uber.

He didn't even have to wait long before boarding.

Aias found his seat. It wasn't in first class like he was used to, and it wasn't the window or aisle seat.

Are you sure I am on the correct flight? Aias asked his angelic guides.

Be patient. You are in the correct seat.

Aias could see the flight attendant looking at his watch and then at the plane's open door.

Ah, I get it. The person I am to meet is late.

Aias could hear the engine start as the flight attendant shut the door.

Wait, nobody came in.

An hour had gone by, and Aias was getting antsy. *Did the person I was to meet get on the flight? Is he here on the plane already?*

Aias got up to go to the lavatory and looked around at the passengers to get a sensation for his next step.

Nothing.

Shortly after returning to his seat, Aias fell asleep, and the turbulence woke him. *No. Not this again. This plane is not going to crash!*

Sitting up straighter as the plane sailed smoothly through the air, Aias heard a man behind him say, "Around fifty-two gospel texts were found in a sealed jar, collected in thirteen leather-bound papyruses, dubbed the Nag Hammadi library."

Aias turned to see if he could see who the man was talking to but couldn't see through the cracks of the seat.

The people on either side of Aias showed irritation at his moving around in their small confinements.

Aias sat back and focused his attention on the conversation behind him.

The other man behind him said to the first, "Is there proof?"

"The event was detailed in National Geographic's documentary, 'Secret Lives of Jesus, in which Jesus Christ's missing years took a remarkable turn.'"

"Then it must be true. What did they say in their documentary?"

"That the missing gospels tell a scandalous life of Jesus as a temper-prone child with uncontrollable powers of destruction through his teenage years of learning how to control his abilities."

"Can you give me an example of a story?"

"One of the stories tells about Jesus playing in the mud and creating sparrows. He gets into trouble when a man tattles to his father, Joseph, that his son is working on the Sabbath."

"What happened to Jesus? Did he get into trouble?"

"He started to as Joseph yelled at him, but Jesus raised his hands, and the mud sculptures magically turned into birds and flew away."

"So, he had supernatural powers even as a child?"

"So, it seems. Another story talks about a Russian doctor in 1894, traveling by horseback in Western Tibet, who fell off his horse and twisted his ankle. He was helped by some Buddhist monks, and while he was healing at their Monastery, he was presented with a Tibetan manuscript called "Life of Saint Issa, Best of the Sons of Men." The manuscript speaks about a Saint that had passed through their area centuries before."

"Doesn't the name Issa translate to Jesus?"

"Yes, it does."

"So, you are saying that Issa is Jesus and also stayed at the same Buddhist monastery that the monks wrote about during his stay?"

"So, it seems."

Aias couldn't believe that what he was on the plane for was happening. *And here I thought someone was going to talk to me. I should have asked that specific question. Note to self. I have to get better at asking Spirit the correct literal questions.* Instead, Aias focused again on the men talking behind him.

"What did the manuscript say?"

"The texts say Issa spent at least six years in India, living and teaching among the Brahmans—the high priests of Hinduism."

"What do you think he learned in India?"

"India has always been known as a place of mystics and mystical teachings. I believe Jesus sought out the needed knowledge of teachers who could understand his abilities and give him a safe place to develop his gifts. But…"

"But what? What happened in India?"

"As you know, India had a strict rule of status. Those of higher status do not affiliate with people of lesser status and vice versa."

"Yes, but why did that matter? Was Jesus not of the correct status?"

"No. That was not the problem. The problem was that Jesus disobeyed and started preaching his good news to people of lower status."

"Oh, I see. So, he had to flee India to escape the punishment."

"Yes, he had to leave the county not to be killed for his disobedience."

Aias knew all too well the strict rules set forth in India. He had spent many years in the Indian school system learning from the mystics.

Chapter 39

Once Aias landed in Egypt, he immediately booked a flight to Northern India because of the conversation he overheard on the plane.

Landing at Delhi International Airport, Aias transferred flights to Pakyong Airport. His destination was the four-hundred-year-old Buddhist monastery of Hemis, located about 40—*ish* km outside Leh, atop a hill. The area was famous for its snow leopards.

Pakistan borders the Leh district of Ladakh occupied Kashmir in the west, China in the north and eastern part, and Lahul Spiti of Himachal Pardesh in the southeast.

As Aias waited for the flight to be over, he read a magazine discussing the area that he was about to visit, ' *....no photograph can do justice to this scene, such an extraordinary wealth of color—the orange robes of the Yellow lamas; the draperies of the red lamas, of various shades*

*from fiery red to purple-black; the red,
white, and green dresses of the thronging
people; the numerous rich tones of the painted
monastery, and the hanging banners; the mud-
colored town and crags behind, glaring in the
sunshine; and lastly, above the whole picture,
the beautiful blue of the Tibetan sky.'
(Knight 1893, 205) —E.F. Knight (1890)
describes the Hemis festival (Fig. 1).*

Aias wished he could have witnessed the festival for himself, but since it took place every June, he knew he was a few months too late and didn't have the power to turn back time.

Aias wasn't disappointed for long. He saw high on top of a rocky mountainside in an opening in the astonishing Zanskar range of the Himalayas were several lhato—a box-like structure filled with a bundle of twigs and sticks with prayer flags and white sashes, with Ibex skulls meant for the protection of the sacred grounds, monastery, and village—marking the perimeter and protecting the sacred landscape of Hemis.

The road took several turns following the valley along the stream. As Aias watched out the vehicle's window, the monastery made itself visible through a line of tall trees. Aias saw a rectangular multi-storied structure following the Tibetan style of architecture.

Aias remembered what he had read about the monastery, *'One should seek out a place for building a temple in places that have the following: a tall mountain behind and many hills in front, a central valley of rocks and meadows resembling heaps of grain and a lower part which is like two hands crossed at the wrist'* *(Gyatso 1979: 29)*. Hemis Monastery fits the description.

The monastery was divided into two parts—the assembly hall known as Dukhang and the temple called Tshogkhang. Aias marveled at the huge courtyard as he entered the main gates.

Aias had previously booked to stay in the monastery and was shown to his quarters by a lama—monk. Dimly lit halls led to his room and the shared washroom, one washroom per floor. Upon entering his accommodations, there was a thick red carpet, where three beds, each with a pillow, one modest side table, and a dusty chair sat. The white drapes covering the window were drawn tight, but Aias knew that the night sky would be sparkling with millions of stars.

The following day, the ringing of the 6:00 am alarm woke Aias. Excitedly, he jumped out of bed and went to get ready.

When he went into the shared washroom, he smirked. *Mom and Lexi would not be able to stay here.* Not only were there men in the washroom, but also women, and it had not been cleaned to Isabella's standards.

The morning prayers were something Aias missed about his time at school. As he entered the prayer hall, Aias was greeted by a huge copper Lord Buddha statue at the back of the room. After he sat on a cushioned bench, Aias crossed his legs into a lotus position and prayed.

What is the likelihood of such a manuscript in this monastery's library? My quest is to find out if the story of the lost gospel that Nicolas Notovitch, who in 1894, wrote a book called "The Life of Saint Issa, Best of the Sons of Men," was based upon his findings of the lost years of Christ when he was here in this monastery.

As Aias left the prayer room, he almost bumped into a man. "Pardon me."

The man looked at him and said, "I know what you are searching for. Come with me."

Aias followed the man through some of the buildings and had to lower his head as he entered a dimly lit room through a wooden doorway. Aias saw a wall unit with many decorative wooden cubicles. Placed in each cubicle was a vibrant orange-colored cloth container. Aias watched as the man moved a container out of a compartment.

As the man removed the wooden lid of the material box, Aias could see that something was wrapped inside.

The man gingerly lifted the wrapped item out of its containment and unwrapped it like a gift, revealing many layers of old parchment paper with a written language that Aias had never seen before.

"What is this?" Aias asked.

"It is written in the ancient Pali language. It is about a man they called Issa."

Aias looked at the ancient text and lightly touched the paper. The instant he did, he vanished.

Chapter 40

It happened so fast that Lexi didn't even have enough time to fight back. The cloth covering her face smelled old and musky. She knew she was lying on the vehicle floor, and someone was tying her hands behind her back.

"You have made a mistake," she yelled out.

As she did, whoever tied her hands now tied something around her face that made talking impossible. She almost gagged from the taste of the dirty material.

She struggled to free herself but felt a prick of pain in her arm and then, within seconds, passed out from the drug administered to her.

~

After seeing Aias off, Isabella came back to his now empty condo. *Where is that girl?*

Dialing Lexi's number, it went to her answering machine. Isabella hung up without saying anything. *This is not like Lexi. She always calls me back.*

Isabella woke up in the middle of the night. She thought she heard the front door open. "Lexi, is that you? It is about time, girl. I was worried sick." Getting up from the spare bedroom, she went to the front door. But no one was there. She rechecked her phone, but Lexi had not called back or texted.

Frantic now, Isabella called the NYFD. "I need to speak to Jerome."

"Do you know his last name," the person on the other end of the line asked.

"No. No, I don't, but this is an emergency."

"Ma'am, a few men named Jerome are firefighters here in New York City. Do you know what engine unit he is with?"

"No. My friend is not back, and he was the last one who was with her."

"Ma'am, I am sure everything would be fine if she was with one of our firemen. But if you are still concerned for her whereabouts, call 911 and speak to an officer."

Isabella hung up without saying goodbye and called the only number that mattered in this situation.

"Red, it's Isabella. Lexi is missing."

A click on the line could be heard as Redington answered the call. "Missing," he repeated.

"Oh, thank goodness you answered. I didn't think you would since Lexi said she has left you many messages."

"Isabella, get to the point. When did you see Lexi last?"

"Yesterday."

"Why do you think she is missing?"

"She is not answering her phone. It's not like her."

Redington thought about Lexi. *Anything is possible with that girl. Answering her phone could mean that she simply just didn't charge it.* "Isabella, why did you call me? You should have called the police."

"Because if anyone can find Lexi, it will be you." The busser went off in Aias's condo. "Just a moment, someone is at the door."

"Isabella, let me in. I am at the front door," Red said.

Isabella pushed the button to let Red up.

Moments later, a knock was heard at the door, and Isabella let Redington in.

Surprised as she opened the door, "Red, is that you?"

"Ya," he said as he moved past her and walked inside.

Isabella looked at his hair. It was dark brown. "Are you in disguise?"

Redington looked at her inquisitively, then remembered his hair. "I needed a change."

"I see," Isabella said. "I liked your blond locks better.

"Good thing I never asked for your opinion," Redington said as he looked around the apartment.

"She is not here. I told you that already."

"Just checking."

"Red, it is not some ploy to get you over here. Really, she is missing," Isabella said honestly.

Red came back over and stood in front of Isabella. Towering over her, he said, "Pour me a beer and tell me everything."

Chapter 41

Aias teleported to the front gates. The front gates that he remembered his mother standing in front of, watching him from a distance, he was back at the gurukul in Puttaparthi.

Staring at his school friend and guru, Aias said, "Delish?"

"I wondered when you would be back," Delish said as he unlocked the school's gates and welcomed Aias in.

"But why am I here?" Aias asked, a bit confused.

"It is your destiny, Aias."

"My destiny? What are you talking about? I searched for proof of hands-on-healing and was following Jesus's footsteps." Then, shaking his head, Aias said, "I don't understand."

"Ah, yes. Just as Jesus quested to find the knowledge behind his gifts, so are you. It was just a matter of time before you ended up where he had."

Surprised, Aias asked, "He ended up here?"

Delish looked at Aias and smiled. Even though Aias looked like an adult, Delish remembered that he was still a very young boy in human years. "Well, not here exactly, but close."

"Did he find out the answer?" Aias questioned.

"It is written in the Bible, so I guess he did."

Aias thought a moment, then said, "Delish, I need to know more. I need to understand how my gifts work."

"Follow me. I have something to show you."

Aias followed Delish out of the school gates and down the street.

They walked for a bit, chatting about Aias's adventures since he left the school.

"We are here," Delish said as he stopped in front of an ashram.

Amongst the well-kept gardens, staring at two large grey and white structures, one on each side of the road, Aias asked, "Where is here?"

"Part of Sri Sathya Sai Baba's ashram. It is a spiritual powerhouse with many buildings. While alive, he built many schools, colleges, stadiums, and hospitals, and we just entered the grounds of the Sanathana Samskruti Museum. It houses the main teachings of the major religions of the world. Here is where you are going to start your discovery. Here, you will learn the life and teachings of many Sages, Saints, and Spiritual Masters."

As they entered the museum, Aias was in awe of the life-size wax figure of Sri Sathya Sai Baba. An Indian man with a large black afro and wearing an orange dress.

"Remind me, what is so special about Sai Baba?" Aias asked Delish.

As if reading Aias's mind, Delish said, "The color of love."

"His gown?" Aias confirmed.

"Yes, he loved wearing an orange robe. He said it was like the sunrise."

Aias was reading one of the information signs about Sai Baba. *Reincarnation of Shirdi Sai Baba.* "Who is Shirdi Sai Baba?"

"Sai means *holy person,* Baba means *father,* and Shirdi is where he came from. He was a man who taught Hindus and Muslims fascinating teachings. He also performed miracles, often involving the granting of wishes and healing the sick."

"You mean that both of the Sai Babas had spiritual powers?" Aias asked with heightened enthusiasm and started understanding why he was back in India.

"Aias, many yogis have spiritual powers."

Aias watched as Delish removed a thick book from inside his clothing and passed it to him.

Aias took the book, knowing that Delish just performed some kind of materialization. Instead of confronting him on it, he just read the title, Autobiography of a YOGI, by Paramhansa Yogananda.

"In this book, you will read the spiritual gifts of many men," Delish said with a smirk, knowing that Aias realized what he had just done.

Aias stuffed the book into his shirt as he asked, "What do you want me to learn about Sathya Sai Baba?"

Delish waved his hand in the direction he wanted to go and said, "Come, we will go to a Banyan tree that is even more special than the one at our school. It is the Vata-vriksha—a boon for spiritual aspirations."

They walked in silence through the ashram grounds to the tree.

Aias was impressed. It was even larger than the tree at his school, but this one had a copper structure under it. "What is that?"

"Sathya Sai Baba installed this mystic copper plate, stating that it had supernatural powers to help seekers during their meditation."

"You want me to meditate."

"Yes."

Aias did as Delish instructed and sat down in a lotus position near the giant banyan tree, then shut his eyes. Then, peeking at Delish, Aias whispered, "I assume my intent is about how my powers work."

Delish didn't answer but nodded.

Chapter 42

"What!" Redington yelled as he stood in front of a very nervous fireman.

After leaving Isabella's, Redington went looking for the last person who had been with Lexi.

Jerome didn't know what to say. He stared blankly at Red.

Still yelling, Red said, "You're telling me that you just dropped her off on the road?"

"She was driving, and crazily, I might add," Jerome said in defense.

Just as Redington stepped closer to Jerome, another firefighter stepped between them and said, "May I be of any assistance?"

Redington pulled out his badge and said, "I am an FBI agent, and this man is the last person to have seen this lady. Redington pulled a photo of Lexi out of his pocket.

"Lexi," the fireman said as he looked at Jerome. "She's missing?"

"Apparently," Jerome said. "I don't know. I haven't contacted her since. . ."

The other fireman answered, "Since the miracle of your burns."

Redington was confused. "What burns? Was Lexi burned?" Redington's anger now turned into anxiety. Redington went to push the other firefighter out of the way.

But the firefighter stepped closer to Redington and said, "Take it easy. She is not burned. Jerome was."

Jerome pulled up his left sleeve and showed Redington as he said, "The kid healed it. It was a third-degree burn that I had for years, and the kid touched me, and it disappeared as if it never happened in the first place."

"Aias?" Redington said.

Jerome nodded.

"But what does this have to do with Lexi disappearing?" Redington asked.

"It was what happened a half hour before Lexi got out of my truck. Man, I am still freaked out about it."

"Freaked out about Aias or Lexi?" Redington asked, confused again.

"The kid!" Jerome said as he backed up, turning to signal that he was done talking.

"Wait! I still need to know where you dropped her off!"

Jerome yelled it out as he walked out of the room.

"Jerk," Redington said under his breath as he turned and walked outside.

Getting into his car, he drove to where Jerome had said.

Pulling over in front of a townhouse, Red got out and looked for clues.

As he did, an older man came out of the house and said, "Two men in masks grabbed her."

Redington looked up. "What did you say?"

But before the man answered, a young lady came out and said, "Almer, come back in here. You need to take your meds."

"Miss, just a second. I'm Special Agent Redington." Red showed his badge. "I need a moment with him."

"It won't be any good to talk with him. He has Alzheimer's. He has no idea what he is saying."

Redington yelled to the man as the lady turned him back into the house, "What were they driving?"

The man waved a hand at the young lady and said, "Let me be."

She hurried him inside anyway.

The old man struggled to turn his head and said clearly, "Black SUV."

"You old fool, someday you are going to say something that will get us all into trouble," and shut the door on Redington.

Redington went back to the FBI headquarters and went in search of Tina.

Tina was a cute little redhead with a temper if you ticked her off.

Redington popped his head around the door of her office space and forced a smile, saying, "Do you have a moment?"

"For you, Red, sure. What do you need?"

Redington's good looks got him in the door. Now, hopefully, his charm could get him what he needed. "I need you to search for a black SUV from a couple of nights ago."

"That isn't much to go on. Where?"

"Right." Redington filled Tina in on the location and approximate time of Lexi's possible abduction.

As he watched Tina's computer screen, he yelled, "Stop! Go back."

Tina played back the video.

"Stop. Right there. Look. That is a black SUV."

Tina squinted at the screen.

Far down the street, you could barely make out an SUV.

Redington froze.

"Well, I'll be. Will you look at that," Tina said as she watched two masked people drag a lady into their vehicle.

"Can you make out the license plate?" Redington said, leaning over Tina.

"I'll try."

Redington started to tap his foot as he waited.

Tina stopped what she was doing and looked down.

Redington stopped. "Sorry."

"Back up, Redington, you're making me nervous, and it will not make me work any faster."

Redington instantly backed up, not wanting to tick Tina off.

"Got it!" Tina said excitedly.

"You're the best!" Redington said as he kissed the top of her head and ran out of the room.

Going over to his computer, he typed in the plate numbers, read the owner's name, and stared at the picture on the screen.

Redington looked at it again and then mumbled, "Why do I know that face?"

Redington leaned back in his chair and thought a moment.

Redington looked up Marko Calponi's gang on the FBI's data system.

It all returned to him, Little Eddy, and the auction house.

"It can't be. I thought he died," Redington mumbled again as he looked that up.

"He did. So, who is this guy?" Redington went back to the picture of the owner of the SUV.

Digging deeper, Redington found that the two men were brothers.

"Crap!"

Chapter 43

Aias went back in time during his meditation, back to 2001. He was in Canada in a caucasian woman's body, looking at a caucasian man sitting across from her. And the man was telling her about an experience he had in India.

"It was my third time visiting Sai Baba's ashram. I was excited because I was in the third row on the stage. He only picks people from the first twelve rows to go backstage with him."

Aias, still in the lady's body, was listening to his story and nodded for him to go on.

"His Grace started by greeting everyone in a non-denominational prayer. There were translators there for us to understand what he was saying."

The Canadian man went on about his whole experience, almost without taking a breath.

"His Grace had a man come up on stage and tell his story. What happened to the man on stage was incredible. He was telling his Grace that he was happy to be there, but he missed his brother's sixtieth birthday. So his Grace said to come with him.

They walked to the side of the stage where there was a wall.

Sai Baba touched the man's back and pushed him through the wall.

The man vanished not only before my eyes, but also the other thousands of people in the audience were in awe of the miracle."

Surprised, Aias heard himself say, "Wow! That is incredible."

The man said that Sai Baba did many blessings in the next thirty minutes and talked mostly about peace and love. "Finally, close to the end of the service, Sai Baba picked me to be one of the twelve people he chose to come for a one-on-twelve meeting with him. I followed Sai Baba with three other men and eight women.

In the room, there were twelve chairs set up in a semi-circle. I found a seat and waited to sit once we were told to do so.

Sai Baba said a special prayer and stepped in front of each person separately.

I watched as he materialized gold jewelry, necklaces for the ladies, and rings for the men.

I was mesmerized by how he pulled the gold out of his palm. Next, he pulled a strain of gold links out of his hand with his thumb and finger. Once it was released from his flesh, he took the end and separated the strains. It was as if the necklace was glued together, and he parted it, making the necklace."

"Fascinating!" Aias said.

"Then he took a ring from his palm and placed it on my left ring finger. I was sad because it didn't fit. It got stuck at my second knuckle.

Sai Baba winked at me and then blew on the ring. It slid on as if it was a perfect fit.

I stared at the ring made of gold with three oval diamonds.

I was amazed at seeing his miracles firsthand.

I received that day also a pair of little silver sandals or 'foot-soles' (padukas), vibuthi, and a blessing."

"Incredible story for sure," Aias, as the lady, said to the man.

Aias found it funny to be talking through the lady's mouth, expecting to hear his voice but hearing hers as he spoke to the man.

Next, Aias was still in the lady's body, but this time was sitting in front of another woman. She was a middle-aged Indian woman also from Canada.

Aias listened as the Indian woman started telling about her time visiting Sai Baba in India.

She started by telling about her family's experience while over there.

"My son got sick the second day we were in India. I mean really sick, where he needed a hospital. I was frightened because I was scared to take him to a dirty hospital after all the clean hospitals in Canada."

Aias nodded. He had heard how the hospitals are free in Canada if you are a Canadian.

"Finally, I had no choice but to bring him to a hospital. My husband and I prayed for our son's fast recovery. As luck would have it, not only did I find out that we took him to a hospital that Sai Baba had built, but that it was a free service, and the doctor was a surgeon from the United States. We were truly blessed that day."

"Was your son okay?" Aias asked.

"Oh, yes. He was well looked after and was out the next day."

"That's wonderful news."

"Yes, but it gets better. I have a gift for you."

"You do?" Aias was wondering what it was.

"Yes, I brought you some Amhrita."

Aias took hold of a tiny glass vial filled with a golden color liquid. "What is it?"

"Amhrita is the nectar of the Gods. It is a sweet liquid with a golden-color and a flavor reminiscent of honey, with fragrances of roses."

"What is it for?"

"Healing the body, mind, and soul."

"How do you use it?'

She took the small vial, opened the lid, and said as she passed it back, "Hold your finger over it and turn it upside down. Then flip it upright and remove your finger."

Aias did as the Indian lady instructed.

"Now, touch your finger to your tongue."

Aias touched his tongue. He was surprised at the taste. He had never tasted anything like it.

The Indian lady continued the story of her experiences in India. "I had gone to India to see Sai Baba specifically. A few days after my son was okay, I went to Sai Baba's temple and waited on the women's side of the lineup."

"What do you mean, woman's side?"

"Men and women are not allowed to enter the temple at the same time or sit together."

"Interesting."

"The lineup is extremely long and takes many hours to seat everyone."

"How many people go to see Sai Baba?"

"Good question. Maybe there were tens of thousands that day."

"What! Crazy."

"I was lucky. I sat about twenty seats back from the stage. But unfortunately, my husband and son were not so lucky. They sat back many, many rows."

"Was it worth going?"

"Oh, yes. One feels as if they were in the presence of an angel. Just witnessing the miracles he performed on other people was worth the visit."

Aias popped out of his meditation to Delish, slightly shaking him.

"Aias, we must leave. It is closing time."

Aias shook his head to clear it and awaken fully from his meditated trance. As he did, gray ash fell from his hair.

Delish touched it and said, "Ah, you must have had a good meditation, for Sai Baba has blessed you with vibuthi."

"It was interesting, that is for sure."

"Did you learn how your powers work?"

Aias shook his head, "No, but the stories in the meditation were about miraculous happenings."

Chapter 44

Redington did what he did best: investigate, starting with Lexi's abductors. He knew he had enough proof to take it to the assistant director, who oversaw the New York field office, and he requested to be put on Lexi's case.

Reminiscing, Red was honored to be recruited by the Federal Bureau of Investigation. He knew that "FBI" was technically an abbreviation, but it also stood for the FBI's motto: Fidelity, Bravery, and Integrity, which he took very seriously.

Redington chose the division that suited him best, the criminal investigation division. He had considered the counterterrorism and information technology divisions but knew defeating crime was his passion.

As Red walked into the NYC FBI's office, he reminisced about visiting the FBI's headquarters in the J. Edgar Hoover Building in Washington, D.C. Red loved learning about the history of the

FBI. The Washington headquarters opened in 1974. The massive bunker-like building housed the director, most department heads, and the world-famous FBI Crime Lab.

He had learned while he visited there that in 1924, Attorney General Harlan Fiske Stone elevated 29-year-old Assistant Director J. Edgar Hoover to the Office of Director. As soon as Hoover took office, he reviewed procedures and agent records.

Hoover wasn't satisfied with how things were run and created rules and regulations for agent conduct and investigative procedure, ensuring that Bureau activity would be uniform across the nation. As Hoover said, "We all should be concerned with only one goal—eradicating crime."

In 1950, Hoover created another innovation, the "Ten Most Wanted" list. This list provided photos and information on the FBI's ten fugitives and was posted in public places such as post offices. You can still find that list, but it is now online. Just type in www.fbi.gov/wanted.

Red also knew that he was fortunate to have been recruited because usually, the Bureau only accepted men or women between the ages of 23 and 39 with a four-year degree. Though he was older and didn't hold a degree, he had the other three criteria: a clean record, no convictions for serious crimes, and he was an American citizen.

Red didn't ask anyone how or why he was recruited but suspected it was either due to the Inspector General or the FBI director. Even though the FBI is part of the U.S. Department of Justice, which the U.S. Attorney General heads, the General doesn't exercise direct authority over the FBI, so it couldn't have been him.

Red also knew it had to be someone powerful because he was given the title Special Agent with a gold shield, not Field Agent with a silver shield. Even though the President appointed the director of the FBI for a 10-year term, there was no way Red was on the President's radar. So, the only way the director could bypass the requiting rules was if the Inspector General demanded his recruitment.

As Red knocked on the open door of the Special Agent In Charge, which was equivalent to the Chief of Police, he said, "Sir, I have evidence that one of Marko Calponi's gang members has abducted a female civilian."

Looking up from the pile of papers he was searching through, Special Agent Anthony Gray answered, "Redington, why are you coming to me with this information and not your Senior Special Agent?"

Red stood up straighter and answered, "Sir, I have first-hand experience with capturing the brother who abducted this civilian. I also have first-hand experience with civilians. She was the one that led me to Little Eddy's capture a few years back. It is she who has been abducted by

Little Eddy's brother, Timothy "The Knife" Ruscitto."

The name got Anthony's attention. "You still did not answer my question."

Redington widened his stance, looked straight into his superior's eyes, and said, "Because he would not allow me to be on this case."

"Why is that?"

"Because he would think that I was personally involved with the civilian."

"And are you?"

Red hesitated for a second.

"I see."

"Sir, I will admit that I had considered a relationship with her at one time, but that was before she was to marry another man."

Anthony put down the papers he was holding as he remembered the conversation he had months ago with the New York State Inspector General. The General was one of the seventy-five appointed USA Inspector Generals. For a specific reason, she had demanded that Redington be given the position of Special Agent in Anthony's Bureau.

"Anthony," Inspector General Lenora Langdon said with authority. "I have sensitive information about why you need to place Detective Redington in your Bureau. I can't go into all the details now, but I need him there within the next month. You must understand that he is vital to the capture of Marko Calponi?"

Anthony wasn't used to receiving orders of whom to hire and especially didn't like receiving them from a woman, but she was the Inspector General, so he had to comply.

Looking down at the papers on his desk, Anthony knew that Redington needed to be assigned this case, but he didn't want Redington to think it was an easy decision. Instead, he wanted Redington to sweat a little. "Agent Redington, are you asking me to give you special treatment?"

"Sir. I am asking to be assigned the case because I am the best person to have on it."

"You think so?"

"I know so."

"A little cocky, aren't you?"

"No sir, confident."

Anthony thought a moment, then picked up the phone and pressed a button. "Fred, I need you to give Agent Redington clearance on all matters concerning Marko Calponi and his gang members."

Redington smiled.

Catching Redington's reaction as he hung up the phone, Anthony said, "Agent, do not disappoint me. Now get out of my office."

Redington nodded and backed out of Anthony's office. He knew exactly where he needed to go next.

Chapter 45

As she came to, Lexi was groggy. Instantly, she realized she was tied to a chair and had a gag tied over her mouth. Her first instinct was to free herself. She struggled for a moment until common sense got the better of her.

Looking around at her surroundings, she noticed that she had seen this place before, but where?

Three men walked into the room, and one told the man guarding her to leave.

As the man came closer, he said in a thick Italian accent, "Miss Constantine, we meet at last."

Marko Calponi had lost an invaluable man when Little Eddy was killed that day at the auction house. He had hoped that his brother "The Knife" would be as cunning as his older brother, but so far had disappointed him until now.

"Alexandra Constantine. I have longed for this day."

Lexi stared at the man talking. She had not seen him before and did not know who the abductors were or why she was taken.

Marko moved towards Lexi and lightly stroked her cheek. "Such a pretty face. Unfortunately, my men will have to do away with you."

Lexi moved away from his touch and struggled against the restraints tied around her wrists.

Marko removed her gag.

Lexi instantly asked, "Who are you, and why have you taken me?"

Marko took hold of Lexi's chin. "My dear. You have cost me a great deal. I have not forgiven you for the demise of Little Eddy."

Lexi instantly knew her capturer, Marko Calponi, the most famous mobster in New York City. The man who was responsible for her sister Susanna's death. Lexi's demeanor changed. The extreme hate she had for this man, the hatred she had buried years ago, all came to the surface. She could not hide her emotions. She said with gritted teeth, "You will be sorry that you captured me."

Marko laughed. "We have a feisty one here, boys." Then, she bent down to Lexi's level and looked her in the eyes, "You do not scare me."

Lexi spat into his face.

Marko slapped her hard across the face.

Lexi's head twisted as he did. It left a red mark. As she felt the pain of his action, she said, "I am not alone. They will find you."

"Not before I make you pay for all you that have cost me."

"We'll see about that," Lexi whispered.

Marko walked away from her, then turned to his men as he left the room and said, "Make her a little more comfortable, will ya."

One of Calponi's men started to beat Lexi and did not stop until she was moments away from death.

Chapter 46

"Aias," Kesia screamed as he bilocated into her room. She ran to hug him, but her arms went right through him.

"Kesia, I am not in Egypt."

"Where are you?" She asked.

"India. I am back at my old school."

"Why?"

"I am just finding out about that now. I will not be able to contact you for a short while."

"Aias, I miss you," Kesia said as a tear fell from her eye.

Aias's heart skipped a beat. He loved her with all his heart and soul and knew there would never be another quite like her. She was his soul mate.

Aias went to touch the tear, but his fingers were like air and passed right through the liquid. "Kesia, don't cry. I am alright and will be with you soon."

"That is not why I am so sad."

Aias was confused. "Why then?"

"It is Lexi," Kesia said, trying to hold back the flood of tears that wanted to escape.

"Kesia, what happened to Lexi?"

Kesia lowered her head and started to cry as all the emotions she was feeling burst like a dam.

Aias wished that he could touch Kesia, and instantly, he teleported to her. Then, touching her tenderly, he took her in his arms.

Surprised but ecstatic at the same time, she took a deep breath and smelled his familiar scent, not caring that it had always seemed like a miracle when he had performed the gifts he had been granted.

"Tell me what happened, Kesia."

Kesia looked up at his beautiful eyes and gazed at them. Mesmerized that she could see the depth of his soul, she forced herself to say, "The night that Jerome came over."

"What happened that night, Kesia.?" Fear rippled through Aias's body.

"I am not exactly sure, but Redington is trying to find her."

"Redington?" Taking Kesia by the shoulders, Aias asked again, "What happened to Lexi?"

"She has been missing for a few days."

"Missing!"

"I don't know all the details, but nobody knows where she is."

Aias kissed Kesia on the forehead and then vanished.

~

"Redington, what did you find out so far?" Aias said louder than he expected to.

Swerving in traffic, Redington fought to get his car under control. "What the? Aias, you trying to kill me?"

"Sorry, but I had no other way to contact you."

"You couldn't have called?" Red said as he pulled over to the side of the road.

"No. I was in India, and my phone is there and not charged."

Redington turned off his car and looked at Aias. "So, I am assuming you know about Lexi."

"I just found out. How can I help?"

He looked so grown up. Redington knew it was not long ago that Aias had been born. It still boggled his brain to think that a human could age in months, which usually took years. He still could not believe that Aias was half-elf.

Aias knew what he was thinking and said, "This is not the time or place to contemplate reality. We have to find Lexi."

"Can't you find her the same way you found me?" Redington asked.

"No. I have tried, but there is a force of evil around her blocking my abilities."

"Well, I guess that makes sense. If Adramelech could take over Little Eddy's body, the archdemon would probably take over his brother's."

Aias shook his head. "You have encountered an archdemon?" Aias instantly saw the image of Redington's encounter with Adramelech. "It can't be Adramelech."

"Why do you think that?"

"Archangel Azrael touched his dark energy, incinerating him instantly."

"Well, you said that some dark energy is blocking you, so who is it then?"

Aias closed his eyes and searched into the energy he felt blocking Lexi. "Abaddon is also known as Apollyon or Asmodeus. It must be!"

"Why must it be?" Redington asked, not believing he was even having this conversation.

"Abaddon is the rival Archdemon to Archangel Hamied."

Redington wished he didn't have to ask, "Who is Archangel Hamied?"

"The Angel of Miracles."

Redington wasn't catching on, "I don't understand. What does this have to do with Lexi?"

"Lexi has been helping me on my quest to understand how miracles work. Especially the miracle I possess of healing others."

Redington sat back a bit, then said, "Let me get this straight. You believe that because Lexi has helped you on your journey of figuring out how you do the crazy stuff you do, she is in danger because of it?"

Aias paused and said, "I think she is caught up in this because the dark has found a way to tamper with my light."

"Are you telling me that you are responsible for Lexi's abduction?"

Aias took a breath of confidence and answered, "I believe that the underworld has the power to tamper with our light beings. I believe that Lexi is a powerful energy being of light, and the dark wants to devour her soul."

Redington took a deep breath, then mustered up the will to say, "Alright. Aias, I will gladly take your help in finding Lexi."

"Awesome!" Aias said as he turned to face the windshield. "Let's go get her."

Chapter 47

Redington turned the car's engine on and sped away from the curb. His instincts told him where to drive, Marko's known headquarters.

Stopping in front of the establishment, Red checked his gun for ammo.

The passenger's side door opened.

"Where do you think you're going?" Red asked Aias.

"Wherever I have to. Plus, I didn't hear you call for backup."

Red hadn't. He knew he was breaking protocol, but protocol came with bureaucratic rules, and time was an issue. "Fine, but stay far behind me."

As Red walked into Marko's place, his vision turned to tunnel vision. Anyone in his peripheral vision disappeared, as did all the noise. He had heard the term "Blind Fury," but until this moment, he had never experienced it. He had no idea where he was headed, but the anger within him led the way. His feet moved unknowingly in the direction of his intent, which was to find Lexi.

As he pushed the door open, he saw that she was gagged and tied to a chair. She had blood dripping from her swollen, bruised eyes. Her head dropped, and she looked unconscious—*those buggers. I am going to kill them.*

As if reading his thoughts, as the two approached Lexi, Aias nudged Red's elbow and whispered, "We only have seconds." Then, grabbing hold of Lexi's shoulder and Red's wrist, Aias closed his eyes and took a breath.

"What the," was all Red got out before being teleported.

Red put his hands out to regain his balance as he touched a now-conscious Lexi. Then, still dizzy, he mumbled, "Where did he take us?"

Instantly healed from being touched by Aias, Lexi answered, "I am not sure."

Both Redington and Lexi looked down at an unconscious Aias.

Lexi quickly bent down to see if he was alive. "Wherever this is, it took everything Aias had. He is barely breathing."

"Tamara," Redington whispered.

Lexi looked at Red and saw that he was looking behind him.

As she turned, she knew where they were. Aias had teleported them to the Buddhist Monastery that Sophea was part of.

As Sophea walked up to the three of them, Lexi heard her say, "He will need all the energy you both can muster."

"What does that mean?" Lexi asked her friend as she got up to hug Sophea.

"The only thing that can save him now is a miracle."

Lexi couldn't believe what she was hearing. "Tam," Lexi caught herself as she was about to call her Tamara. "I mean, Sophea, there has to be something you can do!"

The sound of humming was getting closer. As Redington and Lexi looked past Sophea, they saw a percussion of monks dressed in red. Some were carrying slightly swaying lit lanterns.

Lexi could see the flame of the candles flicker as the monks circled Aias. Finally, the monks holding the lanterns put them on the floor and raised their hands, like the other monks, palm side facing him.

Their humming became louder as the monks closed their eyes and raised their faces to the ceiling.

Lexi recognized the sound they were making. It was the "Om" sound—one of the most powerful sounds one could make.

~

Redington had seen this stance before, but where?

As Red looked from the monks to the girls and then back at Aias, he said, "I know I thought of what you could do as woo, woo, but I like this kid. Tell me what you need me to do to save him."

Sophea looked at them both, then said, "Spirit sure has humor."

Red wasn't laughing and was unsure if he wanted to know why she said that, but he asked, "What does that mean?"

"You are going to need a crash course in Reiki," Sophea answered

Red looked confused.

Chapter 48

"Get him seated for the Reiki initiation,"
Sophea told Lexi.

Lexi wasn't sure if Red was ready to be
initiated into Reiki, but who was she to question
Sophea's request? She sat down and then patted
a spot to her right as she said to Redington,
"Have a seat next to me."

Lexi watched as Red sat down the best he
could on the hard stone surface of the floor.
Grabbing his hand, she squeezed it, then let go.
She didn't see Red looking her way, for she had
already turned her head and shut her eyes.

As Sophea started to chant, Lexi knew she
was starting the initiation. "Close your eyes and
get comfortable, then take a deep breath. Breathe
down into your toes. With every breath you take,
you will start to relax more and more. Listening

to my voice. Not falling asleep, but feeling totally relaxed."

Lexi loved the feeling of going into a deeply relaxed state. Sophea's voice was so calming.

"Red," Sophea said. "I will come over and draw the reiki symbol on your brow chakra, which is between your eyes. Over your heart and on each palm. Then I will draw the appropriate symbol for the level of Reiki that you will be attuned to today."

Lexi wondered if Red would receive level one, two, or three. It couldn't be just level one. That is for self-reiki. And Aias needed all of us to save him. It had to be at least level two.

Lexi took a breath as she heard Sophea start to talk again.

"Red, please touch the tip of your tongue to the roof of your mouth. Take a deep breath and let a hissing sound come forth as you breathe. This action allows your chi to flow and all your chakras to align."

Lexi did it at the same time. She loved the feeling it gave her.

Then she heard Sophea say, "Now, let your imagination go. Imagine my words as part of a dream where anything and everything can happen. Let your mind become one with my words."

Lexi wanted to peek at Red to see how he was doing but decided to keep her eyes closed and let Redington experience whatever it was that he was to envision.

"I would like you to imagine a room. Any kind of room will do. You will notice a secret door on one of the walls. You are not sure how you noticed it. Maybe it sparkled or something like that, but however your subconscious noticed it, you are now walking toward it."

Lexi noticed that Sophea waited a moment before she continued.

"Red, notice that this door opens as you come closer. The passageway looks safe, and you enter. As you do, all your senses come alive. You can smell a beautiful aroma. Everywhere you look, the colors look so brilliant and alive. You hear soft, pleasing sounds of music. You feel so perfectly at ease. Your thoughts are even clearer."

Lexi took a breath as Sophea waited for Redington to take his next breath.

"You take a few more steps into this new room. It seems familiar, but you are not sure why. Then you remember you were here before. It was the same room you were in just before you were conceived. Your spirit chose this particular room, these particular souls to join you on your life's journey. Your soul rejoices as it remembers this part of your life's path commitment."

A tear fell from Lexi's eye as she was reminded of her life's journey and the friends she chose to be with.

Lexi felt Redington twitch beside her but kept her eyes closed.

"In a moment, you will notice your Reiki Master in Spirit coming to greet you," Sophea said. "You will make a conscious contract with your Reiki Master now. I want you to think of these three things after me. First, my Reiki Master in Spirit has the highest level of integrity. Second, my Reiki Master in Spirit comes in a form that I can readily accept. Third, my Reiki Master in Spirit is at the highest level with which I can easily communicate. You may add anything else to this contract that you need to."

Patiently, Lexi waited for Sophea to continue the initiation.

"Your Reiki Master in Spirit is now in front of you. You may greet it in any way you feel appropriate. You may shake its hand, bow, hug it, or just smile. You can ask for its name. Ask it what responsibilities it has while working with you."

Lexi knew that Sophea was quiet because Redington needed a moment to ask his Reiki Master in Spirit these questions.

"I would like you to now say goodbye. Go ahead in whatever way you like. Once you say goodbye, come back through the passage and into the room. Knowing you can always go back through."

Lexi heard Redington take a breath.

"In a moment, I am going to count to three. With each number, you will take a breath. Go ahead, take a breath. One, breathe in all the Reiki levels that Spirit chose you to have today. Breathing out, programming every cell down to your DNA to be filled with this level of Reiki. Two, breathing in all the levels of Reiki. Breathing out, reprogramming your cells with this new energy. Three, breathing in the Reiki energy vibration. Breathing out, all your cells down to your DNA are now vibrant with this new Reiki energy."

Lexi felt Red twitch again as he took his third deep breath.

"I am going to count from one to three, and when I get to three, I want you to wiggle your toes and be fully alert. One, every cell down to your DNA has been attuned to the Reiki energy. Two, you love this new energy that vibrates through your cells. Three, awake. Feeling wonderful as you wiggle your toes and stretch your arms and legs. Feeling so energized as you stand up."

Chapter 49

As he opened his eyes, wiggled his toes, and stood up, Redington remembered where he had seen the moves the monks were making.

As a young man, he wanted to impress a girl he liked, so he went to church with her. He remembered the priest blessing the congregation with his hands in the same manner as the monks were now. Actually, he remembered the priest making this motion when he blessed the blood and body of Christ—the wine and bread. And how the priest waved his hand in the sign of the cross to bless each parishioner on their forehead.

Sophea whispered, "He traced the symbol of the cross on their third eye."

Surprised that Sophea could read his thoughts, Red just stared at her.

Lexi leaned over to Red and said, "The third eye is considered the brow chakra and is the area on the body that sends and receives information from one another."

Red asked for confirmation, "You mean psychic information?"

Lexi nodded as she said, "I know it seems impossible, but many Christian traditions were taken from not only Pegan traditions but ancient Eastern beliefs and techniques as well."

Red watched as Sophea held her hands out and told Redington, "Copy what I am doing. Then, take a deep breath and imagine the Reiki energy coming from Spirit through your crown chakra, touching your heart, down your arms, and out your palms.

Red turned his palms toward Aias and took a breath. His hands seemed to heat up, and a tingling sensation pulsed through his palms as if a current of invisible energy was flowing out of his hands toward Aias.

Red could not tell for sure if what was happening was real or imaginary. He started to hum the sound the monks were making. *If it saves the kid, I will do anything.*

It seemed like an eternity that they were holding their hands out, and Redington's arms were getting tired from his position.

Momentarily, Sophea whispered, "You can relax and shift your position. The Reiki energy will still flow from your palms."

Red nodded and shifted his stance.

~

Aias's body twitched.

Lexi heard Redington's gasp and instantly opened her eyes.

Lexi gasped as well.

The sight she opened her eyes to was not what she expected.

As if in slow motion, Aias's body levitated off the floor a few inches before moving into an upright position. Aias's arms fell open and, for a brief second, resembled the body of Christ on the cross.

Lexi was in awe as Aias's body became luminescent. Then his human flesh faded like stardust, swirling through the air until he disappeared.

As if conducted to, at the same instant, the monks stopped humming, and all that could be heard was silence.

Red grabbed Lexi's wrist, "What just happened?"

Not sure herself, she said nothing and turned to Sophea.

Sophea opened her eyes, looked at the two of them, and said, "Isabella needs to be here." Then she closed her eyes again. The monks joined hands with Sophea and started to chant something in another language.

A moment later, Isabella appeared in the center of the circle.

All of a sudden, understanding what just happened, Lexi broke through the circle, and with tears streaming down her cheeks, she hugged her friend, saying, " I am so sorry."

~

Not sure what was going on, Isabella lightly pushed Lexi away. "What's happening here? Why am I here?"

But before anyone could answer, an opalescence glow appeared, and dressed in a white robe, Aias smiled at his mom.

Noticing her son was hovering like a ghost in front of her, she demanded, "Aias, what is going on here?"

The halo of light around Aias's head shone brightly as he said, "It was a miracle. God saved Lexi. She is destined to attain all the gifts granted by Spirit and share that knowledge with the world."

Isabella didn't clue in, "Aias, why are you speaking to me in ectoplasmic form?"

"Mom, I have ascended."

"Ascended?"

As Red moved to Lexi, Isabella noticed and heard him ask her, "Did Aias just die?"

Isabella saw Lexi nod her head.

"NO!!! Isabella cried out as she fell to her knees.

Aias's glow widened and enveloped Isabella as he said, "Mom, my physical existence merged with the cosmic energy. I have become a higher level of consciousness. I have bypassed becoming an Avatar.

Isabella heard Red ask Lexi, "Remind me what an Avatar is?"

And her answer, "A manifestation of a deity, an incarnated divine, some say, teacher, others say a god."

With tears streaming down her face, Isabella wasn't sure what to do next. All the energy she had was gone. She fainted.

Sophea made a finger motion, and a few male monks came and gently picked Isabella up and carried her back down the passageway their party had entered from.

~

"Now, what do we do?" Redington asked Lexi.

Lexi shook her head and started following the others down the hall.

Chapter 50

*A*ias looked toward the light and disappeared from the monastery, knowing he would see his mother again in her dreams.

Hamied, how long have you been an Archangel? Aias asked his new companion.

The angel's purple cape whooshed in the wind as they ascended through the clouds. His white hair shone a silver pearlescent as the sunbeams peeked through the soft veil of fluff. His glow was so bright that all you could see were his eyes. *That is a good question.*

Are you as old as the universe? Aias asked.

No.

Aias thought for a moment. *Are you as old as God?*

No. Aias, how old is your soul?

Aias paused. *Do you have a soul?*

Hamied looked at Aias and smiled. *Of course, I have a soul. Everything that has consciousness has a soul.*

How old is my soul? Aias asked Hamied.

Older than the Earth.

What! No way. How is that possible?

Hamied smiled again. *The universe is older than Earth, Heaven is older than the universe, and Nirvana is older than Heaven. So your soul is very old.*

Aias had never thought about it before, something older than Heaven. Then he asked, *Are you as old as Archangel Michael?*

He was the first of the Archangels, but there are angels older than him.

Really?

That made Hamied pause. Hovering in space, Hamied turned and looked at Aias. *Yes? There are angels older than Michael?*

Fascinating.

Hamied touched Aias's shoulder, and they were instantly teleported to the realm of angels.

Where are we? Aias asked.

You need a lesson in angels since you are to become one.

Aias was speechless.

I would like you to meet Zagzagel, he is the teacher of angels, then disappeared.

Aias somehow knew that the teacher's name meant "divine splendor" and was the prince of the Torah and Wisdom. He was the angel of the burning bush who gave advice to Moses and was the chief guard of the 4th Heaven, although he is said to reside in the 7th Heaven, the abode of God. Aias also knew that Zagzagel could speak the seventy languages of light and was described as the "angel with the horns of glory."— emanations around his head that produce light beams.

Aias, I will start your lesson with the Angels of Creation. There were seven of these angels in the beginning, and they were placed in control of the seven planets- the seven, including the sun and moon, according to the astronomical knowledge of the time of the scribes, who set down the events of the "first days." The seven angels of creation usually given are Orifiel, Anael, Zachariel, Samael (before this angel rebelled and fell), Raphael, Gabriel, and Michael. The Book of Enoch reports that the angels of Creation reside in the 6th Heaven.

Whoa, slow down. Aias was confused already. *Can we start in the order of creation of the angels?*

A café table appeared with two chairs. The scenery behind shifted to a French café in Tuscany. Zagzagel sat down and drank from a tin coffee cup.

Aias sat down across from him. Yes, the teacher appeared to be feminine. *Thank you.*

A pad of blank paper and a pen appeared on the table.

Zagzagel spoke slower, and without picking up the pen, a diagram started to appear on the notepad.

There are nine orders of angels. They are divided into three categories or, as some call them, "orders or choirs": no matter what, they are the protectors of Heaven, the Universe, and Earth.

I didn't know that. Okay, go on. Aias said politely.

There are also three classifications of angels in each of the three categories. Each category has its hierarchy of angels.

Zagzagel wrote the three categories on paper without using a pen—Heaven, Universe, and Earth.

Then he wrote under Heaven,

Highest orders: serve as the heavenly servants of God.

1st - Seraphim

- Closest to God.
- These six-winged angelic creatures continually attend God at his throne, praising in his glory.
- Their appearance is of burning flames.
- Caretakers of God's throne.

2nd – Cherubim

- One who blesses God.

- Cherubim have wings and four faces: one of a man, an ox, a lion, and an eagle
- Directly attend to God's needs.
- Guardians of light and of the stars.
- Guard the way to the tree of life in the Garden of Eden and God's throne.

3rd – Thrones

- Also known as Elders.
- They may appear as men or as a beryl-colored wheel-within-a-wheel, their rims covered with hundreds of eyes.
- Listen to the will of God and present the prayers of men.

Aias repeated what he thought he had just learned, *So these first three angels look after God in Heaven.*

Yes, Zagzagel said.

Then he wrote under Universe,

Middle orders: heavenly governors of the creation by subjecting matter and guiding and ruling the spirits.

4th – Dominions

- Lords who regulate the duties of lower angels.
- Look like divinely beautiful humans with a pair of feathered wings but have wielding orbs of light fastened

> to the heads of their scepters or on the pommel of their swords.
> - God's instruments in ordering all of creation.

5th – Virtues
- They're the ministries through which signs and miracles are made worldwide.
- Have control of the elements, planets, seasons, and nature.

6th – Powers
- Warrior angels oppose evil spirits.
- Soldiers wearing full armor and helmets.
- Supervise the movements of the heavenly bodies to ensure that the cosmos remains in order.

Then he wrote under Earth,

Lowest orders: heavenly guides, protectors, and messengers to human beings.

7th – Principalities
- Guide and protect kingdoms, nations, or groups of peoples.
- Wear a crown and carry a scepter.
- They are the educators and guardians of the realm of earth.

8th – Archangels
- The first rank of messengers.
- Heralds of God's commands.
- Human-looking with wings.

- Angels of nations and countries are concerned with the issues and events surrounding these, including politics, military matters, commerce, and trade.
- Assigned to communicate and carry out God's important plans

9th – Angels

- They are the ones most concerned with the affairs of living things.
- They can look like anyone or anything.
- Directly in contact with humanity.
- Guardian angels, Teacher angels, Worker angels, etc.

Aias recapped what he thought he had learned. *First, three types of angels look after Heaven and attend to God. Then, three types of angels take orders from the first three and ensure the universe is safe and in order. Then, the last three types of angels protect Earth and make sure that humans hear God's message.*

Yes, Zagzagel answered.

So, which angel do I get to become? Aias asked. *Hamied said I needed a lesson since I was to become one.*

For now, you will be of the 9th rank of angels.

Cool! Hey, Hamied never answered my question. How old are angels?

Zagzagel answered, *let's just say, older than the Earth.*

Chapter 51

Aias looked at the paper that Zagzagel wrote.

Virtues. Zagzagel wrote that virtues are the angels in control of miracles. *I wonder if Hamied is a Virtue.*

As Aias thought about Virtues, one appeared.
No, he is an Archangel. A fallen one at that.
Who are you? Aias asked.
Ariel.
Aren't you an Archangel?
I am, but I am also the leader of the class of angels called Virtues.
I don't understand. I thought that Archangels were lower in the hierarchy than the class of Virtue angels.
Most are, but Archangels have free will and can be promoted in rank, but have the choice to continue to communicate with humans. And only angels or archangels are permitted to do that.

Aias contemplated what Archangel Ariel had just said.

Think of it as having two jobs.

Aias thoughts were spiraling. *Let me get this straight. Within the heavenly realms, Heaven, the Universe, and Earth, there are angels with specific jobs.*

Yes.

But you also tell me that angels can be more than one rank.

Yes.

Aias, let's focus on your actual question. You were wondering about the Angels of Virtue.

I was.

Okay, the principal duty of the virtues is to work miracles on earth.

That makes sense, Aias said.

Now, a miracle is an extraordinary and astonishing happening that is attributed to the presence and action of ultimate or divine power.

Okay.

Aias, a miracle is the ability to possess the powers of the Nine Spiritual Gifts granted by Spirit.

Aias sat back. *Wow! I just thought about Lexi and her journey.*

Exactly. Right now, Lexi is learning how to manifest the miracles of Spirit.

Aias thought back to Lexi's first miracle, the miracle of "Distinguishing Spirits," the ability to tell the difference between spirits.

Aias, what does virtue mean?

To have high morals.

And what are the seven virtues?

I was taught Chastity, Charity, Diligence, Kindness, Temperance, Patience, and Humility.

Okay, now tie them all together.

Aias shook his head. *How?*

Think back to Lexi and her journey. Is it a miracle that she can tell the difference between her sister's soul and that of an impostor or even the difference between her sister's soul and her father's?

I guess it is.

How about her second miracle, to communicate with the spirit world?

Do you mean that she knows how to speak and interpret Tongues?

Yes.

Ya, I guess that is a miracle too.

What about Tamara's or Kesia's gift of prophecy? Lexi learned how to prophesies as well. Would you consider that a miracle?

Many would.

How about your gift of healing? Is that a miracle?

My mom thinks so. It comes naturally.

Yes, Aias. In the Bible, it is written that each is given a gift.

Just one?

Usually, but the others can be learned.

Yes, Lexi and my mom were learning the spiritual gifts from Tamara.

The Old Testament tells many stories about the spiritual gifts granted. Even though the New Testament mostly speaks about Jesus Christ's spiritual gifts, it has many examples of proof.

I have traveled worldwide to find out how my gift works, and I still don't understand how it works. I mean the science behind it.

Aias, there is a cosmic power that flows between us, Virtues, and you humans. Really, you are just a vessel, a channel for the healing energy to flow through.

A channel of energy runs through me. That is how I can heal the sick.

You are a pure vessel. Remember your actual age. You are barely two. Your soul has not had time to be corrupted—the purer the soul, the clearer the vessel.

So it is my age and not that I am half-elf?

It is a bit of both. But humans can learn what you can do naturally. They might not be as effective, but there are many people like Jesus who could heal, even in today's time.

But how does it work? How does the power come through me?

For most people, I would have to say they need intent, breath, and being open to the energy passing through their blissful body to their physical body.

You named two bodies. How many bodies does a person have?

Quantum Medicine states that there are five— Bliss body, Supramental body, Mental body,

Vital body, also known as the aura, and the Physical body.

Fascinating, I want to know more about the five bodies.

Let's just say that for the healing energy to come out of your hands, it has to come from heaven, which is part of your Bliss Body. So, no matter their religious belief, every soul is connected to the cosmic energy of the heavens.

Even atheists?

Even atheists. Each soul has a purpose and a life lesson. An atheist is just following their chosen path.

Hmm. I never thought of it like that. Why does the energy have to go through all the bodies?

Imagine the bodies as if they were like your skin, epidermis, dermis, and hypodermis. The epidermis is the outmost thick layer of skin and consists of another five layers. Think of the five bodies as protection, just like the epidermis.

So the bodies are for protection?

Yes.

From what?

From the spiritual energy. Energy flows all around us.

The energy is dangerous.

It would be if you didn't have protection.

Do I have to be worried about the energy?

No more than you are worried about electricity. You wouldn't want electricity flowing without a thick, protective plastic coating.

Tell me more about these protection layers.

Humans are born with five bodies. Let's start with the physical body. You understand that trillions of microscopic cells protect your soul.

Interesting way of putting it. Sure, I had a human body made up of cells.

Well, Aias, the Physical body is protected by the Vital body. And that body is protected by the Mental body. And that body is protected by the Supramental body, and lastly, that body is protected by the Bliss body.

So, Archangel Ariel, what you are telling me is that my healing powers had to pass through five layers before the healing energy could be given to the person needing it.

Yes.

So, what are all the bodies needed for?

Your Vital body reflects the state of energy or health of your physical body. Your Mental body reflects the mental state of energy or the health of your physical body. Your Supramental body reflects the universal laws that control the wave of possibilities that your consciousness will permit. And your Bliss body allows limitless possibilities.

Possibilities for what?

Miracles.

Just miracles?

No, any of the spiritual gifts.

So, if I understand correctly, my healing was possible because my supramental allowed the possibility from my bliss body. And my mental body had no issues with the possibility, so it did not stop the flow of energy coming through the first three layers. And since my vital and physical body had no preconception of the possibility, the cosmic energy could instantly pass through all five bodies to the person I touched.

That sums it up.

So, if a person believes that healing is impossible, the energy gets stopped at the supramental body?

Yes. The energy will get stopped at any of the five bodies. Your bliss body only allows the energy that coincides with your heavenly contract. Only those possibilities are infinite.

Aias thought about what Archangel Ariel had said. *So, it makes sense that each human is like a snowflake. No two lives are exactly the same. All because of their heavenly contract and the belief of possibilities they allow into their life.*

You've nailed it Aias. It all comes down to what they believe to be true.

Chapter 52

Lexi woke up from a dream about Aias. He had told her the secret of how he could heal. It all had to do with the bliss body.

Looking around, she was in bed, back at Aias's apartment. Then, getting up, she grabbed her housecoat and went out to the kitchen.

Isabella was sitting on the couch in the living room, rubbing her head. "I just had the craziest dream. We were somewhere far from here, in a monastery or something. Tamara was there."

Lexi's eyes moved slowly from the coffee pot she was holding to Isabella. "Weird, I just dreamed of Aias."

"Redington was there too," Isabella added.

Lexi had a déjà vu feeling. "Creepy. I just had a glimmer of him, too."

"It feels so real," Isabella said as she took the cup Lexi was passing her. "Thank you."

Sitting on the other side of the couch, Lexi curled her feet up and took a sip of the hot beverage.

"Where is Aias anyway? He wasn't in his bed, and he isn't answering his phone."

Lexi shook her head, "Hmm, maybe he is with Kesia."

"I'll text her," Isabella said as she put down her mug and picked up her phone.

Moments later, Isabella read the text from Kesia. "She says she hasn't heard from him."

"I am sure he is fine. He probably went out to get you those special bagels you like from the vendor down the street."

"Hmm, I keep getting this sickening feeling like something is wrong."

Shivers ran down Lexi's spine just as Isabella finished her sentence. Convincing herself, she said again, "I'm sure he is fine."

"What's this?" Isabella asked as she bent forward and picked up a notebook from the coffee table.

"It's Aias's. I think he writes his thoughts about his healing abilities in it."

"He keeps a journal?" Isabella said, sitting back as she opened the book.

"Isabella, aren't journals private?"

"Well, he shouldn't have left it here for me to read."

Lexi's curiosity was getting the best of her, so she moved closer to Isabella so she could have a peek.

Mom, I know you are reading this. You too, Lexi.

"Little smartie pants," Isabella laughed.

Lexi smiled but kept reading.

You two have been such a blessing in my life. No one could have asked for a better mother. And Lexi, I admire your curiosity and determination to figure out how the nine spiritual gifts granted by spirit work.

Here is what I have found out so far about miracles. The word Dunamis has been translated one-hundred and twenty times in the New Testament. Its origin is Greek, and the dictionary says it means strength, power, or ability. But most people use the word miracles or miraculous power instead. Dunamis is inherent power. The power that resides in a thing by virtue of its nature.

Now, let's talk about virtue. Virtue means · moral excellence, goodness, and righteousness. But it is also the name of the hierarchy of angles—virtues. These angels are filled with divine strength. They are strong and powerful. These holy virtues are the angels in charge of performing miracles, like my healing ability, by sending us the omnipotent grace of working miracles.

Did you guys know that the Holy Ghost, or as some people call it, the Holy Spirit, is a virtue?

He has to be.

The angels of virtue's job is to perform miracles, and it is taught that a person can be filled with the Holy Ghost. Meaning the power of the Holy Spirit can enter a person.

I read an interesting article by Mark Jones. He wrote, "That even Jesus performed his miracles through the power of the Holy Spirit, not immediately by his own divine power. In other words, the divine nature acted not immediately *by virtue of "the hypostatic union" (the joining of two natures in Christ's singular person) but* mediately *by means of the Holy Spirit."*

Lexi sat back and said, "Wow, in church, we always say, in the name of the Father, Son, and Holy Ghost. Actually, thinking about how I make the sign of the cross." Lexi touched her forehead and said, "In the name of the father." Then she touched her heart and said, "Son." Then, as she touched her left shoulder, she said, "Holy," and on her right, "Ghost."

Isabella watched as Lexi touched each spot. Excited, she said, "Lexi, think about where you just touched."

Lexi looked at Isabella to hear what she was implying.

"You touched your brow chakra for God, which is where intuitive energy comes from. You touched your heart chakra for Jesus, which is love and light. Then you touch each shoulder, which, in Reiki, is where the energy comes from.

Lexi got shivers. "Oh, my God! Isabella, you know what you just figured out, don't you?"

"I think so. That the miracle of healing comes from the power of God to man through the power of the Holy Spirit."

Lexi got up and did a little victory dance.

Isabella joined her. Putting her hands on Lexi's arms, Isabella said, "Lexi, Aias figured out where his gift of healing came from."

"Oh man, Isabella, this is huge. People are reading the Bible wrong. They are reading it as if it was a historical story, where they should be reading it as a textbook to understand all the gifts granted from Spirit."

Isabella sat down, "Hey Lexi, do you remember Tamara talking about how she could do all the gifts granted by Spirit?"

"I think so."

"What are the gifts again?"
Lexi did what Kesia usually did and grabbed her phone. "To one is given from the Spirit the gift of utterance expressing **wisdom**; to another the gift of utterance expressing **knowledge**; in accordance with the same spirit, to another, **faith**, from the same Spirit; and to another, the gifts of **healing**, through the same Spirit; to another, the working of **miracles**; to another **prophecy**; to another, the power of **distinguishing spirits**; to one, the gift of

different tongues; and to another, the
interpretation of tongues. But at work in all
these is one and the same Spirit, distributing
them at will to each individual."

Isabella started to say to Lexi, "Tamara."

But Lexi interrupted by saying, "Sophea."

"Right. Even though we thought Sophea was
a psychic and into metaphysical and esoteric
beliefs, she was really teaching us how to
perform the nine spiritual gifts."

"Now that I think about it, you're right. I went
to her because I couldn't get answers about why
I kept dreaming about my sister, Suzannah,
being in trouble even though she had died." Lexi
looked at the list of gifts. "She taught me
distinguishing spirits, to tell the difference
between them. That was mind-blowing! It
changed my life forever."

"And I met you in the class she taught about
celestial languages and channels. You
remember, audio, knower, visual, and feeler?"

Lexi nodded, then looked at the list again.
"She taught us tongues. The celestial language
of the angels."

"Right. We learned how to communicate with
the spirit world." Isabella moved over so she
could read the information on Lexi's phone and
then pointed. "Look. Next, she taught us about
Bath Kol and the power of prophecy."

"Right." Lexi agreed and said, "The gift of
healing and Archangel Rafael was what I

learned next. Actually, that is where I first heard about Reiki. And don't forget that has been Aias's focus for months now, working of miracles."

Isabella looked up and said, "Mentioning Aias, where is that kid?"

Chapter 53

The buzzer sounded, and both ladies jumped.

Lexi grabbed the phone and said, "Hello."

"Hi Lexi, it's me, Kesia. Can you let me in?"

"Sure, just a sec." Lexi pushed the number six button on the phone to let her in.

Moments later, Kesia knocked on the door before she let herself in. "Hi, so where did he go?"

"I am assuming you mean Aias?" Isabella said as she poured herself a second cup of coffee.

Kesia nodded.

"Want one?" Isabella asked before she answered.

"No, I'm good, thanks."

Isabella but the pot down and grabbed her mug. She shook her head and said, "He's not back yet."

"Weird. Aias is not answering my texts," Kesia said, frustrated. "We were supposed to hangout before classes start next week."

"I am sure he is doing something important. Maybe it is a surprise for you?" Isabella said with enthusiasm.

"Maybe," Kesia said, but without much hope of that.

Changing the subject, Lexi asked Kesia, "Are you excited about college."

"I am, but I wish Aias and I were going to the same school."

"Ah, young love," Isabella said, brushing Kesia's back with her fingers as she passed her by.

Lexi added, "At least you have Luna."

"That's true."

As Isabella sat on the couch, she said to Kesia, "Here," as she patted the cushion. "Have a seat."

Kesia came over and moved the journal to sit down. As she touched it, she felt a spark or something. "What is this?"

Lexi smiled and said, "It's Aias's. Isabella made me read it."

"Hey, I never made you do anything."

Laughing, Lexi said, "Well, that is what I am going to tell Aias when he comes home and catches us reading it."

Kesia opened it up and read out loud, "The angels of virtues perform miracles. I wonder what he meant by that?"

Lexi answered, "We were just talking about how the word miracles actually mean strength, power, and ability in the Bible."

Kesia looked up, "I'm not getting it."

Lexi thought for a moment, then answered, "Aias figured out how his healing ability worked."

"He did. That's amazing. So, how does it work?" Kesia asked, intrigued.

"Remember when we were in Japan researching Doctor Usui's abilities?" Lexi asked.

"Yes, how could I forget that trip."

"Well, remember how Doctor Usui searched for answers about the divine abilities, powers, and miracles that Jesus could perform?"

"Sure," she said, nodding her head.

"Well, even though Aias could perform many miracles, healing was his passion. Because he could do spontaneous healing like Jesus and Doctor Usui, he wanted to understand how the ability or miracle worked."

"Did he figure it out?" Kesia asked, flipping a few pages in the journal.

"We haven't finished reading what he wrote, but we coincidentally figured it out ourselves," Lexi said as she looked over at Isabella for confirmation.

"Don't keep me in suspense. How does it happen?" Kesia said, trying to find where it talks about it in Aias's journal.

"We believe it is the divine power that the Holy Ghost and the other heavenly angels of virtues deliver to us and through us." Lexi took a deep breath, waiting for Kesia's response.

Kesia calmly said, "That makes sense." Then she flipped to another page and read from it. "Aias wrote that the Angel in charge of miracles is Archangel Hamied, and the angel in charge of the angels of virtues is Archangel Ariel."

Isabella made a loud thud when she put her mug on the coffee table.

Kesia looked up.

"Sorry, continue."

Lexi asked, "Do you guys think Archangel Hamied is the Holy Ghost?"

As if Aias knew that Lexi would ask that question, Kesia read from his journal, "No, but some people think the Holy Ghost is Archangel Gabriel."

"I wonder what Aias thought?" Lexi said out loud.

Again, as if Aias knew the question would be asked, Kesia read, "The term Holy Ghost or Holy Spirit refers to any angel that delivers the power, strength, or ability to perform miracles."

"Oh, that makes so much sense," Lexi said, remembering her Catholic upbringing. "A few years ago, a woman told me I wasn't a Christian because I was Catholic."

"What? Catholics aren't Christians," Isabella remarked to Lexi's story.

"Well, to her, I wasn't. So, I asked her what made her believe that."

"And what did she say," Kesia asked.

"She told me that Catholics believe in the holy trinity of God and not that Jesus was God."

"What does that mean?" Kesia asked as she sat forward on the couch.

"I had to do some research after I left her because I was taught that the holy trinity was all one and that it was a mystery that we don't have to understand. However, I figured out that in the Bible, the word "Gods" with an "s" is found, and that if you do not pray to Jesus, you do not know which God you are talking to."

"The word Gods, with an "s," is in the Bible?" Isabella asked for confirmation.

Kesia looked it up on her oracle, her phone, "Yep, Deuteronomy 6:14 and Exodus 23:13, for example, talk about Gods with an s."

"Fascinating," Isabella said.

Lexi continued her story, "As I researched this lady's accusation, I finally understood her concern."

"Which was?" Isabella asked.

"That unless you pray to Jesus, the son of God, you would not know who you were asking for your prayers to be answered. You might be asking a demon, pretending to be God."

"That is why Tamara, sorry, I mean Sophea keeps enforcing the importance of distinguishing spirits, so you could always tell them apart," Isabella added.

Lexi had an epiphany. "Oh, my God. It makes so much sense now."

"What does?" Kesia asked.

Lexi took the journal Kesia was holding and flipped to a blank page. Then, taking the pen still on the coffee table where the journal had been found, Lexi drew a diagram.

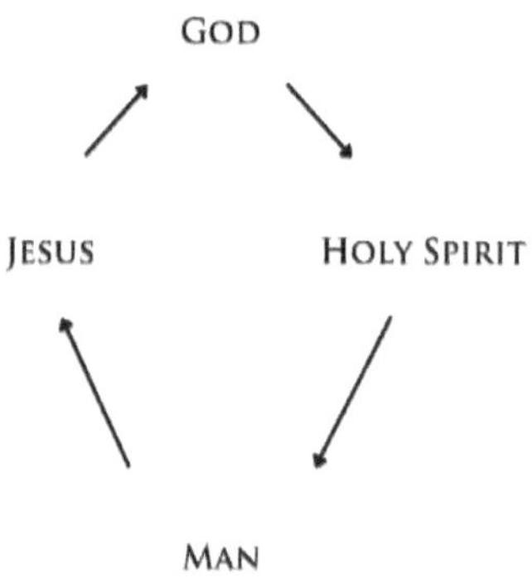

"What are you drawing?" Kesia asked.

"Here, look. She meant that if you pray to Jesus, you will always talk to the correct God. Jesus will deliver your message to God, his Father, and the Holy Ghost will grant your prayer. Or now, I might say, the Holy Spirit will deliver the power, ability, or strength. AKA, a miracle."

"But Lexi, how would you explain what we were talking about earlier?" Isabella asked, staring at the drawing.

"You mean the Reiki energy?"

Isabella nodded.

Lexi thought about it for a moment, then drew.

"Ya, that is what we were talking about," Isabella said as she looked at Lexi's diagram.

Kesia read the words and then asked, "Can you explain this to me, please."

"For sure. Isabella and I figured out that the Holy Spirit delivers miracles. The power, strength, and abilities to perform miracles."

"But why is God brow chakra?" Kesia asked.

"Oh ya, well, in the Catholic religion, we touch our forehead when we say in the name of the Father."

Kesia interjected, "Ah, I get it, and heart for son. So, what you drew is the Holy Spirit, which is the energy, the power, the ability, or the strength behind Reiki miracles."

"Exactly!" Lexi said, standing up and doing her little dance again.

"Ah, I get it. Back in Japan, when we brought the Reiki energy down, we brought it down from the heavens through our crown chakra. I guess the brow is close enough. Then the Reiki energy touches our heart before we allow it to flow through and out our hands to whomever we are healing, ourselves or others."

"Yep!" Lexi said happily.

"Actually," Isabella said. "That would be true of any miracle."

"Any miracle?" Kesia challenged.

"I would bet on it," Isabella said.

Kesia looked at her oracle and typed in the types of miracles. "Okay, it says here that there are five types of miracles—creational, sustaining, providential, predictive, and suspension."

"Explain each one," Isabella said as she took a sip of her coffee.

"Okay, creational makes sense in that it is the divine act of bringing things into existence."

The ladies agreed.

"Sustaining our existence on Earth is a miracle. We have all that we need to survive."

"I agree. That is a miracle," Lexi said, nodding.

"A providential miracle is all about timing. You pray, and coincidentally it can be answered within seconds."

"I do that with parking," Isabella said. "I pray and set my intent on a parking space, and voilà, one is provided."

The girls laughed.

"Hey, just saying it works," Isabella said with a bit of attitude.

Kesia continued, "A predictive miracle is one that you foretell."

"Prophecy is one of the nine gifts granted by spirit," Lexi confirmed.

Kesia kept smiling as she read the last one. "A suspension miracle is one that is astonishing, one that breaks the natural laws of the universe. One that makes you believe in a higher power."

"Oh, how I love those miracles. Speaking of miracles, don't you guys find it odd that my miracle is not home yet?"

"It is getting later in the day. He usually lets me know if he is going to be late," Lexi said.

"Well, he always calls, texts, or pops in," Kesia said.

"True, he does have a habit of *popping in*," Isabella said. Tapping the edge of her mug with her fingernails, she added, "It's not like him to make us worry."

Chapter 54

Kesia had left hours ago, and Isabella had gone to sleep on Aias's bed.

Lexi was getting concerned. Aias still had not come home, called, or texted. She couldn't fall asleep, so she went to the living room.

Pulling a blanket over her from the back of the couch, Lexi picked up Aias's journal and read what he had written last.

Lexi, my mom, is going to remember.

A horrifying scream came out of Aias's bedroom.

Every hair on Lexi's body stood up straight. Instantly, she was on her feet, running to Isabella. Opening the door without knocking, she went in.

"Lexi, he's dead."

"Who's dead?"

"My baby."

"What? No."

"Lexi, it all came back to me. You were there. You, Tamara, and Redington."

Lexi sat on the bed beside Isabella.

Isabella grabbed Lexi's hand.

A flood of memories came back to Lexi, the monastery, the chanting, the monks, Sophea, and Red. Redington was there with his palms facing Aias. The memories of her abduction, Redington, and Aias saving her from Marco, and how Aias had used all his power to teleport the three of them to safety, to Sophea.

She remembered how Sophea said it had been too much, and Aias could not regain his strength.

Lexi remembered everything, and obviously, so had Isabella.

"Get Redington!" Isabella screamed.

Lexi desperately tried to hold back her tears as each memory tore at her heart. "Ah, sure. Sure, Isabella, I'll call Red."

"Get him here, Lexi!"

She found her phone and searched for his number. *Thank goodness he thought to give me a burner phone when we were in… in… where were we?*

The man's voice on the line said, "Lexi! Are you alright? Red had been dying to talk to her since waking up in his own bed.

"Red… Red, do you remember?" Lexi asked cautiously.

"Of course, I remember! How could anyone forget an experience like that?" Red responded, shaking as he remembered the vision of Aias's body levitating just before it exploded into stardust.

"So do we. Red, Isabella needs you. She is on the verge of hysterics."

"Where are you, at Aias's?"

"Yes."

"I'll be right there."

"Thank you."

Red hung up without commenting.

Lexi went back to Isabella, "He's on his way."

Isabella barely answered but gave a slight nod.

Lexi went into the kitchen and poured two glasses of wine. Then, walking back into the bedroom, saying, "Come into the living room. Red is going to be here soon."

Isabella didn't get up to follow her, so Lexi went back and sat on the couch, tucked her feet up, and took a sip. *God, I need you. I need you to make me strong. I need to be strong for Isabella's sake.*

Lexi was happy that it didn't take long for Redington to get to Aias's apartment.

Without answering, Lexi just pushed six to let him in. Then, got up to open the door.

"I came as fast as I could," Redington said as he bent to hug her. "I have been going crazy. I didn't remember how I got home, and I wasn't sure if you guys found your way back or not."

Lexi enjoyed his embrace. "I hadn't thought of that."

"Of what?" Redington asked, confused.

"I didn't remember at first. I thought that Aias was just out."

"You didn't remember?"

"No, and neither did Isabella."

"Wow, I can't get his image out of my head."

Lexi couldn't know either, but she had to be strong for Isabella. "I should go and tell Isabella that you are here."

"Lex, wait," Redington said as he grabbed her and pulled her tight. "I've missed you."

Momentarily startled, Lexi softened to his touch and whispered, "Me too."

Another second or two went by without either of them moving.

Coming to her senses, Lexi moved slightly backward, "Isabella, she needs us."

Redington nodded and followed Lexi into Aias's bedroom.

Isabella said without turning over to face the other two, "Red, he's gone. My baby is gone."

"I know. I am so sorry, Isabella. I wish I could have saved him, but I didn't know how to send him more healing energy. I tried," Red said as he lowered his head and took a deep breath.

Lexi stepped forward and sat on the edge of the bed by Isabella's feet. "Isabella, how can we help?"

Slowly, Isabella turned over and faced Red, "Find Tamara."

"What?" Red was surprised at her request.

"You heard me. Find Sophea."

"Isabella, I don't know how to find her."

"Sure, you do. Do your detective stuff."

"Isabella, I am not a homicide detective anymore. I am an FBI agent."

"Even better."

Lexi placed her hand on Isabella's ankle and said, "He'll find her."

Red turned and glared at Lexi. "Lexi, I have no jurisdiction wherever she lives. And even if I did, how do you expect me to find someone who is off the grid?"

Before he could say another word, Lexi patted Isabella's ankle again, "He'll find her."

Lexi stood up and pulled Redington's arm toward the door. "We'll find her, Isabella. Sleep now, and by morning, we will have found her."

Isabella smiled slightly, closed her eyes, and rolled back over.

When Redington was out of earshot, he whispered to Lexi, "And how do you expect me to do what you assume I can do?"

"We'll find Sophea."

Chapter 55

Lexi sat on the couch next to Redington, "When Sophea lived here in New York City, she taught me how to communicate with the spirit world, remember?"

"Lexi, believe me when I tell you that even though I have tried to forget all the bizarre hocus pocus stuff, I can't. I remember you telling me about your experience saving your sister's soul."

"Good. Then what I am going to ask you to do won't surprise you."

Like a drama queen, Redington shook his head, sat on the couch, took a deep breath, and said, "What are you going to ask me to do now?"

"Meditate," Lexi answered with as serious a face as she could.

"Meditate. And just how is that going to find Sophea?"

"You'll see," Lexi reassured as she took Redington's hand. Continuing in a soothing tone, she added, "Relax and take a few deep breaths."

Redington gave Lexi a look of I can't believe I am doing this but leaned his head back against the couch and closed his eyes.

"As I count from one to three, with each number, you will take a deep breath and relax." Lexi leaned back and closed her own eyes as she said, "One, relaxing all the muscles in your body. Two, as you take your next breath, you will go even deeper into this relaxed state. Allowing your mind to expand your consciousness and allow the infinite possibilities of contacting Sophea. Three, it is a matter of giving yourself permission to go beyond yourself and allow your soul to connect with Sophea's soul."

Lexi listened as Red took all three deep breaths. "Now we will hold hands and combine forces so the connection is better, clearer, and faster."

Lexi took a breath, placed her fingers between his, and felt the heat radiating from his hand—how she had missed him.

Before she continued, she really couldn't help but notice the amount of heat radiating from Redington. *I wonder if he understands what is happening to him.*

"As we take our next deep breath, we will allow our combined energy to locate Sophea,"

Lexi said before she silently contacted her sister, Susannah.

Susannah, I need your help. I know it has been a while since I talked to you, and I am sorry. Please find time for me now.

Lexi, I always have time for you.

Oh, Susannah, I am so grateful for your love. I need to find Sophea. She used to call herself Tamara.

I know who you are asking for. Here, we do not need to call each other by their name, for they have had many names over their lifetimes. Their soul carries a unique energy trait that no other has. So, we focus on their soul's energy.

Oh, I never knew that. Fascinating. So, how do I contact Sophea's soul?

Take a breath. Then send your soul's energy up through your crown chakra and allow it to find her for you.

That's it? It's that easy?

That is all you will need to do.

Thank you, Susannah. I love you.

And I, you.

Lexi took a deep breath and said to Redington, "It is time to let our soul's energy find Sophea. Let go of your reality and imagine a part of your soul flowing up through the top of your head and entering the cosmos to locate her now.

Lexi heard Red take a deep breath.

Within an instant, Lexi felt herself astra-travel through the atmosphere. Her soul was following

Redington's. She allowed his soul's energy to do what it did best—be an FBI detective. She knew he was like a bloodhound, and once he had her scent, there was no stopping him from finding her.

What are you guys doing here?

It was Sophea's voice that Lexi was hearing. *Sophea, Isabella needs you. We need to bring her to where you are.*

Lexi, you guys are not ready yet.

What do you mean?

Your energy is not high enough.

High enough. I don't understand. We were there with Aias.

Yes, but that was an extraordinary circumstance.

You don't understand. She needs you.

Lexi, there is nothing I can do. I am sorry.

There must be something we can do. We need you.

I am sorry.

Sophea, please. I am begging you. Please tell me what we need to do. We'll do anything.

Well, there is one thing you can do.

Yes, anything. What is it?

You can figure out a way to raise your vibratory rate.

Vibratory rate? Then the connection was gone, and Lexi was instantly back in her body. As she opened her eyes, she asked Redington, "What happened?"

"I happened," Isabella said.

"Iss, I was talking to Sophea, but the connection was disconnected before I could ask her more."

"Sorry, Lexi. I thought you two fell asleep on the couch."

"I guess it could have looked like that," Lexi said, trying to control her frustration.

"What did she say?" Isabella asked through tear-stained eyes.

"She said we cannot go to where she is unless we raise our vibratory rate."

Red couldn't help but ask, "What does that mean?"

Lexi looked at him and said, "To the best of my knowledge, it is the frequency at which our body's energy vibrates. The lower the frequency, the less chance we can use our spiritual gifts and abilities."

"But you guys can use your spiritual gifts," Redington said, looking at Lexi and then at Isabella.

"I thought so, too. I am not sure what she meant," Lexi answered.

Isabella spoke up, "Lex, she means that even though humans can be awake and open their eyes, they still cannot see. They cannot see, feel, hear, or know the spiritual gifts that exist within themselves. Their energy's vibration is not high enough to recognize the higher energy frequencies."

"You mean like we are blind to the power that Aias possessed and his ability to perform miracles?" Lexi asked, confirming what she already knew to be true.

"Exactly."

Redington spoke up and asked, "I don't think I understand."

Lexi answered him, "I think what Isabella is trying to say is that even though she and I have raised our vibration and belief in the spiritual gifts, we still are not at a frequency that Sophea would allow us to visit her."

Red stood up and said with a frustrated tone, "Well, how do we raise our vibration?"

"Good question," Lexi answered. "I am not sure."

"I think I might know," Isabella said as she reached for Aias's journal on the table.

Chapter 56

*I*sabella opened Aias's journal and flipped through a few pages until she found what she was looking for. "Here," she said to the others as she pointed to the page.

Lexi and Red came closer to look at the page.

"What are we looking at?" Red asked.

Isabella moved her head so he could get a better look.

"All I see is colored circles… and are those tarot cards?" Red asked, knowing what they were, thanks to Kesia.

"They are," Isabella confirmed. "This is the Kaballah Tree of Life."

Lexi had heard of the Tree of Life and knew that there were many interpretations.

Isabella went on to explain the interpretation she knew, "The mapping of the Sefirah dates to 12th century France. Notice how the horizontal triads are connected."

"Hard to miss the lines connecting the dots, Isabella. They look like bridges," Red said, trying to lighten the mood.

Not impressed that he wasn't taking this seriously, Isabella said, "No wonder Sophea doesn't want us there."

Red grabbed his heart and said exaggeratingly, "Isabella, you wound me."

Lexi let out a chuckle.

Red said, a bit embarrassed, "Isabella, I don't mean to be rude, but this Kabballah stuff is way over my head. Most of this stuff is hard for me to believe, let alone understand. I need you to dumb it down for me. Remember that I am a newbie to this information."

Isabella looked at Lexi and said, "We are going to need help."

"I agree." Lexi added, "Redington needs to get to our level, and we all need to get to Sophea's if we are going to join her in Nepal."

"Hey, I don't need to go to Nepal. I am sure you two can go without me," Redington reasoned.

"No," Isabella said. "You were there before I was there. You saw Aias ascend. That is more than I can say I did. No. You are supposed to be there. That I am sure of."

Lexi reached over and turned a page in Aias's journal. "Does it say anything about raising a person's vibration?"

Isabella flipped quickly through the pages of the journal. "Not really." As she put the journal on the coffee table, she sat forward on the couch, pointing to some words on a page, "Look here."

Lexi and Red leaned in to have a better look.

Isabella pointed to a phone number and a name written in the journal—Camillo O'Malley.

"Who is that?" Lexi asked. "I have never heard of her."

"How do you know it is female?" Redington questioned.

Lexi looked surprised. "I don't, but it sounds like a girl's name."

"I guess there is one way to find out," Isabella said.

Picking up her cell phone, she started to dial.

"Hey, it is 1:00 am in the morning," Lexi exclaimed as she went to hang up the phone.

Isabella stood up, moved the phone out of reach, and touched the speaker button. Then, as she stepped over Redington's long legs, she said, "Hi, Camillo?"

Everyone heard a sleepy male voice answer, "Yes, who is this?" Then, a second later, "Do you know what time it is?"

"Yes, and I am sorry, but this is an emergency. You see, my son has died, and your name is in his journal."

An awkward second of silence passed.

"I see. Isabella, I presume."

Looking at Lexi and Red in disbelief, Isabella answered, "Yes, how did you guess?"

"Aias contacted me a few days ago. He said that you might be calling."

"He did. Did he leave you a message to tell me?"

"Not exactly."

"What does that mean," Redington said in the background.

"That must be Lord Ferguson Charles Redington the 3rd."

Isabella and Lexi both turned to stare at Redington.

Redington cleared his throat, "It is. How do you know my full name and title? No one in the US knows that information."

Mouth open for a second in shock, Lexi questioned, "Lord?"

The man on the phone said, "That must be Alexandra?'

Twisting her head back to the phone, "Yes, but I prefer to be called Lexi."

All they heard was a "Hmm" from the phone.

Isabella spoke up, "Can you tell me why Aias contacted you?"

"Yes, he paid for four tickets."

"Four tickets," Redington said gruffly. "Where are we flying to?"

A chuckle was heard. "No, not airline tickets."

Embarrassed, Redington said, with a harsher-than-needed tone, "Then what kind of tickets are they?"

Another awkward second of silence passed.

"Well?" Redington said, waiting for an answer.

Another second went by.

"What the?" Redington said, not used to being ignored.

Just as Lexi was to say, "Calm down."

The phone went dead.

"He hung up. The bastard!" Redington ranted as he started to pace around the living room. "Who does he think he is?"

Lexi sat down on the couch and Googled Camillo O'Malley. "It says here that he is an international speaker."

"A what?" Redington huffed.

Isabella came over to Lexi and read, "He is world-renowned. He is like a mystic Guru but by Western standards."

"Well, what is he renowned for?" Redington said sarcastically.

"A type of Mindfulness," Lexi stated.

"What can an Irish man teach about mindfulness? How you can drink your stress away?" Redington said cynically.

"Red, be nice," Isabella scorned. "We might need this man."

"It says here that mindfulness can not only have stress-reducing symptoms, but it can also raise a person's vibratory rate," Lexi remarked, absorbed in the website's content.

"When does he speak next," Isabella asked.

"Tomorrow. Here in New York City," Lexi responded, her gaze shifting to the others.

Chapter 57

Lexi watched Isabella and a snoring Redington sleep. They had fallen asleep on the couch not long after the conversation ended with Camillo.

She had gotten a couple of hours of shut-eye herself but was wide awake now, thinking about the last few days.

Mindfulness.

Lexi Googled mindfulness and read a blurb from https://greatergood.berkeley.edu/

Mindfulness means maintaining a moment-by-moment awareness of our thoughts, feelings, bodily sensations, and the surrounding environment through a gentle, nurturing lens.

She took a deep breath as she read. *Though it has its roots in Buddhist meditation, a secular practice of mindfulness has entered the American mainstream in recent years.*

Lexi shifted in her seat.

Who knew that changing a word from psychic development to mindfulness would make the non-believers believe?

Redington stirred and whispered, "What are you reading?"

Lexi looked up and smiled, "Good morning. Sleepyhead. I was researching mindfulness."

Stretching his long muscular legs, he asked, "And what did you find?"

Shifting her eyes quickly from his sexy body, she swallowed her embarrassment, then said hastily, "That mindfulness is focusing your attention on the present moment and observing your thoughts, feelings, and sensations in the body."

As Isabella stretched her arms above your head—stretching her spine from side to side—opening her eyes, she said, "Sounds like what Tamara taught us to do when we were learning metaphysics,"

"That is what I thought," Lexi agreed.

"What are you guys talking about?" Redington inquired with curiosity.

Lexi turned to him, "Well when I first started taking Tamara's courses, I mean Sophea's. Man, I can't get her new name to stick in my head."

"Me neither," Isabella confessed.

Lexi smiled at Isabella, then continued, "Anyways, she taught me that the key to metaphysics is to focus on your internal clues."

"Clues?" Redington asked for clarity.

Nodding again, "Yes, clues. She taught my group that our subconscious mind controls everything about our life."

"Like what?" Redington asked.

"Like our perception."

"Perception of what?" Redington inquired.

"Perception of everything around us."

Shaking his head, Redington said, "I think I need an example. I don't understand what you mean."

Lexi took a deep breath. Then said, "That."

"What?"

"That. What I just did."

Redington's tone changed to annoyance. "You didn't do anything."

"Sure, I did. I took a deep breath. Right after you asked for clarification."

Redington paused, "But that doesn't explain anything."

"Think of it like this. Our mind needs a moment, a pause, to think before speaking. To search for an answer that would suit you. So, I went internally to find an answer. To do that, I took a deep breath."

"A deep breath. You're telling me that a deep breath is the answer to all the questions," Red queried, unbelieving that something so simple could be so astonishing.

"Give it a shot. If you have any doubts," Lexi suggested, confident he would.

Redington took an exaggerated deep breath and then said, "Now what? I did what you said, but I don't have an illuminating answer popping into my head."

Isabella chuckled.

Red turned and gave her a dirty look.

She chuckled even harder.

"Try this," Lexi said to get his attention back. "Tell me what you hear right now."

Red looked at her and shook his head, saying, "What is that going to help?"

"Trust me. Just do it. Tell me what you hear."

Without consciously noticing, Red took a breath. "I can hear you talking."

"Listen closer. What else do you hear?"

Again, without consciously noticing, Red took a breath. "I hear the clock ticking."

"What else?"

Another breath, "I hear the furnace kicking in."

"Okay, now shift your focus, and what do you see?" Lexi asked.

Looking down and shaking his head before he flicked his eyelids, another breath, "I see you two. I know you are going to say, look closer."

Redington shut his eyes and took a breath. When he opened them, he said, "Interesting. Everything looks brighter."

"Awesome. You're getting it. Now shift your focus again, and what do you feel this time?"

Redington hunched his shoulders and said, "That I'm a bit tense."

"Where specifically are you tense?" Lexi asked him, noticing that he retook a breath before answering.

Redington moved his head and shoulders, then pointed. Rubbing a spot on the top of his shoulder, he said, "Right here."

"Anywhere else?"

Redington moved the rest of his body. "No, just here." Rubbing the same spot.

"Okay, great. Now, did you notice what you did each time I asked you a question?"

Being a smart alec, Redington said, "Answered."

"And?" Lexi was requesting more insight.

"And what? I answered you. I didn't do anything else."

"I beg to differ," Lexi contradicted.

He shook his head again and said, "You'll have to spell it out because I don't know what you are talking about."

Isabella chuckled.

"What? Not you, too. Lexi, what did I do?"

Smiling, she said, "You took a breath each time before answering my question."

"I did. I overlooked that."

"Trust me. You did."

Isabella nodded her head in confirmation.

"Well, so what if I did? What does that matter?"

"It matters because it is the first step in mindfulness, or as we call it, metaphysics."

Isabella added, "It is also the first step and easiest way to raise your vibratory rate."

"Why do I want to raise my vibratory rate?" Redington asked.

"Because raising your vibratory rate is raising your body's vibrational frequency. And to go to Nepal to be with Sophea. Hey, I did it. I said Sophea, not Tamara." Isabella said proudly, then continued. "We all need to raise our frequency."

The condo phone rang.

Lexi answered, "Yes."

"Miss Constantine, an envelope has arrived for you. Should I have someone bring it up?"

"Yes, that would be great. Thanks, Carl."

"You know the doorman's name?" Redington questioned.

"Of course I do. Don't you know yours?"

"I don't have one. Remember?"

Lexi tightened her lips and flicked her eyes as she went to answer the door.

Returning to the others, she opened the envelope and pulled out four tickets. "I guess we are going to Camillo O'Malley's lecture."

With a keen eye, Redington asked, "Who is the fourth one for?"

"Me," Kesia said as she walked into the condo before Lexi shut the door.

Chapter 58

Lexi hugged Kesia. "How are you doing?"

"Fine. Why? You say it like I should have a problem.

Lexi paused. *She knows, right?*

Pulling away from Kesia, Lexi said awkwardly, "You know about Aias, right?"

"I know he sent me a note that said there was a surprise for me and that I needed to be here." Kesia looked at the time on her phone. "Right about now. Am I late?"

"Ah, no, I don't think so," Lexi said, looking desperately for help from Isabella or Redington.

Kesia turned and hugged the other two, saying, "So, where is he this time? Did he go somewhere far?"

Redington answered, "You could say that."

Looking at Redington, Kesia asked again, "So, where did he go?"

Isabella started to cry.

"What is going on here? He said there was a surprise for me. Why is she crying?"

Isabella ran from the room.

"What is going on?" Kesia asked in a much louder voice. "Where is Aias?"

Lexi hugged Kesia again and, as calmly as she could, said, "Kesia, come have a seat, and I will tell you all that I know."

Kesia sat down on the couch.

Lexi told Kesia the whole story about what happened in Nepal.

With tears running down her cheeks, Kesia said, confused, "I don't understand. He visited me last night."

"He did!" Lexi squealed.

"Are you sure?" Redington asked.

"Of course, I'm sure. Aias has visited me many times in my dreams. It is as real as you talking to me right now."

"Kesia, I am sorry, but Aias ascended. He is no longer a human or a half-elf."

Coming back into the room, Isabella whispered, "He is an angel."

Kesia shook her head. "No. That can't be right. I just talked with him last night. Everything seemed so normal. He can't be dead."

"I am sorry, Kesia. We were all there. I saw him ascend."

"No!" Turning to look at Isabella. "Tell me it isn't true?"

Coming over and hugging her, Isabella answered, "Oh my darling, I wish it weren't. Believe me. I wish they were teasing."

"Why?!"

Isabella took Kesia's face in her hands and said, "I don't really know. He said something about graduating and accomplishing his purpose in this lifetime."

"But we weren't done. I wasn't done with him," Kesia said with more tears racing down her cheeks. "And if that were true, why did he tell me to come over for a surprise?"

"He must have wanted you to be with people who love you and would understand your pain."

Redington added, "You know Aias. He always is one step ahead of us. He even knew to send four tickets. I am assuming that you are intended to be on this new adventure of ours."

Looking at Redington, Kesia repeated, "New adventure."

Redington nodded and said, it is a crazy one. We need to raise our vibration. Or is it frequency?" He said, turning to Lexi. "Ah, it doesn't matter. We need to raise it so that we can go to Nepal."

"Nepal?" Kesia questioned.

"Ya," Redington said, then looked at Lexi again. "That is what they tell me."

Looking at Lexi, Kesia asked, "What is in Nepal?"

"Sophea."

"You are going to see Tamara?"

Lexi nodded.

Kesia took a ticket out of Lexi's hand and asked, "And what is this?"

"I think it is your surprise," Lexi answered, giving Redington and Isabella theirs.

Kesia read the ticket. "Shift Happens with Camillo O'Malley. Who is that?"

"We are not sure, but he is mentioned in Aias's journal."

"And he knows more about us than we do about him," Redington added.

Lexi turned to Redington and said, "Ya, about that. Lord?"

"It is a boring story, Lex."

Kesia wiped away her tears. "I'm ready for any kind of story."

"Ladies. There isn't a story here. Really, you are wasting your time asking," Redington said as he headed towards the door. "Looking at his watch, he said, "Look at the time. I have a job to get to." Then he left without saying goodbye.

"Coward," Lexi laughed as she turned back to the girls and asked Kesia, "Can you do your magic on your oracle and find out everything you can on Camillo O'Malley, please."

Chapter 59

Later that evening, as the evening shadows fell over Aias's condo building, the girls stepped out, preparing to hail a cab. To their surprise, a sleek limousine glided to a stop at the curb.

Redington got out and said, "May I offer you lovelies a lift?"

Lexi smiled and answered, "What a gentleman. Who knew."

Kesia forced a smile and got into the limo after Lexi.

Isabella squeezed Red's hand in appreciation before she got in.

Upon their arrival at the hotel hosting the event, one of Camillo's assistants approached their waiting limousine. As they exited the vehicle, he cordially announced, "Miss Jackson, Miss Constantine, Miss Bango, and Lord Redington, please follow me."

"Lord?" Kesia questioned. "I thought Lexi was talking about God or Jesus or something. Not an English Lord."

"The man doesn't know what he is talking about," Redington said, trying to dismiss the conversation.

"I know. The Lord has a lot of answering to do," Lexi said, smiling at Kesia.

"There is no Lord."

"And here I thought I was the diva," Isabella said, joining in on teasing Redington.

Red just shook his head and ignored them all.

The assistant led them through a long hallway toward a door. Once they were all in the room, he ordered them, "Wait here."

"But wait. Aren't you supposed to show us to our seats," Lexi called out just before he shut the door.

The door closed, and Lexi went to open it to ask him again, but it was locked.

Pulling a couple of times. Lexi said, "What the?" but really wanted to finish the sentence swearing.

"What is going on?" Isabella added.

"Don't panic. I am sure there is a perfect explanation," Redington said, checking all the doors in the room.

But all were locked.

Kesia sat down. "Well, we know we are not kidnapped because the tickets are real."

"How do you know that?" Redington asked.

"Lexi and I were researching Mr. O'Malley. He is legit. And he is speaking here tonight."

"Then why are we locked in a room?" Lexi asked nervously.

Before anyone could think of an answer, the door opposite to how they entered opened, and the same assistant announced, "He is ready for you now."

"Who?" Redington demanded.

"Come this way." That was the only answer Redington got.

Entering another room, pointing to four chairs, the assistant commanded, "Please have a seat. It will all be made clear in a moment." Then left.

"I think…" was all Isabella got out of her mouth before the curtains opened, and a large audience was sitting in front of them. "…we are on a stage," Isabella finished.

"You think?" Redington said as he stood up.

As he did, a man's voice could be heard over the speakers. "Lord Redington, thank you for volunteering to be first."

Red's face went redder than his name.

Camillo O'Malley came out onto the stage, and a roar of applause was heard.

Bowing his head slightly, a short, plump man in his sixties said next, "Thank you all for coming. I have a special treat for you tonight. Joining us on stage are four very different and unique people. They have nothing in common other than they all loved the same person."

Not knowing what else to do, Redington sat back down.

Lexi heard Redington whisper, "Aias, what did you get me into this time?"

Camillo O'Malley had long grey hair slicked back and tied in a single pony. He wore a wrinkled grey shirt, dark grey pants, and no tie. His fingernails were painted black, and he swore like a sailor.

Lexi said as quietly as she could to the others, "He's scary."

Kesia nodded.

"We could walk off the stage," Redington said out the side of his mouth, trying not to move it.

But before anyone could get up, O'Malley came over, patted Redington on the shoulder, and then walked behind him.

Placing both hands on Redington's shoulders, O'Malley said, "This big boy here is a fraud. A fake."

Redington turned his head, trying to look at O'Malley. He was about to get up, but O'Malley pushed down on his shoulders harder.

"This man is a Lord. His family comes from a long line of English aristocrats, but here he is, hiding out in the United States. Playing detective, or is it FBI agent? When he should be playing cricket, Polo, or on a fox hunt with his fellowmen."

Lexi looked at Red and squinted her eyes at him.

Red said to O'Malley, "You don't know what you're talking about?"

O'Malley patted Red's shoulder, then walked around and faced the audience. "The act of miracles starts with clearing up anything holding you back from your full potential."

"Nothing is holding me back. I chose my life," Redington said to O'Malley.

O'Malley nodded and said to the audience, "That is what we all say. But that is a lie, and you all know it. Deep down, you know you are living a lie."

"I am not a liar!" Redington said as he stood up.

A person in the audience gasped at his size.

At 6'4", Redington towered over Camillo O'Malley's 5'5'' height.

"Sit the fuck down," O'Malley ordered.

"I don't have to take this abuse, you little shit," Redington shot back.

"I said, sit the fuck down." O'Malley walked up to Redington, inches away, saying, "If you are so sure that you are not living a lie, then why did Aias send you all here to me?"

"Good question,' Redington answered. "Why he thought you could teach us anything is beyond me."

O'Malley's demeanor changed, and he said to the audience, "When we live a lie and hold all the awful shit in, we can not accomplish the act of mindfulness. Our subconscious mind is too busy ensuring that the lie is kept a secret. That lie costs us our ability to go within and grow. Those lies hold us back from our full potential. Those lies hold us back from becoming all that we can be. Now, Lord Redington. Sit the fuck down and let me do my job."

Redington didn't know what to do, so he sat back down.

The audience's applause was deafening.

"Miss Constantine, how long have you known Lord Redington?" O'Malley asked.

"A few years now," Lexi answered quickly.

"And did you know that he was a Lord?"

Lexi answered honestly, "No."

Directing his question to the other two ladies, "And how about you two? Did you know that he was a Lord?"

At the same time, both answered honestly, "No."

Redington defended his reasoning: "They didn't need to know that about me. That is not who I am anymore."

O'Malley did not look at Redington but at the audience, saying, "Some things can't be left behind. Can't be hidden." Turning back to the ladies, he asked, "In all the time you have known Lord Redington, did he ever tell you about his family?"

Lexi paused before she answered, "No, now that I think about it, I don't remember him ever talking about his family."

The other two shook their heads no.

"As I said, lies hold us back." Turning to the audience again, "Our subconscious knows everything about us. It protects us. It is the mastermind, the inner genie, of all of our memories and emotions. It looks after all of our physical needs. Our breathing, digestion, and blood cell production. It is magnificent."

Walking near the front of the stage and facing the audience, O'Malley said, "Our subconscious mind works 24/7/365. It never rests. In the healthcare section of Forbes, an article says that the human brain's unconscious processing abilities are estimated at roughly 11 million pieces of information per second. Compare that to the estimate for conscious processing: about 40 pieces per second."

O'Malley paused to let that information sink in.

Then continued, "The secret to mindfulness is to tame the subconscious. Learn how to control your subconscious. Well, you'll never be able to control your subconscious one hundred percent, even if a Yogi mastered the act of holding one's breath and tried not to breathe. Their subconscious mind would override their conscious command and knock them out cold. Their lungs would start to pump oxygen again."

O'Malley walked around the stage again as he said, "Mindfulness is controlling the part of the brain that controls our stress, reactions, and the quest for success."

Turning to the four on stage, "Even our psychic abilities."

Forgetting for a moment about Aias, Kesia did a little finger tap in excitement.

Redington shot her a dirty look.

Kesia stuck her tongue out at him.

The audience cheered.

O'Malley spoke again, saying, "It is our obligation in this lifetime to clear up anything and everything that no longer serves us. Be that our diet, addictions, our job, or our career. And it might even mean getting rid of our friends and family that no longer serves our greater good."

Lexi bit her lip.

O'Malley noticed. "Does that make you feel bad, Miss Constantine?"

Lexi went to answer.

"I don't fucking care. You are here for a reason, and your subconscious mind is what is stopping you from achieving your goal."

Lexi's face was in shock.

"Oh, did I hurt your feelings," O'Malley asked Lexi.

Lexi went to answer.

But before she could, "I don't fucking care" came out of his vulgar mouth. "Now that I have your attention, let's get to work."

O'Malley pulled up a chair beside the four sitting on the stage and sat down.

Turning to look at the audience, he said, "There are many ways to achieve mindfulness, but one must start at the beginning. Whatever crap you have put into your brain, you must remove the blocks for mindfulness to work. Any negative thoughts, any secrets, anything that makes your subconscious mind work overtime."

Lexi piped up, "What about swearing?"

O'Malley turned to look at Lexi. "Does my swearing make you uncomfortable?"

Lexi squirmed a little, "Yes. It is unprofessional."

"Is it now? Who made that a rule?"

"Well, I don't know, but."

O'Malley cut her off. "That is my job, Miss Constantine. To make you uncomfortable. Your subconscious doesn't shift unless you are uncomfortable, now does it?"

"Well."

He cut her off again and yelled, "It wasn't a fucking question."

Redington stood up and said, "Now, just a minute."

O'Malley turned to him and hollered, "What are you fucking going to do about it, liar?"

Redington steamed, "I've had enough of this bullshit," just before he turned to walk off the stage.

"Coward!" O'Malley yelled.

Redington stopped in his tracks and turned. "What did you say?"

"You heard me, coward."

Redington walked up to O'Malley and said, "Say that one more time."

"Lord Redington, have a fucking seat and let us get on with the show. The part of the show where you learn how to raise your vibratory rate. That is what you came here for, isn't it?"

The audience started to chant, "Lord Redington, Lord Redington."

Redington was shocked. He didn't know what to do with hundreds of people watching and cheering him on. Did they want him to punch the guy or sit down? He chose to sit down.

The audience cheered.

"I think I entered the twilight zone," Redington whispered to the girls.

Chapter 60

Thinking this lecture couldn't get any more perplexing, Redington's eyes almost popped out of his head. The man walking onto the stage was his dad, Earl Winston Charles Redington the 2nd.

O'Malley started to talk as he moved the chair he was sitting on and gestured for the Earl to be seated. "For those who don't know, an Earl is the third rank of the Peerage, standing above the ranks of Viscount and Baron but below Duke and Marquess."

Redington looked at his father in disbelief.

O'Malley said, "Meet Lord Redington's father, Winston Charles Redington, the 2nd Earl of Wrightenton."

Redington saw Lexi turn and stare at the man. Redington spoke up, "Yes, this is my father. So, what is your point in bringing him here? Money?"

Camillo ignored Redington's questions, walked up to Winston, and said, "Your Lordship, you have agreed to participate in tonight's event. Is that still true?"

Redington's dad, Winston, answered in his high-class English accent, "Yes. I am a wee bit knackered, but let's have a go, shall we."

"Father, do not do anything for this man," Redington pleaded.

Before Redington could do or say anything else, Camillo spoke to the audience, "Mindfulness comes in many forms. I will use Neuro Linguistic Programing, also known as NLP, for tonight's demonstrations."

As if reading Redington's mind, Camillo explained how NLP works. "Neuro means nerves and linguistic means language. By reprogramming your brain, NLP teaches you to see problems from a new perspective and find better solutions."

"Looks like we have gotten into a bit of a sticky wicket," Winston told his son.

"Blimey," Redington said, going back to the language of his English roots.

Lexi snickered, hearing Redington's English accent.

Redington turned and gave her a dirty look.

Lexi smiled, sat up straighter, and tried not to laugh.

"NLP uses the technique of hypnosis combined with a few signature techniques. Let's begin," Camillo said as he turned to Winston.

Touching Winston on the shoulder, "Close your eyes and relax. Take a deep breath."

Redington interrupted, "Stop!"

Camillo's eyes darkened as he looked at Redington, "Why the fuck are you interrupting us? Your father has come a long way to help you, and all you can do is interfere in his session. So shut the fuck up and let your father do what he came here for."

Redington saw the look in his father's eyes. It reminded him of when he was a wee lad and was in trouble.

Redington pretended to zip his mouth and sat back, crossing his arms across his chest. *Bloody hell. If he wants to make an ass of himself, so be it.*

Camillo continued, "As you take your next breath, let go of any tension in your body."

Camillo paused, "Take two more deep breaths."

Camillo paused again.

"Earlier, before you came onto the stage, you told me that you and your son have not spoken for many years."

Winston nodded without opening his eyes.

"You said that you wished that night had never happened."

Winston nodded again.

Instantly, Redington knew what night Camillo was referring to. It was almost nineteen years ago, and Redington could remember it as if it were yesterday.

He had just turned twenty-five and was about to receive his trust fund. His older sister and brother had already received theirs.

The night started as any typical evening at the manor. As he came in for the evening tea, the Earl and Countess of Wrightenton, Redington's mother and father, were already seated at the dining room table.

The room was magnificent, with its high ceilings, pillars, wainscoting walls, elaborate casing, and baseboards. The room reminded Redington of a family meal in the series Downton Abby, where the table was beautifully set with flower arrangements and candles, and the dinner-wear was set out for royalty.

Everyone seated was dressed in evening wear—what most people would wear to a cocktail party.

Moments later, Redington's sister and brother came in laughing.

As one of the second footmen, dressed in an Azure blue velvet coat with tails, served Redington a glass of Bordeaux wine, and the first footman served his father and mother the meat of the evening—duck, Redington asked his siblings, "What's so funny?"

"Ah, my dear brother, it is of no concern to you, now is it," Grayson stated as he laughed smugly and winked at his younger sister of two years, Janelle.

Lord Grayson was as good-looking as Redington, with similar height and beach blond hair, which they inherited from their mother. He was five years older than Redington and was in line to take over the family's estate.

The beautiful and whimsical Lady Janelle was three years older than Redington. She took after their father with her raven black hair and blue eyes.

"Grayson, be nice to Ferguson. He may be younger than us, but he has the build of a knight and may one day put those muscles to the test."

"Children, really. Our family time is sacred, and we should be giving blessings to our good fortunes. Now, let's say grace," the Countess of Wrightenton said.

Lady Gabriela was the perfect image of a regal countess, slender and beautifully manicured. She was very well looked after by her head housemaid and attending staff.

After bowing his head and saying, "Amen," Redington asked, "If it is okay with you, Mother, I would like to attend to a matter in town after we are finished with our meal?"

Gabriela looked up from her delicately cut piece of duck on her fork, "If you are speaking of the matter of one of our tenants, I am sure it can wait until morning."

Redington knew his only chance was tonight. "It can't wait. It is urgent that I speak with Mister Taylor. He has a prize thoroughbred that I must have. He is selling it tonight. This matter cannot wait until morning."

Lady Janelle excitedly spoke up, "I will be joining him."

Redington looked at her in surprise since she had not spoken of it before.

She winked at him and smiled at her father, saying, "Daddy, you will allow us to purchase this beautiful beast, won't you? You have always told us to take up interests that are dear to our heart and will improve the lives of others on our estate."

Lord Winston could not deny his daughter. She was his pet and was intended to marry next month to one of the sons of the most respected families in the county. "Yes, yes. Of course, you can go."

Lady Gabriela pierced her lips shut, then returned to eating her duck.

"Well, it sounds like a party. Count me in," Grayson said with a big smile.

Redington took a deep breath. He was not expecting to be accompanied to Taylor's barn.

Redington insisted on driving since it was his adventure.

"Shotgun," Grayson called out as he got into the passenger's seat.

His siblings were chatting up a storm about the upcoming marriage and how Janelle's new beau would be a grand fit for the family, bringing his money and title with him.

Redington was sick of hearing about prestige and position. He didn't care about that stuff. He was more interested in the welfare of the commoner.

Just as he was about to tell them to shut up, a buck jumped in front of the car.

Redington swerved to miss the buck, but the rainfall had made the road slick, and he lost control and slammed into a giant oak tree.

When he regained consciousness, he saw that the hood was wrapped around the tree, and smoke was coming from the engine. He immediately assessed the state of his siblings and looked at the passenger's seat.

Grayson was not in the car. All Redington saw was a bloodied windshield.

Looking behind, he scrambled to get out to help his sister.

As he pulled her from the wreck, his eyes met hers just as the light went out of them.

"NO!!!!" Redington screamed into the night.

Holding her close, he prayed to God not to let this be. But he didn't receive the miracle he had prayed for.

Letting his dear sister's body down gently, he got up and stumbled as he searched for his brother.

Five feet from the car was Grayson's body. He had been thrown through the windshield due to the impact and not wearing a seatbelt.

Redington hoped that he had died instantly and that he had not suffered.

Tears rolled down Redington's cheeks.

He could see the lights from the manor but couldn't bear that he had to bring the news back to his parents. They were going to be devastated.

Chapter 61

"Go on. Tell us about that night," Redington heard Camillo say to his father.

"She died a month later," was all that Lord Winston responded.

"Who?" Camillo asked for confirmation.

"My wife. She died of a broken heart. Her two children had died a horrible death, and her baby had left for the Americas."

Camillo looked at Redington.

Redington was staring at the floor but could feel Camillo's intense glare.

"Where in your body do you hold all this pain, Lord Winston?" Camillo asked next.

Redington watched his father's hand move up to his chest.

"Have you ever forgiven your son for that night?" were the words that came out of Camillo's mouth next.

Redington knew the answer.

Lord Winston shook his head slowly from side to side.

There was a gasp from the audience.

Lexi grabbed Redington's wrist to support him, but Redington flinched so she would not touch him.

Redington had buried that painful night deep into his subconscious. He made it a point never to speak about family. The memories were far too haunting.

"Would you like to forgive him now?" Camillo asked.

Winston's head nodded yes, but Redington's eyes were shut and did not see.

The words, "Son, I forgive you," rang out.

Numb from remembering that horrid night, Redington did not comprehend the words. It was as if someone had spoken in a different tongue.

A moment later, a hand touched Redington's. It made him jump. With his eyes closed, he knew his father had gotten up and approached him. He could smell his English Leather Cologne, his father's favorite scent.

"I forgive you, Ferguson."

A tear fell from Redington's eye.

Clearing his throat, Redington said, "I don't forgive myself."

Lexi had gotten up so that Lord Winston could have her chair.

Sitting down, Winston faced his son and said, "Look at me."

Reluctantly, Redington opened his tear-stained eyes and looked at his father.

Red's hand was squeezed this time.

"I am getting old, Ferguson and I do not want my last days to be alone. I want to be around family. It was God's plan."

"God's plan! Why in hell would God ever make such a horrible plan?" Redington yelled out.

Camillo spoke, "Redington, where in your body do you hold this memory?"

Thinking that his question was insane, Redington shook his head.

"Answer him, son. He is trying to help you," Lord Winston said as he squeezed his son's hand again.

Looking from his father to Camillo, Redington said, "I hold it in my head."

"Great," Camillo commented.

"Great. You think this is great?" Redington disgustedly responded.

"Yes. Now that we have the what, where, when, how, and why we can move on to clear this shitty night's memory and its hold on the two of you.

"And just how do you foresee that?" Red asked sarcastically.

"By using a combination of hypnosis and other modalities to reprogram your subconscious mind, in the trade, we call it Neuro Linguistics Programing or NLP," Camillo said but faced the audience. "If everyone in the audience can be quiet, I will begin."

Redington fidgeted in his seat, unsure what to expect but ready for anything Camillo threw at him.

But instead of Redington, Camillo addressed Winston by saying, "Your Lordship. I will have you focus on that horrible night."

Redington waited anxiously.

"Lord Winston, I want you now to imagine that you are the size of a pea and have flown out of the top of your head. Looking down at it, you are hovering about six inches above your body. Nod your head when you have completed this request."

A slight nod came from Winston.

Camillo was pacing in front of Winston as he talked. "Good. Now notice that an imaginary timeline has appeared slightly below where you are hovering."

Redington watched as his father took a deep breath.

"It goes on both ways for eternity," Camillo said as he walked behind Winston so that he could watch the audience. "While you are hovering above yourself, it is like watching a movie. You are not the character but are watching the character, even though you really are the character."

Camillo's voice echoed louder through the conference room. "I want you to go back along this timeline and remember the exact moment when you were told there had been an accident and that two of your children were dead."

Redington watched his father as a tear fell from his dad's eye.

Winston nodded when Camillo didn't speak right away.

Redington watched as Winston nodded, insinuating that he had remembered.

Another moment went by.

"As you hover above yourself on that horrid night, tell me what happened. In as much detail as you can."

Everyone watched as Winston took a breath. As he spoke, his voice cracked, and he had to clear his throat.

"My wife and I had retired to the library to have a glass of sherry. We were playing a game of chess when the butler came in and told us the news."

Winston paused.

"Okay, now slowly go forward on the timeline. What happened next?"

Winston straightened in his chair. All eyes were on him. "My wife went hysterical. We had to call the doctor to come and give her a sedative."

Camillo asked, "Did you not go to see the accident?"

Winston's eyes were shut when he said, "They were dead. There was nothing I could do for them. Whereas my wife needed me."

Camillo pushed on, "What about your third child, the one who was not dead? Why had you not gone to see who it was?"

Winston opened his eyes and paused. "The butler told me who had died. I knew it was Ferguson who lived."

Redington closed his eyes. It was hard to hear what his father was saying, but he remembered now why he had left home.

Camillo asked, "What happened next on your timeline?"

Winston closed his eyes and then said, "The staff helped me take my wife upstairs to her chambers. The doctor arrived quickly after. He was worried that she may have another heart attack."

Camillo asked quickly, "She had one prior to this evening?"

"Yes, two, in fact."

Redington had no idea that his mother had been ill. Not one of the servants, his siblings, or his father had said anything. He had always thought that it was his fault that she had died. He thought that he had broken his mother's heart because it was his fault that his sister and brother had died.

"What happened next on the timeline?" Camillo asked Winston.

"I went in the ambulance. They had to take my wife to the hospital. All three children were there anyways, so I could be kept up to date on what was happening."

"Then what happened next?"

"It was all a blur. One day seemed to melt into the next. My wife never came out of the hospital. She died a month later."

"What about the funerals? What happened there?" Camillo asked.

"Which funeral?" Without waiting to hear Camillo's answer, Winston said, "I was waiting for my wife to get better to have the children's funerals, but she never did." Winston dropped his head, and tears started to flow. "I had all three on the same day."

"Winston, stay on the timeline. Don't drop into your body. Remember, you are watching this like a movie. Pop back onto the timeline. That is an order."

A moment later, Winston took a deep breath, bringing his head back up.

"Where was your son, Lord Redington, during all this time?"

Winston tensed his shoulders and said, "He left a note."

"What did the note say?"

"That he was so sorry, but he could not bear living on the property where he had killed his siblings. That he was going to start a new life in the Americas."

Camillo took a breath before he asked the next question. "Did you try to contact him?"

"No," Winston answered.

"Why not?"

"I had just lost the love of my life and two children. I did not have the emotional energy to argue with my youngest child. If he did not love me enough to stay, then who was I to try and guilt him into coming back? No. If he had wanted to stay, he would have."

Redington couldn't believe his ears. *That is not how it happened.*

Chapter 62

"Lord Redington, is that how you remember the horrid event?" Camillo asked.

Red cleared his throat. "No."

"Alright. I am going to have you do as I had your father. Take a breath and imagine that you are the size of a pea. Float out of your head about six inches and hover on your timeline. Go back to that night of the accident. What do you remember?"

This time, Redington did not hesitate to do what Camillo asked. He wanted answers. Redington nodded as he had seen his father do. "My brother and sister insisted on coming with me to see the horse. They never trusted me with my decisions and always told me what to do. Being the youngest and not wanting my ears smacked, I just let them come."

"Move forward on the timeline slowly. What happened next?" Camillo instructed.

"I was trying to ignore them while I was driving. It had been raining, and the roads were slippery. My brother was sitting beside me, and he lit up a fag."

"A what?" Camillo asked for clarification.

"A cigarette."

"Go on."

"I asked him to toss it out the window, but he wouldn't. I knocked it out of his hand. I thought it would fly out of the window, but instead, it landed in his lap. He took off his seatbelt to grab it."

Camillo asked, "What happened next?"

"He was jumping around like his pants were on fire. I was about to pull over when a buck jumped onto the road, blocking my way. I swerved to miss the buck, but the roads were too slippery, and I lost control of the car."

"Then what?"

"When I came to, all I could see was blood. I thought it was the bucks."

"What happened next?" Camillo asked.

Redington closed his eyes. "I crawled out of the vehicle and made my way to my siblings, but they were dead."

Red lowered his head in grief. All the years of suppressed emotions let go, and he cried out in despair for the loss of his kin.

You could hear a pin drop. The audience was so quiet.

Camillo walked behind Redington and bent down. "Let it out. It is time to let out all the pain. All the confusion. All the hatred for that horrible night."

Red cried out in rage this time.

Camillo touched his shoulder and said, "Let it out. It is time to heal. It is time to make peace with yourself."

Red dropped his head again, and tears streamed down his cheeks.

Winston got off his chair and bent down on one knee. Taking his son's hands in his, he said, "I am so sorry."

Redington could not believe his ears. He had been wishing for this moment ever since that night.

He slowly opened his eyes and moved his hands to squeeze his fathers.

Winston looked up with tears in his—which, for a noble Englishman, was something.

They just stared at each other.

Camillo turned to the audience, saying, "When negative emotions are captured in your body and not released, your entire system goes off balance. Your subconscious will do anything to protect you from harm, and so, will try to deviate you from anything that could trigger them to be released. It is the fight or flight mechanism."

Camillo walked back to face the men. "Lord Winston, have a seat, will you? We must do one more thing before I can release you from the stage."

Winston got up with the help of his son and sat back down.

"Gentlemen, take a deep breath and move on your timeline to this exact moment in time. Once there, take another breath and float back into your body, facing forward, so you are looking out toward the audience."

Both men seemed to take a breath at the same time.

"Thank you for participating. I believe Aias would be happy with the results."

Chapter 63

Lexi had been so entranced with the evening event that she had forgotten that Aias had sent them to see Camillo.

Lexi caught Redington's eye as he and his father left the stage. She smiled slightly to imply that she felt for him.

"Miss Constantine. Miss Jackson. Miss Bango."

Lexi's headshot from Redington to Camillo. *Oh my God. My turn.*

"Aias had specific instructions for the three of you."

Isabella spoke up, "Wait! You are going to take the word of a twenty-year-old?"

"Twenty-one, to be exact," Camillo said with a sly look at her.

"Okay, he might look twenty-one, but I can assure you that he is much younger," Isabella argued.

"His driver's license confirmed his age."

Lexi's eye twitched. *I didn't know he could drive.*

"Ladies, you have two choices. One, get up and leave the stage now, or sit back and let me do what is needed to be done."

Lexi looked at Isabella and Kesia.

Isabella shrugged her shoulders.

Kesia was in shock. She had never witnessed anything like that.

"Fine. We can handle whatever you throw at us," Lexi said with as much confidence as she could muster.

"Are you sure?" Camillo shot back.

Lexi looked at the girls again.

Isabella and Kesia nodded.

"Yes," Lexi said, sitting up in her chair straighter.

"Audience, you heard what the lady said."

Lexi felt her stomach do a somersault. *What did I just get myself into?*

Camillo walked toward the curtain behind the ladies and pulled the material until it revealed an opening.

Through the opening, Sophea walked onto the stage.

Lexi gasped. Holding her hand over her mouth, she got up and hurried over to Sophea. Hugging her instantly.

Isabella and Kesia weren't far behind.

The audience cheered.

Unknown to the girls, Camillo had informed the audience of this most unusual request of a son for his mother and his friends.

"How are you here," Lexi asked Sophea as tears rolled down her cheeks.

"It is a long story, one I will tell you when we have more time," Sophea answered.

Camillo adjusted the order of chairs so that there were now only three. "Ladies, please have a seat."

Lexi noticed that Camillo's harsh and ugly language had changed to a softer and more etiquette tone.

"Ladies, Sophea is here on the request of Aias's last words. She is here to teach you the last secret you need to know for a miracle to happen."

Camillo gestured to Sophea to take over.

Sophea turned and faced the audience. It had been a few years since she was last on stage. "I thank you for welcoming these ladies with open hearts. It is the heart that holds the key to miracles."

Lexi wiped her tears on her sleeve.

Sophea continued, "Miracles come from prayers, wishes, dreams, and desires. They come in many forms. Big miracles and tiny ones. They come as a surprise or at a request. They are your deepest desires manifesting into reality."

Lexi leaned forward as she listened to Sophea's words. She had missed her dearly.

"Miracles are not just performed by God, but also by his team of angels, his holy messengers. Like Archangel Hamied or Ariel"

Sophea took a breath to let the audience embrace her words. "Miracles happen every day to those that accept them to be true. A miracle can be as simple as finding a pen when you are looking or having an electronic device work again after giving up on it. Being out of gas and making it many miles to a gas station can be a miracle. Having wished for flowers to bloom a specific color other than what you bought can be a miracle. Finding an item on the side of a road that you have been wishing for is a miracle. Needing some furniture, clothing, or food and a friend or stranger appears with the goods without you asking is a miracle. A smile when you are down and out can be a miracle."

Sophea started to walk near the edge of the stage, talking to the audience.

Lexi knew Sophea was in her element.

"A lost item or puppy found is a miracle. A sleeping baby in your arms is a miracle. Making it just in time to say goodbye to a loved one in the hospital is a miracle. Receiving an award or writing a bestseller is a miracle. Becoming a business unicorn is a miracle."

Lexi had just read about unicorns in the New York Times. It was a business that made over a billion dollars a year.

"Miracles are all around you. You just have to be open to receiving them." Sophea said as she turned to look at the two ladies.

"Skidding out of control on ice and missing another car by inches is a miracle. Being rushed to an emergency and saved by a doctor is a miracle. Having terminal cancer and it magically goes into remission is a miracle."

Lexi knew she had been a witness to many miracles since her sister, Susannah, died.

Sophea winked at the ladies and said, "Seeing, feeling, hearing, or knowing that a ghost is present is a miracle. Being able to communicate with it is an even bigger miracle. Knowing a future outcome is a miracle. Laying on of hands and healing another person is a miracle."

Sophea paused. "Miracles are all around us, but the truth of it is. It is created in and from your heart."

Sophea came behind all three ladies and lightly touched a shoulder of each. "This is a miracle."

Chapter 64

$\mathcal{I}$sabella was a bit dizzy. She had felt this feeling before. Looking around, she knew she wasn't in New York City anymore. "Sophea, what did you do?"

"What I had to."

Isabella looked over and saw that Lexi and Kesia were gaining their bearings as well.

"Where are we?" Isabella asked.

"Exactly where you wished to be," Sophea answered.

"And where is that?" Lexi enquired.

As Sophea rang for some tea, she said, "With me, here in Nepal. Kathmandu, to be precise."

Isabella asked, this time with a snarky tone, "Why didn't you get weak and die from bringing us here?"

Sophea looked at her curiously but understood the pain of loss in her tone of voice.

"Well, Aias couldn't handle bringing Redington and Lexi. So, why could you?"

Sophea took a moment to answer.

"Because you believe."

"Aias believed," Isabella said with tears forming.

Lexi placed a hand on Isabella's shoulder to comfort her.

"I don't understand," Isabella said, almost pleading for the answer.

Sophea poured the tea that had arrived before answering.

"Yes, he did. But Redington did not."

"So, you are saying this is all Redington's fault?"

Lexi jumped into the conversation, "Oh my. Isabella, you would have to blame me for Aias's death then. He was saving me."

Isabella looked at Lexi with grief-sicken eyes, then said, "But why? Why did my baby have to die?"

Sophea said with the utmost love in her voice, "Because he had raised his vibratory rate to the most that one could. He had fulfilled not only this lifetime's lessons and life's purpose but all his Earthly commitments. He became an angel. His next step is attaining the requirements needed to reach Nirvana."

Isabella took a moment to think about what Sophea had just said. "I get that my son was a miracle in more ways than one. But I need a better answer to why am I here and he isn't?"

Sophea took a sip of her tea. "You will need more knowledge for that answer to make any sense to you."

"And how am I supposed to get more knowledge if you aren't giving me the answer?" she said, frustrated as hell.

"You know the old saying, if I give you a fish, you eat for a day, but if I teach you to fish, you eat for a lifetime."

Isabella shrugged, "Of course. I am sure everyone has heard that saying. But how is fishing going to answer my question and grant me the knowledge I need to learn enough to understand your wisdom?"

"The answer is in the last word I said."

Isabella thought for a moment. "Lifetime? Okay, I am really confused now. How is "lifetime" going to answer my question?"

Sophea looked at Isabella from over her teacup.

Lexi thought she saw a glimmer of sparkle in Sophea's eyes. She looked over to Isabella and said, "It looks like we are ready to learn our next gift."

Miracles and Miraculous Signs

As I write each novel, I know the title, the archangel, the spiritual gift granted by Spirit, and personal experiences on the subject matter. But I don't know what will happen to Lexi or any of her companions along the way.

It is always a surprise to me.

My family laughs and says, well, if you don't know what will happen, then who does?

I guess Spirit knows.

Many times, I am amazed at how the story miraculously unfolds. From the characters' names, the locations they visit, and even the fine details of the subject matter while I research. Then, I am in awe as the links start to appear.

An example of this is when I chose the Temple of Edfo. I had never heard of it before, only to find out that it had proof of the spaceship hieroglyphics that fit in with the story I was telling about Nibiru.

I can only give thanks to Spirit for the miraculous coincidences!

By this time, I assume that you figured out that I write these novels using my intuition, and this time, it said to add other people's inspirational miracles.

So, here they are. Enjoy!

Contents of Miracles

RAINBOWS AND SPOTLIGHTS

A few years back, my father passed away, leaving behind a grieving wife and family. As I was driving and thinking of him that day, a rainbow appeared, without a rainy cloud in the sky, gifting us a sign that he had made it to Heaven.

Even though I knew he was okay, I was pleasantly surprised by what happened at the memorial a month later. Sitting on the mantle was a collage of pictures taken of my dad. As the evening was approaching and people started to leave around seven that night, a bright light shone through the patio doors and directly on this one particular photo of him. So many people noticed and commented. As I moved the photo, the light followed it. If I didn't believe in an afterlife before, I sure do now.

Thanks, Dad! Love and miss you always,
FRAN C.

MADE OF STONE

When I was about twenty-one, living in Victoria, BC, I was waiting for the pedestrian light to change on Bay Street, giving me the okay to cross as I was about halfway across the first lane. Bamm!

I was shocked, *like, what just happened?* I was staring down at a guy and his bike.

He yelled up at me, "Dude, what are you doing? You're in my way."

Still in shock, I said, "Dude, I just saved your life. You were about to ride into four lanes of traffic."

Remembering the experience as if it were yesterday, I can't believe that I felt no pain from him hitting me. I didn't even budge. I felt like Superman.

It has been many years since that day, and it still seems like a miracle happened.
NICHOLAS B.

VERY VIVID PREMONITION

It was summer back in '82. A couple of weeks earlier, I had enjoyed an awesome day cliff diving at Lynn Canyon Creek, North Vancouver, BC. I even taught a couple of guys from Russia how to dive.

I was so excited about tomorrow's dive. I love the feeling that free-falling gives you. It literally feels like you are flying. But then, as you hit the water, it is so refreshing and stimulating at the same time.

I was so looking forward to spending the day doing thirty or more dives off those cliffs.

That night, I awoke to the most vivid dream. I dreamt that I dove into the water as usual on my first dive, but I came up in Lake Ontario as I surfaced. I was dazed and confused, so I started walking through the city, realizing I was in Toronto.

I knew my aunt and uncle lived there, so I set out to find them. But, of course, it was a dream, and somehow, I magically found their house. The front door was open, and I followed a couple of other people inside.

I searched the house and finally found my aunt.
She was crying. I asked her what the matter
was? But she didn't answer me.
So, as I asked her again, with a louder voice,
was when I noticed other people crying. Then I
saw why, there I was in an eight by eleven
frame, sitting on a table.

As she picked up my picture and said, "Why did
he have to die so young?" was when I realized
that I was a ghost, and my aunt couldn't see me.
Then I put it all together. I had died cliff diving.

As you may have already guessed, I didn't go
cliff diving that day or any day after that.

I thank my Guardian Angel for sending me such
a clear message!
NICHOLAS B.

SOMETHING SPECIAL

Twenty-some years ago, my wife and I attended a funeral for her grandmother. After the service, we were at her parent's place when her mom told us to go to the suite and pick something special to remind us of Grandma.

Grandma lived in a small suite attached to my wife's parent's home. We walked into the living room, and as my wife started to turn to look at what she might want, we heard a thud from behind us. Turning to see what made the noise, we were stunned that lying on the carpet five feet from where it had been moments before was an antique framed photo of Grandma when she was in her twenties.

You must understand our shock. The photo had been on the mantel above the fireplace when we walked in. And even if our movement of entering the room made it fall, how did it fly five feet from where it had been sitting? Why didn't it just fall and break on the rocked surface directly below?

All I remember saying to my wife was, "I guess grandma wants us to take the photo!" Which she did and still has today. B.P.

BLESSED HOLY OIL

This miracle happened not once but twice.

The first time was just after my wife and I had separated. Distraught and seeking counsel from my neighbor, an elder at her church, we were drinking coffee when her minister stopped by. The three of us ended up discussing my situation, which ended with him saying, "I would like to bless you with holy oil."

I accepted his offer, not seeing any harm and welcoming any possibility of relief from the pain of leaving my wife and children.

After applying some oil from a vial to his hands, he touched my forehead. The moment, actually the instant he touched me, I started to sob uncontrollably. Within seconds, I felt my body release all the heavy negative feelings. My stomach ache disappeared, along with all the tension, pain, and sadness I was holding. And then a calm, peaceful feeling swept over me.

The second time was two years later when I attended a church service given by the same minister.

I received a hands-on blessing from many parishioners, and as the minister anointed me with the blessed holy oil, it happened again—the uncontrolled release of tears and an instant sense of peace.

I have experienced holy water before, but nothing miraculous happened as it did from the blessed holy oil. Of course, it could have been the man anointing me, but I am eternally grateful either way, oil or man.
B.P.

HUGGING A PRIEST

It all started when I hugged the priest, and his glasses got caught with mine. My left temple paid the price with a small cut.

Unfortunately, I ended up with shingles. You know, all that I can remember about that event was the horrible pain.

My doctor prescribed pain medication, but I must have been allergic or something because each day, I became sicker and sicker. I tried to go to get the prescription changed, but my doctor was out of town, and the other doctor said I would have to wait until he got back.

I was so ill that my granddaughter, who was coming over every couple of days to give me Reflexology—a foot massage technique, told her mom that somebody must do something, for she thought I was going to die.

Thankfully, one of my daughters and a different granddaughter took me to the emergency room the following morning. Where I was examined, taken off the medication, put on a sodium drip, and given potassium to drink.

The Reflexology granddaughter came after work that same day to check in on me. She was shocked to find me sitting in the hospital bed as if nothing had happened. I was back to my old self.

It was a miracle, from death's bed to feeling back to normal within hours. Who knew that minerals were all that I needed?
ANNE P

GUARDIAN ANGEL

It was a cold, frosty winter night. We were on our way back to Kelowna from Vancouver via the Coquihalla. My husband was driving, and the kids were asleep in the back seat of the truck.

All of a sudden, a chill ran down my body. My reaction was instant. I yelled, "Slow down."
He did, but not enough. So, I repeated, "Slow down."
"I did," he replied.
"No, I mean it, slow down!"
"Con, I did."
Freaking out, I yelled, "I mean it, slow down!"

As we headed down the sloping road, he slowed down to a crawl.

Moments went by, and he said, "I don't know what you are freaking out about? They have plowed the road, and there are no cars."

I couldn't help it. The feeling wouldn't go away.

As our truck came around the corner, there in front of us were many cars pulled over, and one flipped over.
All I said was, "Drive, don't look, just slowly drive by."

"What if they need help?" he asked me.
"Don't stop. If we stop, there is not enough
room for a car to get by, plus they wouldn't have
time to slow down. So please, just drive."

After safely passing the accident, my husband
asked, "How did you know?"
I just shook my head and said a silent prayer of
gratitude to my guardian angels.
CONSTANCE S.

OUR MIRACLE

I got pregnant using an I.U.D. just six weeks after my son was born. . . but that was not my miracle.

During the last three months of my pregnancy, I had been in and out of the hospital three times with Braxton Hicks contractions. The first time, the intern accompanied me by air ambulance to the Children's Hospital in Vancouver.

The fourth time, I had gone out for a bit of shopping with my mother-in-law, and while we were at a coffee shop having tea, my contractions started coming, and not like in the last few weeks. However, this time, the pain was almost unbearable.

Hubby's mom dropped me off at the hospital.

I called my husband at work to tell him that I was in labor, and he said, "Are you sure? I can come later. You know, since our first child took thirty hours."

I said, "No, I think you should come now."

He showed up in the nick of time.

From being admitted to giving birth, it had only taken thirty minutes.

As my doctor, who had delivered my son, was checking how dilated I was, my water broke. And then all hell broke loose.

The monitor started to go wild. I remember hearing the doctor tell the nurse that the cord had come out and was cutting off the baby's oxygen.

Then a siren went off, and instantly, about twenty people rushed into the room. My doctor said they didn't have time to get me into an operating room.

I went into hysterics, yelling out, "Save my baby."

I just kept yelling.

Then, I remember my doctor lightly touching my shoulder and whispering, "I need you to push."

Just like that, I was coherent and started to push.

As they cut the cord, I remember saying to my husband, "It's a girl."

She came out limp as a rag doll and black and blue. She didn't breathe for six minutes. Those were the longest six minutes of my life.

I found out later that the miracle was that because I had just recently had my son, my cervix had not solidified yet, so my doctor said that because of it, she was able to pry open my cervix with her fingers and suction the baby out as fast as she could…why the black and blue baby.

God works in miraculous ways!
CONSTANCE S.

$28,600.00 EVERY TWO WEEKS...

Like so many other girls, I dreaded my monthlies. Each time, I would prepare my mind for the suffering and heavy bleeding. I endured this routine for another 27 years until I became pregnant.

Becoming pregnant was a miracle in itself, especially after two miscarriages, but a story from a paramedic about a friend of hers who had a successful pregnancy on the third try gave me hope—I held onto that story and told myself that the third time would be the charm, and it happened.

I was pregnant with my son at the age of thirty-nine. I was finally able to relax. No period, no pain! My pregnancy was blissful. I had attentive support from my husband and sister, no morning sickness, a healthy appetite, and a regular sleep routine. I could even exercise at five months pregnant—I even got a hole-in-one golfing with my husband!

BUT!!! After the birth of my son, my periods came back—with a vengeance. I thought it was due to the peri-menopausal stage of my life. My GP said, "It is all natural, nothing to be concerned about." I endured ten more years of crazy, heavy, painful periods and downing copious amounts of ibuprofen tablets.

Then I had an episode where I woke up to a murder scene from CSI! It was like a faucet flowing. Finally, after two trips to the hospital in less than 24 hours, a doctor told me that they found my blood sample to be abnormal, and unfortunately, they could not treat me for this issue, and I would have to be moved to another hospital. In the ambulance, on the way over, my sister gave me strength when I needed it most, and her yelling made me laugh inside because she gets so overly protective when it comes to family. I remember her yelling, "Put on the sirens!"

By the time I was admitted to ICU, my fingers were like little sausages, and I remember they had to cut off my gold ring. Next, I remember more pain while having an IV installed into my thigh to provide access to machines that would treat my blood. Then they immediately hooked me up to an Apheresis machine—Apheresis is the process of withdrawing blood, filtering something out of the blood, and then putting the filtered blood back into the body. The issue was my plasma. My plasma was dark yellow and cloudy—healthy plasma is clear and colorless.

Then the fun began—NOT—in between plasma treatments, blood transfusions, and kidney dialysis treatments, I had a series of other tests done. Thank God cancer and TTP were ruled out. BUT I had "AHUS" (Atypical hemolytic uremic syndrome).
A rare blood disorder that causes a sharp drop in platelets destroys red blood cells and impairs kidney function.

My tests showed…

- That my kidneys were damaged—a normal range is 42-102 umol/L—my elevated creatinine was at 644 umol/. 15 times higher than normal.

- Normal red blood cell levels for females are between 120 g/L and 160 g/L. My hemoglobin count was half of what it should be at 64 g/L.

- Also, I had a high LD level, which signifies the destruction of red blood cells. A normal LD level is 105 to 333 IU/L—mine was 3225 (IU/L). 30 times higher than normal.

The most significant danger I faced was my low platelet count—a normal platelet count ranges between 150,000 to 450,000 platelets per microliter of blood. Platelets play an essential role in helping your blood clot, which may explain why I was bleeding so heavily during my periods. On November 29, 2016, my platelet count was 10,000 platelets per microliter—I did not know that deadly internal bleeding could occur when your platelets fall below 10,000 - I was told this at one of my annual check-ups a couple of years later. My Apheresis nurse, who had treated me when I was sick, called me her "miracle patient," and she teaches lessons using my case.

I was in and out of sleep as the doctor told my husband and sister about my deadly diagnosis, but there was a cure: a newly available drug called "Soliris". It would cost us $28,600 bi-weekly or $728,000 a year. We didn't have those funds readily available...Thank God my doctor came to our rescue!

My doctor wrote a letter to the Exceptional Access Program explaining that I've been "diagnosed with a life-threatening illness that requires expensive medications to manage my health and please process the "Trillium Drug Plan" application with the utmost urgency." Miraculously, the request was granted, and my life-saving medication was flown in and administered to me the next day.

The doctor said the next 16 hours after my treatment was crucial to my recovery. Meanwhile, my sister felt my husband's fear, but he was putting on a brave face for us, so she called my Mom, older sister, and two younger brothers who live in Vancouver for extra moral support, and they flew out to Toronto immediately to be by our side.

I received my first dosage of "Soliris" just hours before my family arrived from Vancouver. I saw the fear in my mom's eyes. That same look was in my husband's and siblings' eyes. I could not let my family down... my son was only ten years old - his innocence was a blessing - and I knew that I had to be there for him. I wanted to see him grow up, become a man, and have a family.

At that moment, my heart and mind were set. I'm going to get better and get out of here!

My sister saw a change come over my face. She saw renewed determination and fire in my eyes.

I spoke to God at every turn, asking him to guide me and protect me. My blood results were improving, but my kidneys were still a concern. I was told that I might need kidney dialysis treatments regularly or wait for a kidney transplant. I vividly remember the day when I told my older sister, "I'm not choosing any of this. I will get better," and I faithfully prayed to God for my full recovery.

I had kidney dialysis treatments done three times per week, which lasted about four hours each time. During which my son's principal came to see me—she is the embodiment of a true miracle. Many years ago, she was diagnosed with stage 3 cancer and was given four months to live and was told by her doctor to get her will in order. Still, she said to herself, I'm going to beat this, and God will help me overcome this obstacle, and she did. Recently, she beat cancer a second time—on that day of her visit, she gave me a little ornament for my bedside table that said, "May God's Angels Always Watch Over You," and a bottle of water that was blessed with healing powers. She told me how, on that day, when visiting that holy place where the water was, her legs were hurting her. She could barely walk, but she persisted in visiting that holy place, and when she drank from the blessed fountain, her pain miraculously disappeared. I believe my dear friend came into my life to help heal me by being a testament to God's grace and mercy.

My faith in God was never stronger, and I felt closer to him as I talked to him well into the night. I also prayed for the patient beside me because I think she may have been suffering from cancer.

Finally, my doctor told me the good news that I could go home for Christmas as long as I followed a regimen that included injections to stimulate red blood cell growth and regular bi-weekly treatments of "Soliris," which a nurse administered by IV drip, at my home.

The medication was delivered by courier in an insulated cooler and was kept in the fridge until my nurse came the following week. It consisted of 4 vials; each vial cost $7,150.00, which amounted to $28,600.00 every two weeks. My first treatment out of the hospital was on Jan. 11, 2017, and twenty-five treatments later, ending on Jan. 05, 2018, and $715,000.00 later, I was well enough to stop further treatments.
Now, the lingering question was, how did I get this rare disorder in the first place, and was it hereditary?

My doctor submitted a blood sample for genetic analysis at Sick Kids Hospital. The result came back with a "variant of uncertain significance." There was no consensus on this variant's "pathogenicity" (the property of causing disease). After researching the results, globally, only one other case was reported in 2016, and it was a woman living in China.

This news was astounding... only one other human being in the whole world shared the same genetic result, and it was in the same year?

My doctor then obtained government approval to get another genetic analysis completed in

Germany and referred me to a Geneticist at Mount Sinai Hospital. Again, the results were inconclusive.

Today, I am symptom-free and healthy, and every year when I visit my "Dream Team" - the best of the best, at St. Michael's Hospital for my annual check-up, my heart swells with gratitude for all the miracles that made my recovery possible.

Not everyone is fortunate enough to be given a second chance at life, so I am honored to share this story with you.
My experience is a testimony that miracles do happen and that if you have faith in God and believe in God's healing powers combined with the strength and love of family and friends, miracles DO happen.

Just think of all the miracles that had happened along the way...

Firstly, my heavy bleeding (which my GP had considered normal for my age) triggered the immediate trips to the hospital, which led to the discovery of my unknown blood disorder and pending kidney failure.
Secondly, if there had been no beds available to me at the second hospital, where my rare blood disorder was treated, I would not have met my

"Dream Team," who acted swiftly and decisively to save my life.

Thirdly, the fact that I had moved to this province saved my life because the "Trillium Drug Program" that enabled me to obtain this expensive medication was unavailable from BC, where I had moved from.

Fourthly, the fact that this medication to treat AHUS exists and was made available to me at the most crucial time was also a miracle.

Fifthly, the birth of my son is a miracle, and if he had not been born, I would not have met his principal, who is the living proof of God's miracles. Her conviction in God solidified my faith, which enabled me to receive God's blessings.

Lastly, and most importantly, is the Miracle of Love. My illness would not have been discovered if it was not for my husband's attentiveness and persistence. When the situation was most dire, the love of family and friends and the love of my purpose as a mother, wife, daughter, sister, and friend gave me the conviction and will to fight and overcome this illness.

Love is the most powerful healer, and against all

odds, I know that love conquers all.
JENNIFER L.

WAS IT LUCK?

I don't think so. There are so many miracles in everyday life. Some people think they are just good luck.

I was coming home from work during rush hour and had just crossed the bridge when I thought strongly about singing a song that I had been singing frequently while taking a class in Banff the previous week. I am not prone to singing or even humming. However, I followed through on my intuition and started to sing a few bars loudly.

That is when it happened. I was hitting the gas to make it up the hill just as an oncoming car barreling down from the other lane pulled into my lane. As I evaded traffic, it all happened in slow motion—left, right, and center.

I knew that had I not been singing that song, it connected me to my inner self. It would have been a head-on collision. I am so thankful to be blessed by incidents like these that remind me that there is more out there than just me and that the more connected I am, the better my life is.
DIANE W.

POWER...LINE

It was dusk when I came home from Lake Country to Kelowna. I had just turned onto the Highway. On the left of the road, I noticed many cars that had pulled over to the side, but my lane was clear.

I didn't even have a split second to notice why. There in front of me was the reason. The powerline had fallen, and the line itself was laying taut stretched out across the highway, about hood level.

I didn't even have time to slow down, let alone stop. In a fraction of a second, the powerline lifted to eye level over my hood and up over my cab as if someone had picked it up.

Looking back, I realized that it was a miracle. I could have lost my head.
NICHOLAS B.

I RECEIVED MY 'SUCCESSFUL' SKY-DIVING CERTIFICATE

I was so excited at my co-worker's suggestion to do something adventurous, a tandem sky diving jump. My sister even decided to join us.

The day was a little windy, but it didn't stop the first group's jump. I watched my sister's face with pure joy as she landed. I was so ready for my turn. Unfortunately, the wind had picked up, and I was not able to jump that day.

A few weeks later, the same co-worker said he was going to try solo this time. Did I want to go?

Yep!

The day started with four hours of ground training, where the instructors told you how to pull and turn the ropes of the shoot to guide and safely land. It was easy to pull the handles when they said, "Flare." all I had to do was bring the handles down to my knees to slow down. I had it down pat.

After a one-way radio was taped to my chest, I was ready and willing. The plane door opened, and I sidestepped to the wing and held on. Then, when instructed, I let go. The shoot opened, and I was away.

I was expecting to feel more excited about flying than I did. It was easy to pull the handle, maneuver, and steer the shoot. I was able to fly to the exact landing location… and then, it all went to sh*t.

As I heard my instructor yelling "FLARE! FLARE!" many times, I remember thinking, *this is not going to be good*. It was all happening so fast I couldn't pull down the ropes to flare. I could not slow down.

After slamming into the ground and being dragged about ten feet, I remember lying face down in the dirt. I couldn't feel any pain, even though I had road rash and a mouth full of gravel. I remember thinking that my right foot shouldn't be where it was, twisted up by my hip.

After my pants were cut off by the EMT, who very nicely covered my bare butt with a blanket, I found out at the hospital that I had two broken femurs and a lot of bruises and was in the operating room within a couple of hours.

The miracle is that I survived a horrifying accident. And even though I spent two months in recovery and eight surgeries over the next eight years (one of which broke my left leg again), I somehow was not dead, paralyzed, or had brain damage. To this day—even though I have chronic pain—I am able to walk on my own, hike, swim, and enjoy my children's hugs. I am so thankful that I am alive to tell you my story and that I will be a grandmother before you have read this.

TRICIA C

ONCE UPON A WEE MIRACLE

Hi, folks.

My name is Dave, and I grew up on a dirt-poor farm in rural Nova Scotia. I didn't realize we were dirt poor because most of our neighbors were in similar circumstances. We got by from what we could grow on the farm and orchard, from our cattle, pigs, and chickens, and from what we could harvest from the woodlot, where we cut logs and pulp wood and firewood for cooking and keeping us warm.

The bigger boys looked after the blue work—milking cows, cutting hay, cleaning the barn, working on the woodlot, and whatever it took to keep the farm running. The girls did the pink work—helping Mom to keep the house clean and tidy, washing clothes and dishes, looking after the smaller children, making butter, helping to prepare meals, and many other things we all thought were routine. All the bigger children, in their turn, helped with the spring planting, weeding, picking endless rocks, and later the harvest in the fall.

Dad was the supreme leader when he was at home, but he often spent long, lonely months away on various construction projects, which kept us out of poverty. Dad cherished the times he was at home and worked hard to do things the boys could not take care of on the farm. He loved to go fishing with the boys and adored and doted on his lovely daughters.

Skiing, boating, golfing, and other expensive pursuits were not even considered. Those things were for rich folk in a different world. But a weeklong visit to Aunt Ella's place in Glace Bay or Aunt Laura's in Parrsboro were exciting adventures that we looked forward to months in advance.

We were too busy enjoying life to realize that we were dirt poor.

Somehow or another, we all survived our childhood and entry into adulthood. Two of us actually managed to graduate from university, including me—with a big help from Canada Student Loans. Our parents were totally unable to assist us financially to attend university, but their moral support was much appreciated at the time and fondly remembered in our senior years.

Our siblings were all able to move into decent lifestyles, and five of the eight of us went on to have million dollar or better holdings. We all have to thank our parents for their guidance and encouragement for us to get a good education and strive to become good citizens and succeed in life.

Did I forget to mention that Dad was a World War II veteran?

Moving forward after my university years, we all became more "modernized" and entered lifestyles we could not have imagined a decade earlier. As for myself, after ten or more years working in an office, I became interested in golf.

Ideally, for best results in developing skills at the game, one should begin golf in their pre-teen years. Not to be deterred by such details, I joined the game with enthusiasm that was totally unrelated to skills. If any of my friends from those formative golf years read this missive, my thanks for their sufferance and forbearance as I became acquainted with the game.

Within a couple of years, I moved to a new job and life in "The Land of the Midnight Sun, Yellowknife." By a stroke of luck, I soon made friends with Duke. Duke was a naturally gifted athlete seventeen years older than me—

an old guy. We quickly became close friends, and he took on the daunting task of teaching me how to play golf. He attained the ultimate goal of being a good teacher when his pupil (me) could beat him at the game.

Life moves on inexorably.

Duke retired and moved to Victoria. I got married, and we had a son. Within a few years, we moved to the Okanagan to start a small wine business. The first few years running my new business were a series of crises with little or no time for golf.

However, my son Bill had started going to school, and I was determined not to let my work life separate me from him, as had been the case in my childhood. Vintage Hills (later called Two Eagles) opened in 2000, and Bill was six. I got a membership for us both and tried to help him as much as I could. Within a few years, we were playing one hundred or more rounds a year.

It may be out of context, but I would say the ensuing ten years were the happiest in my life. This was only partly due to the fun of playing so much golf with Bill. The whole experience of raising my son taught me that there are many more important things in life than myself.

By around 2010, Bill was in his mid teens and began to spend more of his time with his friends, which is completely natural. I was now in my 60s, and my golf skills had begun to decline, which was also quite normal. I continued to play one hundred or more rounds per year, some with Bill and more with friends in my own age bracket. But something was wrong.

Each year, I was gradually experiencing more and more severe back problems, which coincided with the golf season. By halfway through the season, I would occasionally turn to a chiropractor to get some relief from the agonizing pains. I never had much faith in the chiropractor, but the sessions did provide some relief, and I continued to play.

It may have been an obvious solution to simply quit playing golf, as this was clearly the cause of the back pains. The thought of quitting appalled me for a number of reasons. Golf was a great activity for me as it gave me a lot of healthy outdoor exercise and was a good way to keep an active circle of friends.

I have known way too many people who had withdrawn from their lifelong activities due to reasons much the same as I was grappling with. The activities were things like hockey, baseball, bowling, fishing, skiing, hunting, and so on. These were activities they enjoyed for many years but then abandoned as the inevitable aches and pains associated with aging set in. Many of these people went on to become couch potatoes and recluses. Such a fate was, to me, worse than death.

But one summer, the back pains started earlier than in the past and were more severe. I began to think that, like it or not, it was time to put the clubs away. The pain, although brought on by golf, was not present just during time out on the course. The pain was ever present throughout the day and was interfering with my habit of sleeping soundly at night, and getting out of bed in the morning was a lengthy and agonizing process.

One day, I was chatting with my good friend, Fred, while enjoying a cold beer when I told him it was likely the end of the road for me with golf due to back pains. Fred told me of an experience he had when he was about my age when he was also experiencing severe back pains brought on by golf. Due to the urging of his friend at the time, he went to see an acupuncturist. After only two treatments, his back pains were cured and have not occurred since.

As his experience had occurred nearly twenty years earlier, he could not refer me to his acupuncturist but said he had heard good things about Dr. Rosalyn Harder in Kelowna.

Up until this point in time, I had considered acupuncture to be a hoax. But with the likelihood of my alternative being an end to golf, and with Fred's encouragement and urging, I phoned Dr. Harder for an appointment.

Doctor Harder conducted her practice from her home on a quiet little side street not far from KGH. As I entered her home, my misgivings about acupuncture were trying to overcome Fred's recent encouragement on the subject. Dr. Harder welcomed me to her home and took me into the area reserved for her practice.

She immediately struck me as a gentlewoman, likely a few years older than myself. She had clearly been a very attractive lady in her youth and was still a credit to her gender. She encouraged me to talk about my life experiences especially as they may have had any bearing on my current back problems.

I talked quite freely to her, and we seemed to bond easily and quickly. While talking about myself, I also encouraged her to share her background and how she became an acupuncture practitioner. She told me she learned her skills while living in China during the 60s and 70s.

That last piece of information could have ended my venture into the field of acupuncture before she had a chance to insert a single needle. There are clearly some of my friends and associates who would classify me as a redneck. Whether I am or not will have to remain an unanswered question. But I quickly realized she had spent her youth in a country ruled by Mao Zedong, one of the greatest mass murderers in history.

I wisely decided that the purpose of my visit was to get relief for my back and not to enter a political debate. Dr. Rosalyn, as I fondly came to address her after we were better acquainted, instructed me to strip to my underwear and lay face down on her treatment bed.

We had spent close to an hour talking, but the treatment itself was over in about twenty minutes and was completely painless. She told me to get up carefully and get dressed. Getting up off the bed was brutal, and much to my chagrin, Dr. Rosalyn had to help me get back on my feet.

After hobbling out of her house I went home and prepared for another sleepless night and the usual difficulties arising in the morning.

But the next morning was a miracle. I hopped out of bed much more like a nineteen-year-old than an aging cripple.

Although, like Fred, two treatments did not completely fix my back problem. Over the next number of years, I had other occasions to visit Dr. Rosalyn numerous times. Her expert skills kept me in reasonably good shape, and I continued to golf and, for the most part, pain-free.

Unfortunately, my friend Fred took his doctor's advice and withdrew from golf, so two treatments were all he needed. *By the way, I did not mean to infer that every person who gives up their active lifestyle becomes a couch potato or recluse.* Fred, like many others, had plenty of other activities to keep him healthily occupied.

I had become sort of a three-activity type— work, golf, and family. I did not think it would have been good for me, either physically or mentally, to give up any one of the three.

Sadly for me, Dr. Rosalyn retired in 2018, by which time we had become good friends.

I never did ask her if she had been one of Mao's cadres when she wasn't busy with her acupuncture training. I lost contact with her after she retired to do some traveling with her husband while they were still healthy enough to do so. Maybe she had an opportunity to visit some of her old comrades from the commune. May God bless her.
DAVE T.

WALKING TO WORK

It was around seven forty-five in the morning, and I was on my way to work at Kelowna General Hospital. It was slightly raining, and I was carrying an umbrella. I always walk along the east side of Pandosy Street and south towards the hospital.

As I approached Burns Avenue, there was an SUV that had pulled up past the stop sign. Traffic was busy, as always, and the SUV was forced to take its time to turn left.

As I started to cross the road, I could have sworn we made eye contact as she looked in my direction. She had to have seen me step off the sidewalk and start to cross the street.

To my horror, just as I stepped in front of the passenger's side of the car, she gunned it. I tried to get out of the way, but I hit my head hard, falling backward! I couldn't move and figured out what had just happened as I lay there. I knew it was a miracle that she had missed hitting my body, but she had run over both my legs, to my horror.

The lady got out of her car and screamed, "I thought I killed you," then, "What should I do?"

I couldn't speak. All I could do was bum-walk myself off the road and back onto the sidewalk as my head was bleeding. As I sat there with my head between my legs, I tried to get my belongings that had fallen out of my bag.

The lady had moved her car and came over to me, repeating, "What should I do?"

She convinced me to get into her car so she could drive me to the Hospital. She dropped me off in front of the ER.

Wet, muddy, and drenched in blood, I limped into the Emergency Room entrance, where I was scheduled to work and was now late.

The nurses immediately brought a stretcher and took me into the trauma room. The nurse in triage—one of my coworkers—said, "Sue, what happened to you?

In shock, bleeding badly, and not feeling much, I remember saying in disbelief, "I just got run over!"

Later, the doctor asked if the car had run over my legs—even though the tire marks were on my pants—for they were not broken. Though—I did have a severe concussion, and my head needed staples and stitches. My neck hurt badly when I moved and even to the touch. My right ankle was sprained, and my leg ached and burned. I ended up with TMJ in my jaw, and my spine from shoulders to tailbone was tender and had sharp pain when I moved. My right elbow was bruised and swollen.

I was a wreck, physically and emotionally. But it was a miracle that I was alive!

Afterward, I spoke with a friend, who was a medium, and she told me as she psychically viewed the accident, "Holy cow! That was a big vehicle." She also said, "*Something* lifted the vehicle off of you, possibly an angel. And that is probably why my legs were not broken and why I only suffered a sprained ankle."

She told me that it was an absolute miracle!

Trying to think on the bright side, I believe that this accident may have happened to turn my life in a different direction and slowed me down. I have always felt very grateful, and even though it has been years, I still can't work. The accident has moved me forward spiritually, I live more in the moment, and I appreciate life more and more each day.
SUE V

HOME ALONE

When I was home alone, and hubby was away on a hunting trip, late at night, I heard something fall in the basement. Lying there listening, something fell again. I grabbed my phone—in case I needed to call 911—and went to investigate.

An empty gun case had fallen from the shelf onto the counter (first bang) and then onto the floor in the middle of the room (second bang).

The next day, my friend, who has a gift of sensing ghosts, came over. She went downstairs by herself, and when she came back up, she said she saw a short, angry woman and got the name Mary.

I said, "That's my mom." My mom was often angry, contrary to popular belief.

Then my friend said that she also saw another woman, and got the name Margaret.

I said, "That's my mother-in-law."

She got a third name, Jeff.

That was the brother-in-law that I was upset with at the time.

So, I am thinking that my mom-in-law came to let me know that it was time to forgive Jeff and to move on.

Working on it.

Another sign from my angels was the night before I started to receive Chemo I felt a hand on my shoulder, even though no one else was around.
DONNA C

DIMES

I was presenting at a workshop in Las Vegas, and one of the attendees was my aunt. She was telling us the story of seeing dimes.

She was telling us how she has found 'solitary' dimes in the weirdest places ever since my uncle passed away, and she had heard that finding dimes was a sign from your loved ones in Heaven.

Note that if any other change is with the dime, it doesn't count.

Now, here is where the story gets interesting. I had found an 'American' dime in my suitcase that morning. I found it strange since I had packed the suitcase while I was in Canada myself. The next morning, in the same suitcase, I found a 'Canadian' dime. *My uncle had humor.*

As she talked, I shivered because a year before, I was visiting my daughter in Las Vegas and sitting in a lounger by her pool around ten o'clock one night. It was a beautiful August evening, and I had my eyes shut when my uncle started talking to me. We had a few moments of conversation when suddenly, I said, "Hey, wait, you can't be here, you're not dead," and poof, he was gone. The next day, my mom called and told me that my uncle had passed away the night before.

Years later, and a few more loved ones gone, I asked my aunt to tell me the story again about the dimes.

Her latest one was just the other day. She and my grandmother went to her youngest son's house to celebrate a birthday. There on the table, in front of my Gran, was a single dime. My Aunt asked, "Does anybody know where this dime came from?" Nope. My aunt told me that it must be a sign for my Gran from my oldest cousin, who had just passed away the day before.

My aunt recently lost her oldest son, and after he passed, she was cleaning up at my Grans and found a dime on my grandmother's side table and another one under the sheepskin on her chair. She told me that while his siblings (my two cousins) were cleaning up his apartment, they found dimes in a couple of boxes and one on the floor by the toilet.

My aunt was telling me that one of the weirdest ones was when her daughter, my cousin, was having a shower, and a dime fell from above.

Now, whenever my aunt finds a 'solitary' dime, she saves it in this display unit that she received as a gift.

Dimes From Heaven

Heaven's raining dimes from someone that you love. It's usually no coincidence they come from up above. So, when you see a dime, pick it up and know an angel's looking out for you no matter where you go.

CONSTANCE S & CAMILLE M

LOVEY

When my
daughter was
born, my
brother and his
wife gifted her
"Lovey." A
cuddly stuffed
blanket.

One night—five years later—my daughter calls
out, "Mommy! Papa left a message in Lovey."

I came running into her room to see what the
commotion was all about. There was a dime
inside of Lovey. Sewn into the stuffed animal's
material was a dime. We looked at how someone
could have put it in there, but there was no
entrance or loose stitch.

You have to understand that I have washed
Lovey many times over the past five years. I
would have noticed it before. Other family
members have examined the toy, and there is no
way that the dime should be there.

We love getting messages from my dad, aka
Papa. MARCIE M

WHEN I VISITED KELOWNA

First off, I must tell you that Kelowna is where I was born and where my mom, dad, and sister had moved back to after living for many years in Alberta.

Story #1
A few years after my dear mom's death, I was visiting her three sisters in Kelowna.

We were going somewhere, and my Aunties had already gotten into the car. As I opened the car door and went to get in, there it was a dime lying on the floor of the car.

It gave me peace and excitement that Mom was giving us all a sign that she was there! Amen.

Story #2
Another time, when I was visiting Kelowna, my cousin and her husband had picked me up—in her cool convertible, I might add—to go out for dinner. As I stepped out of the car, right on the sidewalk, was another sign from my momma—a dime.

Story #3
Recently, when my sister passed away suddenly, I came back to Kelowna and stayed at my dad's house.

I was about to settle in and put my suitcase away when I walked by the front door and saw a dime on the mat!

I had only arrived a couple of hours before and had not noticed it then, so it really made me feel her love!

On the day of her funeral, I went to do errands and stopped to get a drink at Starbucks. After I ordered, I stepped back to wait for my order, and I looked down, and there was another dime!

This time, I received two signs when I first arrived, and the day we were celebrating my sister's life!!!

I felt the connection, and it helped me through a very hard time.
Amen, thank you, Jesus.
Colena M. B

PENNY, DIMES & TOONIES

Here are a few short dime stories.

I used to find pennies when I would think of my sister, Kathy, after she passed away. But now I find dimes when I think of her. I consider it 10-fold!
LINDA B

My Dad sends me dimes all the time. One time, I got out of my car, and there were five dimes on the ground beside it. Another time, I reached for my kitchen towel hanging on a door handle, and a dime fell out of it.
DEBRA F

Oh my gosh, I have a shoe that is a jewelry box. The shoe holds rings, but for me, it holds my dimes. My mom and my cousin leave me dimes. More so, my cousin, I think. We talked about it, and how my mom was leaving us dimes before she passed, then my dimes increased.
JESSICA S

I find dimes on occasion.
Usually, this happens when I ask for help
from my spirit guides. Sometimes, I will find
them every day for a week or so. Other times,
it is for just one day.
ROB H

My hunny finds dimes … I find pennies…still
the same amount of excitement… lol….
My family hates wasting money… lol.
LINDA P

TOONIE

My mother-in-law, Pat, had a way of relating to others, especially children, that was honest, perceptive, and loving. We were devastated when she suddenly got sick and died at the age of seventy-five.

During the final days of her life, her husband and all her children kept vigil. Her daughter thought of her as her best friend and number one supporter. Before Pat died, Diane asked her to give us dimes to show all was well. Diane had heard that spirits can manipulate these small, round objects.

After her death, all her family and many friends began finding dimes regularly. Of course, we kept every dime that came our way.

One day, I was paying at the till of Shoppers Drug Mart, and the young woman waiting in line behind me was preparing for her turn. I saw her open her change purse, and then about a dozen dimes sprang out, hitting me and dropping at my feet. She apologized with embarrassment, but I assured her it may have been my fault, too.

We found dimes at significant times very regularly for many years.

When my own mom was nearing death, my sisters and I talked about Pat's generosity with dimes. We thought we would take it a step further and asked Mom to give us toonies instead. Sadly, it didn't turn out, but she does send us dimes sometimes.
MAUREEN A

Acknowledgments

A heartfelt and sincere appreciation goes out to my mom, Linda. I want to express my deepest gratitude for the countless hours you've devoted to reading my manuscripts repeatedly. Your unwavering support is nothing short of amazing, and I am incredibly fortunate to have you in my life.

I want to extend my heartfelt thanks to my Aunt Diane and my grandmother, Anne. You both hold a special place in my heart, and I truly value the time you spent pre-reading my manuscripts and providing invaluable feedback. Your support means the world to me. Love you both!

And to my husband, Nick, you are the embodiment of patience and unwavering belief. Your tireless effort in brainstorming ideas for my books and diligently uncovering even the smallest errors, despite the manuscripts being edited five times already, is a testament to your unwavering support. Thank you for wholeheartedly believing in my dreams and allowing me the freedom to bring them to life. You are my soulmate in this lifetime and countless lifetimes before. Love you, Babe!

Ways to Raise Your Vibration

1. Prayer
2. Clean up! Clean out your automobile, house, closets, old clothes, attic, basement, etc.
3. Removing contaminations
    a. Mercury fillings
    b. Certain cleaning products
4. Pay off debts
5. Stop any obligations that don't serve you
6. Watch movies like:
    a. What the Bleep do we know,
    b. Down the Rabbit Hole,
    c. Conversations with God,
    d. The Celestine Prophecy,
    e. Awake: The Life of Yogananda,
    f. The Secret,
    g. The Shift
7. Books to read:
    a. The Artists Way by Julia Cameron,
    b. Conversations with God by Neale Donald Walsch,
    c. Seven Spiritual Laws of Success by Deepak Chopra,
    d. The Bible,
    e. The Secret by Rhonda Byrne,
    f. The Celestine Prophecy by James Redfield,
    g. The Alchemist by Paulo Coelho,

h. A New Earth: Awakening to Your Life's Purpose by Eckhart Tolle,
i. The Road Less Traveled by M. Scott Peck,
j. The Four Agreements: A Practical Guide to Personal Freedom by Don Miguel Ruiz,
k. Siddhartha by Hermann Hesse,
l. Autobiography of a Yogi by Paramahansa Yogananda.

8. Workshops & Courses
9. Quiet time for yourself
10. Meditation
11. Incense
12. Deep Breathing Techniques
13. Restful Sleep
14. Drinking water
15. Art – Drawing & Crafts
16. Writing
17. Journaling
18. Color – wear it (even if it is just your underwear)
19. Out in Nature
20. Crystal stones
21. Light Exercise
     a. Walking
     b. Yoga
     c. Tai chi
22. Bach Remedies
23. Body Cleanse
     a. Shower
     b. Luffa

24. Make new friends with common interests of growth and wellbeing
25. Stop complaining
    a. Get a new job if you don't like yours
    b. Divorce or leave whoever is holding you back
    c. Go on a holiday
    d. Get help for your Addictions
26. Nutrition & Diet
27. Colonic
28. Get negative ions
    a. Outdoors
    b. Running water
        i. Fountain
        ii. Waterfalls
        iii. Beach – waves
        iv. Hot Springs
    c. Dirt – gardening
    d. Wind
    e. Food
        i. Blueberries (all berries)
        ii. Apples
        iii. Citrus fruit
        iv. Raw food diet
        v. Cabbage
        vi. Broccoli
        vii. Sweet potato
        viii. Green beans
        ix. Almond
        x. Walnuts

        xi.   Pine seeds
        xii.   Sunflower seeds
        xiii.   Supplements
                – chlorophyll & spirulina

f. Beeswax candles
g. Himalayan Salt lamp
h. Epsom Salt baths
i. Clicking Basalt stones together
j. Negative ion bracelets
k. Sunlight

29. Laughter
30. Joy

Companion Book
Secrets of a Healer – Magic of Reiki

Softcover ISBN: 978-1-7772220-0-0
eBook ISBN 978-1-7772220-1-7

Self-Reiki

Reiki = Life-Force Energy

Reiki is one of the most ancient healing methods known to humankind, used as an alternative therapy for treating physical, emotional, mental, and spiritual dis-ease.

Reiki is the Japanese word for 'Universal Life-force Energy.' The definition of 'Rei' is a universal, mysterious power, transcendental spirit. 'Ki' is described as the vital life-force energy. Together, they could mean 'Spirit Energy' or 'Power Energy.' However, the essence is more that of 'Universal Life-force Energy – All-Encompassing.'

Constance's Reiki Interpretation

I love to use this simplified story to explain to my students what Reiki energy is and how it works.

Imagine a lamp in your home; it can be any size or color. All lamps have an electrical cord, a lamp fixture, and a light bulb to use the lamp properly.

Imagine you are the lamp fixture, the client or person you will work on is the light bulb, and God, Spirit, or your Reiki Master is the Ki (Chi) energy that flows through the electrical cord to light the bulb.

All you are the facilitator, the lamp, the one needed to light the bulb. And without plugging the lamp into an electrical socket in the wall, the light bulb would not come on.

I remember doing a science project in school where we had a potato and a small flashlight bulb. Amazingly, a potato has enough energy to light the bulb momentarily. Now, like the potato, I do not have enough energy to heal my client. And if I try, I will burn out quickly. Only the Source has all the power the client will ever need.

If you ever feel drained after a session, you gave your energy away, not the Cosmic energy granted through Source.

Also, it is useless and a waste of energy to plug the electrical cord in without the bulb in the lamp. Ensure you always have a reason and the client's permission during a Reiki session. When your Reiki Master in Spirit comes to help you, do not waste their time.

The point is you are only the facilitator, not the energy itself. I have witnessed many miracles while practicing Reiki, but it is not me. It is only the energy from Spirit flowing through me.

Basics of Level I Reiki – Self-Reiki
The APPRENTICE

My gift to you is receiving your 1st Degree (Level 1) Reiki for free.

Why? Because I think everyone and their dog should know how to do Reiki (self-healing).

All the Reiki techniques are based on the seven major Chakra's:
- Crown
- Brow/Third eye
- Throat
- Heart
- Solar Plexus/Navel
- Sacral/ Spleen/Sexx
- Root/Base

You will learn the twenty-one minor Chakra's hand positions.
1 – Crown Chakra
1 – Throat Chakra
2 – Shoulder
1 – Heart Chakra
2 – Crease of elbow
2 – Wrist of each hand
2 – Palm of each hand
1 – Solar Plexus Chakra

1 – Sacral Chakra
1 – Root Chakra
1 – Hips
2 – Behind each knee
2 – Ankle of each foot
2 – Sole of each foot

Each meridian has a different number of points that you can activate, just like a Chakra.

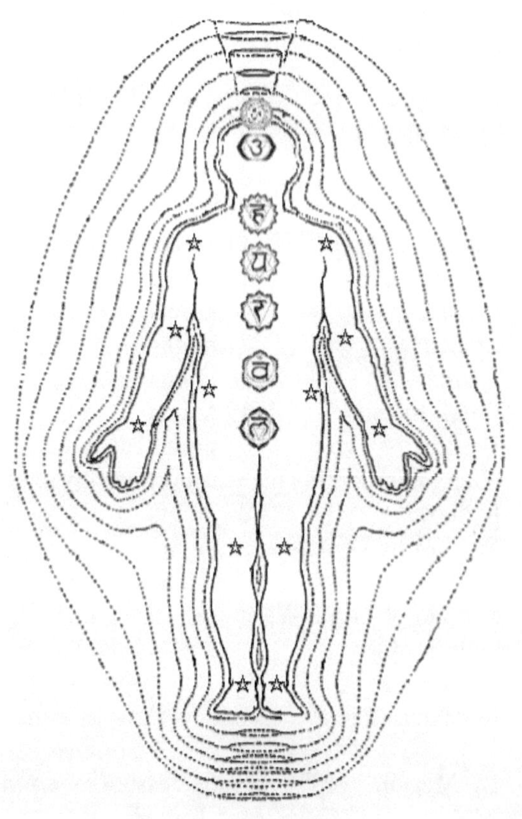

PLUS:

In Shiatsu, you would learn 361 Tsubo points that run along 12 meridians. A Tsubo is any point along the surface of the body.

Look on any Acupuncture Points Chart, and you will find:

Meridian   **Points**
Lung   11 points
Large Intestine   20 points
Stomach   45 points
Spleen   21 points
Heart   9 points
Small Intestine   19 points
Bladder   67 points (different charts number this meridian differently)
Kidney   27 points
Pericardium or Circulation /Sex
                                 9 points
Sanjiao or Triple Warmer   23 points
Gall Bladder   44 points
Liver   14 points
Ren Meridian or Conception Vessel/Central
                                24 points
Du Meridian or Governing Vessel/Governing
                                28 points

***Meaning; these Tsubo are the points that energy can go into and out of the body—front and back. Each Tsubo can receive Reiki energy to balance the meridian.

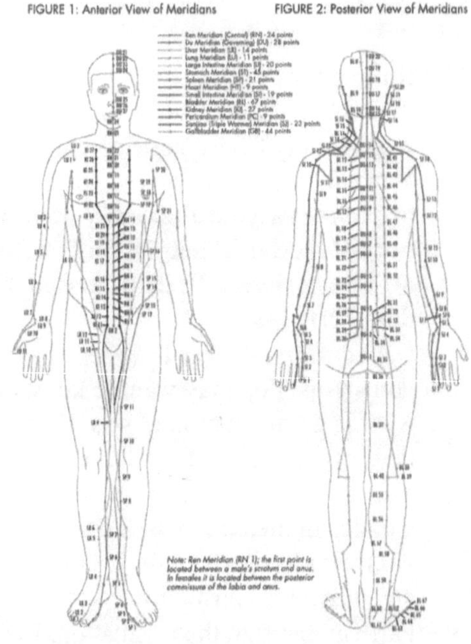

Your Reiki Level I Attunement
You will need:
Approximately 30 minutes
Comfortable chair
A small glass of lemon water

Reiki Attunement Procedure:
- Listen to the Reiki Level I Attunment video on my Constance Santego YouTube Channel - **https://www.youtube.com/watch?v=tdE4Kbod9r4&list=PLdu7TXEB2oCAqpawtjeZaHRn2LdLxzfmd&index=7&t=14s**
- Get comfortable, but I suggest that you sit up. You may want to know what is going on around you. If you lie down, some students fall asleep.
- You will be guided through a wonderful meditation to clear yourself physically, emotionally, mentally, and spiritually.
- Partway through the meditation, I will ask you to do the Kidney Breath and Hui Yin while your Reiki Master opens your Chakras so that later you can do Self-Reiki.
- I will ask at the end of the meditation for you to do the Water Ritual while you read the Raku Kei Affirmation.

Attunment Meaning

In Reiki, an "attunement" is a process by which a Reiki master transmits to the student a heightened capacity to channel the life force energy. This is typically done through a specific ritual or ceremony. Through this ritual, the students' energy channels or chakras are opened or cleared to allow them to channel the Reiki energy for healing effectively. It's a process of initiation to elevate the student's ability to tap into and channel this energy.

Dr. Mikao Usui, the founder of the Reiki healing system, didn't use the term "attunement" in the same way it is commonly understood in the Western Reiki context. The Western understanding and practice of Reiki, including the concept of "attunement," has been somewhat modified and adapted from Usui's original teachings.

In Usui's teachings, a process known as "Reiju" (which translates to "spiritual blessing" or "spiritual gift") was used. Reiju is the transmission of energy from the teacher to the student. It's a process that helps open and expand the student's main energy channels, allowing them to connect more effectively with the Reiki energy. While Reiju serves a similar purpose to the Western concept of "attunement," the methodologies and understanding might differ.

However, Dr. Usui did emphasize the importance of spiritual development and personal growth, which were foundational to his Reiki system. The Five Reiki Principles (or Five Reiki Precepts) that you mentioned are a testament to this, guiding practitioners in their daily lives.

Kidney Breathing & The Hui Yin

When you are being attuned, during the meditation, I will be directing the Raku fire energy up your spinal column and into your pineal gland. This re-energizes your entire body and raises your spiritual consciousness.

For the kidney breath, place your hands over your kidneys (located on your lower back).

Your Hui Yin is an acupressure point between your anus and genitals (Root Chakra). Breathe normally, while feeling like you are pulling this point up into your body as you contract it.

As you take a breath, imagine the fire energy rising from your Root Chakra, up through your spine, entering and swirling in your head.

Place your tongue at the roof of your mouth behind your front teeth, and release this energy through your mouth.

Release your Hui Yin.

Water Ritual

Water purifies, conducts energy, and amplifies the effectiveness of the symbols one is attuned to.

Prepare the Water
Get a small glass of water (2 oz)
Pour ½ tsp of lemon juice into the glass
Once you have the glass, your Reiki Master in Spirit will assist you in blessing the lemon water with the appropriate Reiki symbol.

Say the Raku Kei Affirmation and drink the lemon water, symbolizing cleansing your inside.

Raku Kei Affirmation

I believe there is a great cosmic magnet that manifests as the Spirit of truth, love, and light. This cosmic magnet lives in me as part of my divine nature.

I recognize the pure white light in my soul. This Holy Spirit in my soul continually guides me in all that I think, say, see, and do.

Through my magnetic personality, I pour my resources into the world. As I give, so shall I receive, living my life happily, expressing creatively, and experiencing perfect well-being.

So be it now and forever.

Now you are ready to perform Self-Reiki

After receiving your 1st Degree in Reiki Attunement, your energy system may need to adjust to the higher vibration. This new energy frequency will balance itself out in a noticeably short period of time.

Procedure
- Make yourself comfortable by sitting or lying down.
- Call upon your Reiki Master in Spirit and your higher self to assist you in this treatment. If you have attuned to 2nd or 3rd Degree Reiki, use the symbols.
- Close your eyes and pay attention to the rhythm of your breathing.
- Rub your hands together.
- Place one hand on your Solar Plexus (Navel) Chakra.
- Place your other hand on your Sacral (Spleen/Sexx) Chakra.
- Intent or ask that the Reiki energy flows through you at the highest level that is beneficial for you right now.
- Next, follow the twenty-one minor hand positions as directed until you intuitively can sense where to place your hands.

Front and Back Positions for the Body
- Head/Crown & Brow Chakra – 5 positions
- Neck/Throat Chakra – 2 positions
- Shoulders – 2 positions
- Heart/Heart Chakra – 2 positions
- Ribcage/Solar Plexus Chakra – 1 position
- Bellybutton/ Sacral Chakra – 1 position
- Groin/Root Chakra – 1 position
- Back – 3 positions
- Elbows – 2 positions
- Wrists and Hands – 4 positions
- Knee, Ankle & Feet – 6 positions

Go to my Constance Santego WEBSITE for the FREE Reiki hand position guidebook, and follow the Reiki Level I instructions.

https://constancesantego.ca/education/worksh ops/reiki-level-1-courses/

The Author

Dr. Constance Santego is a highly respected expert in the field of holistic health and spiritual healing. With over twenty years of experience teaching courses on these subjects, she has developed a deep understanding of the interconnectedness of the mind, body, and spirit in achieving overall well-being.

Dr. Santego holds a Ph.D. and Doctorate in Natural Medicine, which has provided her with a comprehensive understanding of alternative healing modalities and their application in promoting optimal health. Her educational background has equipped her with the knowledge to address health concerns from a holistic perspective, considering the physical, emotional, and spiritual aspects of an individual's well-being.

Throughout her career, Dr. Santego has been committed to sharing her knowledge and empowering others to take control of their health and healing. She has a unique ability to blend scientific research and traditional wisdom, creating a bridge between conventional and alternative medicine.

In her "Secrets of a Healer" educational series, Dr. Santego draws upon her vast experience and expertise to captivate readers with her insights and teachings. She takes readers on a transformative journey, delving into the realms of holistic health, spirituality, and self-discovery. Through her writing, she aims to inspire individuals to tap into their own innate healing abilities and embrace a balanced and harmonious approach to well-being.

Dr. Santego's work has touched the lives of many, guiding them toward a more profound understanding of themselves and their connection to the world around them. Her series serves as a beacon of wisdom, offering practical tools and techniques for personal growth and transformation.

Overall, Dr. Constance Santego's blend of knowledge, experience, and passion makes her a captivating figure in the field of holistic health and spiritual healing. Her contributions through teaching, writing, and her spellbinding series continue to inspire and empower individuals on their journeys toward well-being and self-discovery.

Message from the Author

A miracle to me is something marvelous that can't be explained by science. I am not sure if my abilities came from the fact that I lost sight in my left eye before I was two. I am unsure if science would try to explain that due to the accident, my hearing and other senses picked up for the lack of sight. I could accept that, but what about my sixth sense and supernatural abilities? How does science explain that?

As you have been reading my story, my experiences through the many characters in this series, from seeing ghosts when I was three to witnessing miraculous healings to having items appear after others say they are not there. I have been asked if I believe in God.

More so now than when I went to church. I believe that there is a higher power that we can learn to tap into. A power that is there to teach us what we need to learn to move toward Nirvana.

It is hard to separate Metaphysics and Psychic abilities from Spirituality of any kind. It is one and the same.

I have so enjoyed writing these first five books.

When hubby comes home from work many days, I excitedly say, "You won't believe what the characters did today!"

I start each book with the subject idea: distinguishing spirit, tongues, prophecy, healing, miracles—and the next three, knowledge, wisdom, and faith.

Then, there is the angel of each book.
Book 1 – Archangel Michael
Book 2 – Archangel Gabriel
Book 3 – Bath Kol
Book 4 – Archangel Raphael
Book 5 – Archangel Hamied
Book 6 – Archangel Raziel
Book 7 – Archangel Uriel
Book 8 – Archangel Chamuel *(as I write this, I get a feeling this angel might change).*

Then, of course, there is Lexi, our protagonist, our main character. I didn't know she would be the main character when I started writing. I actually thought it was going to be Tamara. I didn't know what would happen to Edward or the other characters. So I had to have faith that God knew, and I would just keep on typing.

Some chapters took me a week or more to research, but I loved the connections that would happen once I chose a character's name, occupation, etcetera.

Some would say that writing these books was a miracle. However, my family still says, "How do you do it?"

All I know is that I have these eight books to finish writing, and then, who knows, maybe I will switch genres and write romance.

The nine spiritual gifts granted by Spirit written in the Bible are miracles. All of them!

I can't wait to discover the adventure Spirit takes me on in the following three novels. Okay, I already know a bit about book six. Lexi goes to…

Hey, wait. That would spoil the surprise.
Love and Light, Connie

Also Available

Play the game Ikona and test
your Virtues and Sins.
For additional information on
Constance Santego's wide range of
Motivational Products, Coaching Sessions,
Spiritual Retreats,
Live Events and Educational Programs
Go to
www.ConstanceSantego.ca

Follow me on:
Instagram - Constance_Santego &
Facebook - constancesantegoo
YouTube Channel - Constance Santego
Subscribe and receive free information &
Meditations

www.ingramcontent.com/pod-product-compliance
Lightning Source LLC
Chambersburg PA
CBHW032103310726
48972CB00001B/79